THE CENTAURI SURPRISE

a novel of T-Space ™

Alastair Mayer

Mabash Books

For Mary R. M. Mayer, 1923-2019,
for putting up with more than she should have had to.

CONTENTS

THE CENTAURI SURPRISE

Previously . . .

Spoiler Warning: the summaries below necessarily reveal some details of the earlier books

In *The Chara Talisman*:

Archeologist Hannibal Carson finds the remains of a high-tech talisman in a primitive tomb on the planet Verdigris, in the Delta Pavonis system. A ruthless cult, the Velkaryans, believes it may be a clue to a lost cache of alien weapons. Homeworld Security enlists Carson, together with a starship pilot, Jacqueline "Jackie" Roberts, and Carson's timoan partner, Marten, to decipher the clue and find whatever it points to before the Velkaryans do.

On a planet orbiting the star Chara, thirty light years on the far side of terraformed space, they find a mysterious pyramid and its high-tech contents. After several run-ins with the Velkaryans, gaining an ally named Rico, they manage to return, but some of what they found was destroyed.

In *The Reticuli Deception*:

Captain Jackie Roberts uses the star patterns inscribed on several similar talismans to discover that they were drawn from a common point-of-view, a point somewhere near the Zeta Reticuli star systems. Carson recalls a legendary UFO encounter, the Betty Hill Incident, after which Ms. Hill drew a star map she claimed to have seen while aboard the alien craft. That map showed "trade routes" from Zeta Reticuli to our sun and other nearby stars. But the records of the map are second and third hand, virtually illegible.

Roberts, with Carson and Marten, takes her ship, *Sophie*, to Zeta Reticuli. Rico and another Homeworld Security man,

Brown, go to Earth to try to retrieve the original UFO reports. Everyone runs into trouble. A Velkaryan team, led by a man named Reid, also wants those files. Rico is shot and left for dead, but Brown escapes. En route to Zeta Reticuli, Roberts and company are initially refused landing on Verdigris, but land anyway. They find another pyramid, this one already broken into.

They continue on to Zeta Reticuli, where they have a close encounter of the third kind with a mysterious alien and another run-in with Velkaryans in the person of a man named Vaughan and his ship *Carcharodon*. The aliens temporarily isolate the Velkaryans, while our heroes return home empty-handed but for their knowledge of the encounter.

In *The Eridani Convergence:*

A Timoan starship pilot, Tevnar, finds a wreck on a planet orbiting Kapteyn's star, a red dwarf.

Vaughan and the *Carcharodon* awake in deep space, leaving Zeta Reticuli. They set course to Tanith, orbiting 82 Eridani, to refuel and make minor repairs.

Jackie Roberts has resumed her cargo and courier business, and at Tau Ceti gets a message from Ducayne of Homeworld Security that he needs something picked up on Tanith. There, she meets up with Ducayne's agent, Jordan Burnside. He still hasn't retrieved the package, a possible artifact. Worse, she sees the *Carcharodon* in port.

Carson has a run-in on Sawyers World. Ducayne, to get him away and wanting someone to validate the artifact, sends him to 82 Eridani also.

Tevnar found the artifact in the wreck at Kapteyn's star. Vaughan wants it too, but is recalled to the planet Verdigris. He attempts to grab it before leaving, but after a gun battle, ultimately departs without it. Burnside wants to pursue him to find out what was so urgent. He goes with Tevnar. Carson and Roberts take the *Sophie* to Kapteyn's where they briefly examine the wreck, then head home. Later, Tevnar reports that Burnside stayed on Verdigris to investigate further.

Chapter 1: The Sleeper Wakes

Elsewhere.

RICO OPENED HIS eyes, or thought he did; it stayed dark. There was a faint smell, like a mix of medicinal and electronic odors, and he could hear the faint hum of machinery. Where was he? He tried to remember. There had been the firefight at the Denver Spaceport. Brown had already boarded the ship when Reid and the others showed up. Rico had been covering Brown's escape with the files he'd retrieved. He remembered seeing the ship lift; Brown had gotten away. Then pain, and everything had gone dim. He'd been shot. Rico now knew where he was. *In a traumapod. Again.*

Crap. Maybe the Velkaryans who'd been shooting at him had left him for the police to find, but it was more likely that it was the Velkaryans who had managed to get him to the traumapod. Their intentions wouldn't be friendly. He'd almost rather be held by the police. Any third option was unlikely. He groped around the pod's interior, surprised that he wasn't restrained. He wondered if there were any way to get out of the pod, and then escape from wherever the pod was, without being caught. The release button should be about—

"Ah, Mr. Lee. Or should I say Rico?" the voice came over the traumapod's internal speaker. "I see you're finally awake."

Well, so much for plan A, thought Rico.

The head end of the traumapod opened up and Rico blinked against the bright light. The platform or cot on which he was lying slid out, and Rico saw his . . . captors? Rescuers? The two of them didn't look like cops. One was garbed in something that looked like nurse's scrubs, he must be the med-tech. The other wore plain civilian clothes, not too casual, like office wear. Both looked to be tough, no-nonsense types. Not uniformed cops, but the guy in civvies might be a detective, or an agent for some bureau. Or, they could be Velkaryan agents.

"How are you feeling?" the plain-clothed man asked. The question was asking for data; there was no empathy in it.

Rico took inventory. He remembered bruises down his left side from the car he'd deliberately crashed, and gunshot wounds to his right thigh and left shoulder. Had there been another one? He didn't remember. All he felt now was the general weakness from spending time out cold in the pod, and some itching where he'd been shot. The rapid cell regrowth, no doubt.

"I've been worse, especially considering," he said. "How long?" Then he added, "And who is Rico?"

"I'll ask the questions. And nice try, but the government DNA tagging doesn't hide who you really are, it just tells the ID scanners not to ask. What happened to Hopkins? We have reports that you were working for him."

Really? Interesting. Hopkins had been Rico's boss before they had gotten involved with Carson and that disastrous trip to Chara III. The truth couldn't hurt here. "No, he's dead. Malfunction with one of his ship-to-ship missiles. I don't know all the details. I was in the back of the *Starhawk*, Hopkin's ship, flash-blinded from an earlier explosion, when something blew up. We must have crashed. I came to later with a massive concussion. A couple of folks had stumbled over the wreckage and got me into a traumapod. I don't know if anyone else survived, but I'm pretty sure Hopkins didn't." Okay, so it wasn't the *whole* truth.

"What was with the shootout at Denver Spaceport?"

Interesting. 'Denver Spaceport', not 'the spaceport'. So they weren't in Kansas, or Colorado, anymore. "Ask the other guys, they started it. *Aaugh!*" His abdomen cramped as something delivered a sharp shock to it.

"That's what you get for lying. It was actually you who fired the first shots. So, why?"

Rico wondered if they had some kind of lie-detecting technology built into the traumapod, or if they already knew more than they were letting on. Possibly both. "If you know that much, you can guess why. He tried to run me down with his car, and then he was reaching for a gun." Close enough to the truth. "Don't I get a lawyer or something?"

"A lawy—? Oh, no, we're not the police."

He'd figured as much; his question had been a diversion. On the other hand, there was something vaguely cop-like about the guy, not what he'd expect from the Velkaryans or any of the thugs he'd been around when running illegal artifacts for Hopkins.

"Then who—"

"I'm the one asking questions. The people you were exchanging shots with, who were they?"

That was a surprise. "You don't know?" Maybe they weren't Velkaryans either. Then who?

The man just frowned at him, saying nothing.

"Okay, one of the guys was named Reid." Rico paused, considering how much to say next. "Uh, you know my name, and about Hopkins. I think Reid was in the same line of business." Well, sort of. Rico braced for a shock, but it didn't come.

"Artifact smuggling? You were shot in the parking lot of a courier outfit, but the only business they were doing that day was off the planet, not receiving anything. Was it something stolen from an Earth collection? What?"

Rico chose his words carefully, not wanting to invite another shock. "As far as I know there were no alien artifacts, stolen or otherwise, being shipped out. Certainly I didn't steal any. Maybe Reid did," he said. It had been stolen files, not alien artifacts, and apparently nobody had yet made the connection to a missing shipment from the Steel Mesa storage facility. "Are you sure you're not cops?" Because they definitely weren't asking the kind of questions a Velkaryan might.

The other ignored the question. "Where did you get your DNA tags?"

That had been Quentin Ducayne's doing, just before this little expedition to Earth. Ducayne was a very secretive guy, as was his organization, connected with Homeworld Security. "I don't think I'm allowed to say."

The other glanced at a display and grunted. "Huh, well that seems true enough. Was it government?"

Rico figured that lying about it would just take them down a pathway he didn't want to follow. "Yes."

"All right, we'll take that at face value for now." He looked over at the med-tech. "How's he doing?"

The tech scanned a readout on the traumapod, which was obviously still monitoring the sensors stuck to Rico's body. "Better than I'd have expected, but he should go back in the pod for a while longer."

"Okay Rico, back to bed. We'll talk more later."

"Wait. You're not a cop, and you're not an, uh, associate of Reid. Who are you?"

"I'll get back to you on that." With that he turned and left the room.

Rico considered overpowering the med-tech and making a break for it, but the guy had a good fifteen centimeters in height and twenty kilos mass advantage over him. In his still-weakened condition, and not knowing where he'd be making a break to or from, it was best to wait. He lay back on the cot. "Okay," he told the tech, "go ahead and tuck me in."

The tech's eyes narrowed, but wordlessly he touched a control and the cot slid back into the pod, which closed itself around him.

What the fuck *is going on here?* Rico wondered as he heard the slight hiss of anesthetic gas introduced to the chamber. It came to him just as his consciousness faded. *Oh no. Not more spooks.*

Chapter 2: Talisman

Drake University, Sawyer's World

DR. HANNIBAL CARSON, Professor of Exoarcheology, heaved a sigh and looked up from his desk monitor and gazed at the wall. On the screen was yet another in a stack of virtual papers, the mid-term tests of his Archeology 201 class. They had already been checked and graded by his assistant, but he was the final arbiter and it was his responsibility to enter the grades into the records system. It was mind-numbingly tedious work, and he hated it. It wasn't the tediousness per se, he could be diligent about meticulously excavating a site with a brush and trowel, it was the office he hated. He would much rather be in the field. Even hacking through the jungle on the planet Verdigris, mosquitoes and all, was preferable to this.

He turned his attention back to the mid-term. He updated the student's entry in the grading sheet, closed the file, and opened the next. The knock at his door was a welcome reprieve.

"Come in," he called.

A young woman entered, green-haired, and dressed casually in ship coveralls. "Well, this is different," Jackie Roberts said. "I'm not used to seeing you doing desk work."

"Jackie! I haven't seen you for a while. What are you doing here?"

She held up the small package she was carrying in her left hand and waved it. "Special delivery. It's not really, I just saw your name on it and decided to bring it over myself. I just got back from the Solar System and it was among the packages I was carrying."

Jackie Roberts owned and operated a small starship, the *Sophie*, and was a licensed courier.

"Solar System? You were on Earth? I thought you hated the place."

"Technically I was on Luna, I never set foot on Earth. Ducayne asked me to give Regina Elliot a ride, and this package was one of a handful waiting for carriage back here. I got lucky on the timing."

Carson reached for the package, but Roberts pulled it back. "You need to acknowledge receipt."

"Oh, sure." Carson scanned his omniphone over the package, and the two exchanged digital signatures. Somewhere on the network, a database updated to indicate his receipt. Roberts released her hold on the small package. "Who's Regina Elliot?" he asked as he took the package.

"Haven't you met her? She's Ducayne's deputy assistant, or whatever her official title is. His second in command."

"Oh. No, I don't think I have." He looked the package over. It was about fifteen centimeters square and five thick. It could have been a book, except it was unlikely anyone would go to the trouble and expense of shipping a book this far. He wasn't expecting any packages. He examined the shipping label. It was indeed addressed to him, care of the university, but the sender information was a coded address that he couldn't figure out.

"Help me out here, Jackie. Where's this from?"

"I picked it up on Luna," she said, taking it back to read the label. "It had just come in on another flight, I'm not sure where from." With almost no exceptions, any flight coming in from another star landed on Luna first, still technically enforcing the quarantine regulations set down fifty years earlier, although these days that amounted to little more than a document and customs screening and changing to an Earthbound shuttle. Jackie scanned her omni across the package then read something off its screen. "My, my. It's been transshipped a few times, originally it came from—" she scrolled down the display "—Wolf 25, by way of Eta Cassiopeiae. One Doctor Peterson, just care of the spaceport on Wolf 25 II." She handed the package back to him. "Someone you know? Artifacts or something? I better not have just smuggled in something illicit."

He flipped the package over, looking at it curiously. He didn't know any Dr. Peterson that he could recall. "It's still sealed, wouldn't your courier status protect you?"

"It would, and I was joking. The whole cargo was scanned and inspected anyway, so you don't have to worry about that being a bomb, either."

He glanced up at her sharply. He had been running into unsavory characters lately, and had escaped a kidnap attempt not that long ago. Would somebody want him dead that badly? "A bomb?"

Roberts rolled her eyes. "No, I just told you. Lighten up, Carson." She paused, then grinned and added, "But wait until I leave before you open it, okay?"

"Funny. Very funny. Just for that—" he tore the package's plastic wrapper open.

A smaller package, an opaque, padded, specimen bag, fell out of the envelope. There was also a sheet of paper. He unfolded it and read the text printed on it.

> "Dr. Hannibal Carson," it read,
> "I heard you were looking for things like this. Sorry, but I don't know the provenance of any of them. I inherited these as part of a collection of alien artifacts, most of them probably illegally acquired, which is why I choose to remain anonymous. The rest are going to other archeologists or museums.
> Best regards, A Friend."

"What does it say?" Roberts asked.

"Someone is getting rid of a collection of illegal artifacts they inherited, and thought I might be interested in these. We get such things from time to time. Unfortunately, with no provenance it's not going to be very useful. But let's see if I can at least figure out what planet they originally came from." So saying, he opened the specimen bag and slid out a small folded cloth bundle onto his desk. He unfolded it to reveal handful of artifacts.

"Oh, my," Roberts said when she saw them. Carson himself was speechless.

There was an obsidian arrowhead, a woven bracelet with small embedded shells that Carson recognized as coming from a planet orbiting Gliese 68, and a pair of small abstract figurines that looked to be made of fired clay. They were irrelevant. What had caught his attention, and Jackie's, was the largest item in the small collection.

It was about ten centimeters square—if the rounded shape could be called a square—and looked like it was made of stone, with a scattering of embedded cabochon-cut gemstones connected by engraved lines. Carson and Roberts had seen its like before. It was a talisman, just like—except for a different pattern of gems—the one they had used to both locate, and to open, the alien pyramid on the planet St. Jacobs, also known as Chara III.

∞ ∞ ∞

"Is it real?" Roberts asked in a hushed voice. The network-wide search that Carson had run looking for items similar to his original find had turned up several others, a few of them fakes. With a demand for alien artifacts, suppliers weren't above selling a few counterfeits. What could the buyers do, complain to the authorities?

Carson glanced at the other items. They looked real enough, although the best fakes would. He picked up the talisman and hefted it. It was heavier than its stone appearance would suggest. If it were a real Spacefarer talisman, it would have sophisticated circuitry inside powered by a very long-lived technetium battery. This felt like other, real examples he'd held. The pattern of gems and lines—a star map—looked authentic too, but he wasn't the expert on that. He held that up to show Jackie. "What do you think, does this look like a real star map?"

"It does look similar to the real ones. I won't know without running a comparison against my star charts. I wonder where it points to?"

"I wonder where it was originally found," Carson said, "but that's a more difficult question. Anyway, run your analysis against a picture of this one and we'll know where it points to."

"Sure," Jackie said, and used her omni to photograph the talisman from several angles. "Since I'm heading back to the *Sophie*, do you want me to take this one to Ducayne? He's beginning to get quite a collection."

She was right. The partial talisman he'd found on Verdigris, and three others that had turned up in his earlier network search were now in Ducayne's possession at Homeworld Security "for safe keeping". Another, the talisman that Carson and his colleague, Marten, had found on a different dig, was now also in Homeworld Security's care, with the team currently examining the pyramid on Chara III, to which that talisman was a key. It irked Carson that he was getting sidelined from following up on the discoveries he himself had made. He made his decision. "No," he said, "I'd like to examine this one first. In fact, I'd appreciate it if you didn't mention it to Ducayne just yet."

She looked at him and cocked her head, eyes narrowing. "What are you up to, Hannibal?"

"Nothing, yet. I just want a chance to do some investigation of my own, without Ducayne's 'mission priorities' getting in the way. For one thing, these other items might give me a hint as to where this came from." That is, if they were all from the same planet, but as far as he knew, figurines like that did not come from Gliese 68.

She peered at him for a moment, as if trying to read his intentions, and then relaxed and shrugged. "Okay. Not really my business, I'm just the delivery girl. They're your artifacts. But I'm curious, so let me know what you come up with." She grinned, and added, "Especially if you want me to tell you where the map points to."

"Fair trade. I just want to avoid any arguments with Ducayne about who gets to hold onto this," he said, picking up the talisman, "which is easier if he doesn't know about it." He glanced at the time. "Anyway, I have a class to teach soon, and I really should finish up grading these mid-terms." He folded the artifacts back into their cloth, put them into the sample bag, and put it away in a desk drawer. "Thanks for coming by, Jackie. I'd much rather talk to you than do this," he gestured at his monitor, "but duty calls."

"All right," she said. "I need to get back anyway." She opened the door to leave, then turned to him, adding "I'd tell you to stay out of trouble, but I know that's asking too much." She winked at him and, before he could utter a reply, left.

Chapter 3: Ricardo Questioned

Elsewhere

THE LIGHT CAME on and Rico's pallet slid out of the trauma-pod. He definitely felt better than when he'd last awakened, whenever that had been.

"So, Ricardo, shall we continue our conversation?"

Ricardo? Nobody had called him that in a long time. "You keep coming up with these names. Who is Ricardo?"

"You are. The Lee alias aside, more usually known as Rico. But you were born Ricardo Alvarez Chang."

Shit. The name brought back uncomfortable memories. "Never call me that again."

His questioner must have caught the edge in his tone. He looked at Rico and raised an eyebrow. "We'll call you whatever you want if you cooperate with us, Rico."

"Cooperate with who? You say you're not cops, and you're not Velkaryans. What's your name, and who are you?"

"You don't need my name, and we're the good guys, Rico."

"Everyone is the good guy in their own story. Who are you really?" Rico decided to call the guy Agent Friday. He had no idea what day it really was, but the guy acted like some kind of agent.

"Department of Homeworld Defense," Friday said.

Ducayne's outfit? That didn't make sense. They'd know who he was and probably why he was here. Or was it Ducayne pulling the scam? Rico suddenly felt like a man out on a frozen lake who had just heard the ice crack under his feet.

"I wasn't aware the home-world needed defending. Who from?"

"No, you need to answer some of our questions. Those guys you were trading shots with, who were they?"

"I don't kn..*OWW!*" Rico flinched at the shock. Damn, he'd forgotten about their lie detector.

"Try again."

"Okay. I don't know for sure, but I think they were Velkaryans."

"Who or what are Velkaryans?"

"Don't tell me you don't know that," Rico said. "They have a freaking political party. And you didn't ask when I mentioned them earlier."

"What we do or don't know is irrelevant," Friday said. "I want to know what you know."

"Geez, all right." Rico gathered his thoughts. How much, or rather, how little could he get away with telling? "Also known as the Church of Divine Providence, they don't like aliens, and they think that T-Space planets were terraformed for humans. I guess technically the political party is separate from the church. They hired my boss Hopkins to retrieve some alien artifacts. Talismans."

"And did he? And you?"

Technically no, not talismans. "No. We ran into problems. Maybe that's why Reid was shooting at me."

Agent Friday frowned at the display, then looked at the med-tech, who shrugged. Rico tensed, anticipating another shock. "I think you're lying, but there's an element of truth there."

"So why," he continued, "are the Velkaryans interested in alien artifacts if they don't like aliens?"

"Beats me," said Rico. "Know your enemy?" That was weak. "Maybe they're looking for something to prove aliens are danger-ous? You're Homeworld Defense, *are* there dangerous aliens out there?"

"We're asking the questions. What do *you* think? Are there?"

"The most dangerous alien I've ever seen was an angry tim-oan, so no, not really. Although I've heard stories about what a squad of irritated tree-squid can do, and it's not pretty."

"Tree-squids and timoans don't have spaceships." The latter wasn't strictly true, but timoans had purchased those.

"Nobody does but us humans," said Rico. "The Terraformers are as extinct as dinosaurs."

"Perhaps."

"What is that supposed to mean?"

"Nothing. But I think you misunderstood. We're not Earth's Homeworld Defense, or the *Union de Terre*'s Homeworld Security."

The med-tech spoke up. "Flicker on that last, sir," he said, still watching his instruments.

"Oh? You know something about Homeworld Security? Does the name Ducayne mean anything?"

Rico tried to evade the question. "What do you mean, 'not Earth's'?" Earth, via the *UDT*, also patrolled the settled planets. Except, wait, Alpha Centauri? Sawyers World? But that was where Ducayne's headquarters were. Unless that was just a field office. . .Rico realized he didn't know as much as he ought to about the outfit he was working for. The alternative had been jail.

"Another flicker on Ducayne, then a burst of activity. I think he's figuring it out."

Agent Friday looked at the med-tech then back at Rico. "Really? And what conclusion did you come to?"

Rico realized he didn't have any cards to play, so he just asked. "Does the Treaty of Alpha Centauri mean that Sawyers World has its own defense force?"

"Interesting question. I'll even answer it. Yes. Most people know it as Space Guard, and it's generally confined to law enforcement and space rescue in and around Sawyers and Kakuloa."

"So you guys are the freaking *Coast Guard*? What are you doing on Earth?"

"Not quite. And why do you think you're on Earth?"

"But, that's where I was shot!" If he wasn't on Earth, he was on some other Earth-like planet, from the gravity. Or in a ship in warp, except that there were none of the usual background noises of that. Then who had scooped him up from the spaceport?

"That's probably enough for now. You were in pretty bad shape, so a little longer in the traumapod wouldn't hurt. We'll have you out of there before long." He signaled the med-tech, who activated the retraction of the cot.

"But—"

"Next time."

As Rico drifted off under the influence of the traumapod's anesthetic, it occurred to him that the Space Guard could merely be the most visible side of Sawyers' Homeworld Defense, and if they were involved in anti-smuggling—and Rico knew they were, from experience—they probably had undercover operations as well. Is that what this was about? They wanted him to work an anti-smuggling operation? That still didn't answer how they'd got hold of him, though. He was out before he could pursue that line of thought further.

Chapter 4: Paleography

Drake University, Sawyer City, Sawyers World

HANNIBAL CARSON STRODE across the campus from his office to the Student Union building. It was one of the busier buildings on campus, and he could usually find an autocab that had just discharged its passengers there. Since the incident a few weeks ago, when a hacked autocab had tried to kidnap him, Carson was wary about using his own omniphone to summon a cab. *Ducayne's professional paranoia has started to rub off on me*, he mused. At least he'd been off-planet for part of the time since then.

A cab was letting someone out just as Carson reached the building.

"Hold the cab, please!" Carson called to the young man who had just stepped from it.

The student looked at him in surprise, then turned to the still-open door and instructed the cab to wait.

"Thanks," Carson said as he slid into the seat, more to the student than to the cab, but the former was already on his way into the Union.

"*You are welcome*," the cab said in its slightly mechanical voice. "*Destination?*"

Carson shook his head. *Stupid robot.* "Sawyer Spaceport, main building," he said, and tapped his omni to authorize payment. That should be safe enough.

The UDT Homeworld Security office where he was headed was located somewhere under the spaceport, built as part of the original infrastructure and accessed through an aging hangar building. At least, that was the entrance Carson knew about, but he suspected there were others. Having the cab drop him at the main building was just simple cover; it was a short walk from there to the hangar.

He wasn't going there to see Ducayne this time. Doctor Malcom Brown — Carson knew Brown wasn't his real name, but that's how they'd been introduced, and it sufficed — had called to let Carson know that he had "some interesting results regarding the paleography of two recent artifacts." To anyone overhearing the call, that would have sounded like just the sort of discussion of written languages that might interest Carson but would bore any non-archeologist. Carson, however, happened to know that the artifacts in question represented advanced technology and were found many light years apart.

One artifact had been pulled from the remains of a crashed ship on a non-terraformed planet orbiting Kapteyn's Star. The other, actually a group of artifacts, was millennia-old debris recently discovered on the seafloor off the coast of Belize, on Earth. Any comparison of the writing found on both would be very interesting indeed, archeologist or not.

∞ ∞ ∞

Sawyers World, UDT Homeworld Security

Carson found Brown in one of the conference rooms in the underground facility at the spaceport. The room, originally a simple briefing room with a large table, a dozen chairs and a wall-mounted combination display and sketchboard, had been converted to an archeology lab. The conference table now served as a lab bench, sporting several microscopes, cleaning tools, a camera stand, and other paraphernalia. Against one wall was another, smaller table on which sat chemical and spectrographic analysis machines. There was also a large locked cabinet that probably secured the artifacts when not being examined. Carson felt sure that this use of the room was something the original builders had never remotely anticipated.

"So, what have you found so far?" he asked Brown.

"Quite a bit, actually," Brown said, looking pleased. "Take a look at this." On a desktop monitor, he brought up a pair of side-by-side images. Each showed a grid, the cells of which held close-up images of parts of the artifact and wreckage which showed what they believed was writing. Each cell displayed a different glyph, arranged so that matching glyphs from each source occupied the equivalent location in either grid. There were many gaps, but the common subset was obvious.

"So the writing matches?" There were minor differences, but Carson guessed they could be attributed to the equivalent of font differences, or perhaps stylistic changes over the years between the two. "And have you determined an age for the Kapteyn's artifact?"

"I'd say the writing was a close enough match to say both objects were built by the same culture. Best guess on the Kapteyn's age is about seven-hundred years, considerably younger than what was pulled out of Belize. But there's more." He put another image up on the screen, showing side-by-side comparisons of two spectrographs, and of two mass-chromatograph readouts. They were remarkably similar.

"Again, the left side is Belize, the right side Kapteyn's. We analyzed samples taken from bits of metal tubing. The metallurgy is almost identical."

"That's surprising," Carson said. "Even if the tubing served identical functions in both ships, over a span of—what, twelve-hundred years or so?—you'd expect some differences in manufacturing processes."

"That's what I thought too. So either the composition is the absolute optimum choice for the function, or—"

"Or the culture made little technological progress over that time. I'm not sure which interpretation I like better."

"But it does definitively prove they *were* made by the same culture," Brown said.

"It proves the tubing was," Carson said, "but there could have been two cultures and one bought the tubing from the other in trade. Arguably the stylistic differences in the glyphs are due to cultural differences, but with similarities that indicate strong influences—such as trade—between the two."

Brown frowned. "All right. I'll grant that academic rigor means raising that as a hypothesis, but Occam's Razor says the opposite. There's still the difference in age. For that matter, the later device could have reused tubing salvaged from something older."

Carson shook his head slowly, more in bewilderment than negation. "My gut says no, but I can't point to any proof. We need a lot more data before we can start reconstructing the history of the civilization, or civilizations, that made these."

"And that's not what our focus is. That's the archeologist in you talking, which is fine, but it doesn't help us figure out what the Kapteyn's artifact actually did." Brown paused, then grinned and said, "And if you give me some archeologist crap about ritual objects or religious icons, I'll belt you one."

Carson chuckled. "Maybe if these were from a pre-technological society, I would. But no, I'm sure it was primarily functional. Where have you gotten with analyzing the internals? Any obvious functional subsystems or components?"

"As a matter of fact, yes. The electrical power distribution was pretty obvious. A conductive path is a conductive path; there are only so many variations on wires, circuit traces, or grounding you can make. Of course, that doesn't help when the circuit leads in and out of some featureless block which may or may not have other leads from it. And we've discovered all kinds of interconnection methods. Obvious electrical connections, of course. Also optical, with both fiber optic and some kind of integrated optical path."

"What do you mean?"

"Like the metal traces on a circuit board, but transparent and acting as a light conduit. Our opto-electronics guys say it's highly transparent and internally reflective. I'm still waiting on definitive chemical analysis, but they think it might be modified diamond or a lossless fluoride glass. The advantage over fiber is that it allows sharp corners where the signal is reflected around with low loss. Try that with fiber and you'd get a lot of leakage, assuming the fiber didn't just snap first."

Carson took a moment to digest that. He understood the words, but not the implications. "So, technology we don't have yet?"

Brown hesitated. "Not exactly. The guys think it could be reproduced at laboratory scale—probably they're working on that now—but nothing like that in mass production."

"What was the tubing for?" Carson asked.

"Some of it seems to have been for signal paths, like microwave conduits. Some of it seems to have been for cooling. Not all the tubing was the same composition, though. What I was referring to earlier was just certain samples that matched between the two artifacts; there was other tubing and conduit that didn't."

"Oh, okay." Carson had been wondering about that.

"There are some other pipes or tubes that we have no idea what they were for. Heck, most of what's in there we have no idea about. Take the blocks on the circuit boards. They range in size from rice-grain to a couple of centimeters on a side, so in some ways similar to something you'd find in any piece of human equipment, although with enough differences in sizes, shapes and layout as to look strange."

"How do boards between the two sources compare?"

"Well, we haven't found much in the way of intact boards from the Belize wreckage. It looks like whatever the pieces came from was pretty thoroughly destroyed even before sitting on the bottom of the ocean for twelve hundred years. We found some shock patterns suggestive of a forceful explosion. But a few large pieces were recovered."

"And?" Carson prompted.

"Like the tubing. There are some similarities, in fact externally they're virtually identical, but other parts are unique. Of course, we won't know how similar the identical-looking parts are without microscopic analysis. Could you even tell a millimeter-sized resistor from a capacitor from a diode just by looking at them? And the unique pieces may have totally different functions, rather than being different designs for the same thing."

"So still not answering the question of different cultures," Carson said.

"Quite. But it does tell us one thing."

"What's that?"

"Some of the artifacts were, well, not one-offs, but probably low production volume items. They're not hand-crafted. Actually, even with our gear, very little is hand-crafted, we'd use a fabber. Anyway, one of my tech guys said that, even without knowing what they did, there were details that suggested they weren't de-signed for mass manufacture. For example, there was lot of the circuitry that could probably be reduced to a single integrated chip."

Carson understood. Devices produced in high volume—like the omniphone on his wrist, for example—had almost all their functionality in a single large chip, and the rest integrated into the smart materials that made up the display, morphable case, and any added unique gadgetry. Even something as complicated as a fusion unit or warp module, from what Carson had understood from talking with Jackie, was largely built up as a massively three-dimensional integrated device. By comparison, the first warp modules, of the sort used by Finley's first expedition, had been considerably larger and at least partly hand-assembled.

"So these were, if not prototypes, something not widely used, then?" Carson said.

"Very likely. Now, the Kapteyn's artifact is like that throughout. The pieces from Belize are a mix of parts that look mass-produced and things that look more like prototypes. We have fewer of the latter, and the pieces are smaller. But it's curious. How did we luck out on finding these instead of something more common, more mass-produced?"

That was a good question. Odds of randomly finding something rare were low. The more common something was, the more likely to find a discarded or broken version of it. Unless . . . .

"These were both found in crashed spacecraft, assuming that's what the Belize find is," Carson said. "Perhaps the more common version—later versions—were in spacecraft that didn't crash? Could these be related to why the spaceships crashed in the first place?"

Brown frowned. "That . . . sounds reasonable. But two different spacecraft a thousand years different in age? That doesn't make sense."

Carson had to agree. There was some factor they were missing. Did the Kesh just have phenomenally bad luck with developing new starship technology? The only actual flying Kesh ships Carson had seen had both been large, pyramid-shaped vehicles. There had been the wreckage that was spotted on an asteroid in the Epsilon Eridani system; it might have been the remains of a pyramid ship. Too bad it had been cleaned up before Ducayne's team had returned to recover the debris. What game were the Kesh playing?

His musings were interrupted by the room's intercom.

"Malcolm, this is Ducayne. If Carson is there with you, have him stop by my main office when you're done."

Chapter 5: Velkaryans

Church of Divine Stellar Providence Headquarters, Earth

THE EXECUTIVE PROJECTS DIRECTOR of the Velkaryans, a man named Hubble, looked at Reid across the elaborate, fossil-embedded surface of the conference table.

"We have a new assignment for you, Reid," said Hubble.

"Oh? What now?"

"You're going back to Sawyers World."

"Ah. I see." Reid had been transferred back to Earth several months ago, and his first assignment, to intercept certain files that Homeland Security seemed interested in, had gone badly wrong. "Is this by way of punishment?"

"No, not at all," Hubble said reassuringly. "Of course, we all wish the Blue Book exercise had gone better, but it wouldn't have happened at all if you hadn't recognized Rico aboard ship. Anyway, this assignment may be connected."

"Oh? How so?"

"The system that we had the *Carcharodon* follow Carson and Roberts to, Zeta Reticuli, is mentioned in one of the more infamous Blue Book UFO incidents. Anyway, since he returned, Hannibal Carson has been talking to members of the Original Eight. Elizabeth Sawyer herself several weeks ago, and more recently we've heard that he's trying to arrange a meeting with Peter Finley."

"They're still around?" Reid knew the names, of course, but as historical figures. They were part of the crew of the *USS Poul Anderson*, the first ship to land on the planet, stranded there for four years until the return mission. Still, they couldn't be much past their mid-eighties now, so there was no reason for them not to be still alive. They just stayed out of the news. "Carson, he's the archeologist, right? I take it you don't think he's just asking them to fund an expedition."

"If he is, we'd like to know just what expedition. But one of our analysts had a thought. Both Sawyer and Finley were geologists. We think there's a connection."

"Go on."

"There's a structure on Sawyers World near the *Anderson* landing site that Finley visited. It's called Pete's Peak, an ancient volcanic plug. The thing is, the original mission reports on it are scarce, likewise any investigation since. It's hard even to find good pictures of it online."

"I think I've heard of it. What's special about it?"

"We had some pictures taken from orbit. It's remarkably square for a volcanic neck."

"You think it might be a pyramid? Sawyers World doesn't have natives." Reid said. As far as he knew, any other worlds with pyramids had, or had in the past, alien primitives.

"Not now, as far as anyone knows, but old arrowheads and spearpoints have been found. They're probably at least a hundred thousand years old. But we think Carson is planning to investigate this peak. He must think there's something interesting there."

"I take it that you want me to go and see what he's up to."

"Exactly. If it *is* a pyramid, then we need to get whatever's inside it before anyone else does. *Especially* if there's the chance to get our hands on another communicator."

"That doesn't sound too hard. The *Anderson* landing area is a long way from any civilization, aside from the local museum and visitors site. How far is this peak from that?"

"About sixty-five kilometers, but there's an added complication. The pyramid, or peak, is smack in the middle of the Anderson Wildlife Preserve. It's the only known habitat of Finley's leopard."

"What kind of bullshit is that? A wildlife preserve? For a leopard? Sawyers World is still mostly wild areas. Do they even know if it's endangered?"

"Probably not, and it's the only such preserve on Sawyers World. Oh, there are designated wilderness areas, but that's different. It's more likely that this preserve is a cover story."

Reid didn't like the implications. "That would mean the Sawyers World government knows about the pyramid, wouldn't it? That does complicate things."

"The official story is that they were worried about the leopard being hunted for its fur. The furs *did* fetch a very high price during the first few years of interstellar trade. And we've seen nothing that would indicate the government overall is aware of the alien pyramid-builders. It is possible that a small inner circle does. That kind of information would be kept quite secret."

Reid nodded. Nobody—not the UDT government, not the Velkaryans, and probably not the Sawyers World government—wanted the general populace being aware that there were space-faring aliens out there whose technology seemed to exceed, by far, that of humans. The Terraformers were so long ago that the man-on-the-street could easily write them off as semi-mythical, or a bizarre hypothesis dreamt up by planetologists who couldn't otherwise explain how the planets got the way they did. The official Velkaryan position was that God created them that way for humans to occupy. Space-travelling aliens were something out of science fiction, or were otherwise primitive species who had been given technology by misguided humans. *Traitors to their own species*, Reid thought, disgusted.

"But if it's a wildlife preserve, surely they're not going to let Carson or anyone else do any digging."

"Ordinarily, no. But Carson seems to have some influential friends and can be very persuasive. Maybe nothing will come of it, but Carson seems to have crossed our path a few times in the past year. It's worth keeping an eye on him; he might be working with Homeworld Security, at least part-time."

"Those bastards. I owe them one." Reid had been wounded in a shoot-out with what were probably *UDT* agents at the Denver Spaceport. They'd managed to get away with the files he'd been after, but they'd had to leave one of their own, Rico, behind, riddled with bullets.

"Regardless. Anyway, take the next ship out and report in to local headquarters."

"That would be Maynard, right?" Reid had come here to Earth from Sawyers World, but that hadn't been his main base, just his last stop.

"Not anymore. He and his ship, the *Star Wind*, disappeared a year ago. Carson may have been involved, but we're not certain. You might ask him if the opportunity arises. Anyway, the man in charge now is Deitrich. The details will all be in your orders. Pick them up on your way out."

"Deitrich. Got it." Reid rose to leave, already thinking about the mission. It should be interesting.

Chapter 6: Meeting Arranged

Ducayne's office, UDT Homeworld Security

CARSON REPORTED TO Ducayne's office, the one hidden below ground rather than the public one in the hangar, and found Jackie Roberts there too. "You wanted to see me? What's up?" he asked, looking from one to the other, wondering if Roberts had said anything about the new talisman.

She may have guessed his thoughts, because she shook her head slightly and said, "Don't mind me." She began to rise from her seat, "I was just on my way out."

"You can stay," said Ducayne. "This isn't anything you don't already know about." He turned to Carson. "I wanted to let you know that your meeting with Peter Finley has been arranged."

"Finally," Carson said. He had been waiting for this for a couple of weeks now. "When?"

"He's invited you out to his estate tomorrow. I know that's short notice but—"

"But tomorrow is Thursday, a day I don't have any classes to teach," Carson said, wondering if Ducayne had access to his personal calendar. It wouldn't have surprised him.

"Exactly."

"Have you made any progress on tracking down who hacked the autocab that tried to kidnap me?"

Ducayne shook his head. "That's more of a Sawyers World matter. I've referred it to the local authorities, and they'll keep me posted. We have an understanding."

Carson looked over at Jackie. "Does your offer of giving me a ride out there still stand? I think I'd prefer even your bike to an autocab." The kidnap attempt had been immediately after his meeting with another of the legendary first landing team on

Sawyers World, Elizabeth Sawyer herself. He had managed to escape from the moving cab, but with some loss of skin and a cracked rib.

Jackie smiled back at him. "Of course it does. Do you think I'd miss a chance to meet one of the First Landers?"

Carson shrugged. "You've been a first lander yourself on a number of planets."

"Mostly when I was a kid," she said, "and none of them humanity's first venture out of the Solar System."

"Be that as it may," Ducayne said, "there's no need to take Jackie's bike. You can use one of our aircars."

Carson and Roberts looked at each other, then back at Ducayne. "Sure," they both said.

"Is there a catch?" Carson asked.

"Probably," Roberts said before Ducayne could answer. "I'm still paying him back for the work on the *Sophie*."

Ducayne frowned. "Your ship repairs and upgrades were the result of a fair agreement, Captain Roberts," he said, "not 'a catch'." His expression softened, and he added, "Anyway, all I want from Carson is a post-meeting debriefing."

"That, I can do." Carson said.

∞ ∞ ∞

Jackie Roberts and Carson left the office. As Ducayne's door closed behind them, Carson asked her, "Were you *trying* to piss him off? What was that all about?"

"What?" *Where did* that *come from?* she wondered. "He wasn't pissed off, just playing along. Believe it or not, Quentin Ducayne does have a sense of humor."

"Really? I've never known him to crack a joke, as such. But I suppose you're right. I've seen him angry, and he wasn't anywhere close to that."

"He doesn't joke often, but I've seen it. Maybe I know him better than you do."

"Just how well *do* you know him?"

That wasn't just asking for information. To her, it felt like there was something accusatory about the question. Was Carson jealous? Of *Ducayne?* Her incipient anger turned to amusement. "Carson, while you're off at your university teaching, I've been here either supervising repairs and upgrades to the *Sophie* or helping them understand the alien technology we've encountered. And half my off-planet runs are couriering for Ducayne. Of course I know him."

"You're helping with alien technology? Since when are you an archeologist?"

Jackie stopped and wheeled on Carson. "*Archeologist?* Is *that* what you think it takes to understand this stuff? You and Marten would still be in that pyramid on Chara III if I hadn't figured out their language from that periodic table of the elements." That wasn't quite how it had happened, but it got her point across. "That stuff is high tech, not stone relics. Let me remind you that I grew up around starships, my mother is an astrophysicist, and I pilot a starship of my own. I just might know a bit more about alien technology than you do."

Carson stepped back, his hands raised. "Whoa, I'm sorry, I didn't mean anything by it. You're right. I think of those things as archeological artifacts. Ducayne wants to know what they're supposed to do and how they work."

"Exactly," she said, calming down. "Look, Ducayne and I work together, sometimes. Technically he's one of my clients. I'm on a retainer for the work he had done on *Sophie*, and I'll be happy when I'm free of that." With a smirk, she added, "You have nothing to be jealous about."

"Jealous!" Carson sputtered. "Who said anything about—" He saw her smirk broaden into a grin. "Ha, ha. Very funny," he said.

But Jackie heard a hint of protesting too much in his tone.

Chapter 7: Finley

Outside Sawyer City

HANNIBAL CARSON WAS unreasonably nervous about this meeting. Peter Finley was almost as legendary as Elizabeth Sawyer. Like her, Finley had been aboard the *Chandrasekhar*—the original, *Anderson*-class ship, not the Drake University Sapphire of the same name—for the first landing on Kakuloa, and of course was one of the Original Eight who landed on this planet in the *USS Poul Anderson,* over fifty years ago. He ranked up there with the Apollo moon-walkers, and that was aside from the not-inconsiderable influence over affairs on Sawyers World that he and his family had. He was an original signer of the Treaty of Alpha Centauri, after all.

Carson and Jacqueline Roberts were in Ducayne's aircar, cruising toward Finley's estate outside of town. Roberts was at the controls, focused on her flying, while Carson looked out the window. As he gazed out over the terrain, a dark spot against the sky caught his eye. He looked away, scanning the horizon, and then looked back. It was still there.

"Not to make you nervous," he said to Jackie, "but there's another aircar that's been at our five-o'clock position for the last few minutes."

Roberts glanced back over her shoulder. "I'm not seeing it. How far away?"

"About two kilometers," Carson estimated, eyeing the tiny speck. A quick glance would have missed it. "It's been keeping a constant distance for as long as I've been watching. Do you suppose it's following us?"

She glanced back again. "Okay, I've got it now. There's not much else in this direction," she said. "So it's unlikely to be a coincidence. Want me to find out?"

He knew Roberts was a good space pilot, but he'd never flown with her in an aircar. Since they were usually as self-contained as autocabs, he wasn't even sure what she could do. But he trusted her flying skills, and this *was* one of Ducayne's cars. This could be interesting. He cinched his seat belt tighter. "Go for it," he said.

"Hold on." She reached under the dash and flicked a concealed switch, then immediately tilted the aircar thirty-degrees to the left while bumping up the throttle. The car took off sideways at high speed, the rotors now both lifting and pushing them laterally. Carson felt himself partly hanging sideways in his seat, trying not to crowd Jackie, who wore a huge grin on her face. He looked back again, to see the speck now moving closer and turning to intercept.

"Yeah," Carson said, "I'd say they were following us."

"All right then, let's get them lost, shall we?"

∞ ∞ ∞

Jackie settled in for some serious flying. The previous maneuver had just been to confirm that they were being followed. She checked the instruments and looked out, around, up and down. Plenty of room.

"How are we going to lose them?" Carson asked. "There's not exactly anywhere to hide out here."

"Wrong," she said, and pointed upward. They had been flying at about a thousand meters above ground level, with visibility an easy twenty kilometers before ground haze obscured it. Two thousand meters above them, the sky was half-obscured by a broken cloud layer.

Carson leaned forward and looked up through the forward window. "Seriously?"

"Have you ever known me to joke about flying?" That should shut him up. She had to concentrate. She increased thrust, the rotor whine building to a scream, and the car rose like a fast elevator.

She looked back and glanced at the mirrors, but couldn't make out the other car from that angle. "Carson, where are they?"

He managed to look back and down out the side window. "They're trying to follow, but you've got an edge on speed," he said.

"Copy that."

They were almost at the cloud layer. The view out the window disappeared into a foggy whiteness, and she cut power to maintain level flight.

"We're going to stay in this?" Carson asked. "I thought you were going to climb above it."

"It's the only way to stay hidden," she said, turning the aircar to a new vector.

"What about radar?"

Aircars were equipped with collision-avoidance radar, Carson must be thinking they could track her with it. Fat chance.

"If theirs is standard, it will have limited range," she said. "But just in case. . . ." She reached under the dash for another of Ducayne's hidden switches, and flipped it. There were advantages to aircraft that belonged to an intelligence agency. "There. Scrambled."

Carson was looking out the window, although there was nothing to see beyond the car but milky white. "So how long do we stay in this stuff?" he asked.

Jackie scanned the instruments. The navigation system was perfectly happy listening to satellites and its own internal inertial sensors, it didn't need to see to know where they were going. "I can stay here until Finley's place. The only concern is. . ." she touched a screen on the dash, and the display changed to show the outside temperature. Hmm, that could be a problem.

"Is what?"

"Icing conditions. That cloud out there is like heavy fog. Condensation will just blow off, but if it starts to freeze. . . ." She didn't finish the thought.

"But the car has heaters for the rotors, right?"

That was the problem. A little ice on the body was no big deal, the car had plenty of reserve lift. But ice on the rotors would change their shape and disrupt the airflow, and they'd lose lift quickly.

"No, too much drain on the batteries," she said. "These things aren't designed to fly into icing conditions. One of these days we'll get fusion units that will fit in an aircar, but not yet." She kept the concern out her voice, thanks to long practice with not upsetting the passengers. The one compensating factor was that the high RPMs of the rotors would tend to fling any water off before it froze, at least until they got so cold that they didn't. She kept checking the temperature display. She became aware that Carson was watching her do so.

"We've probably lost them," he said, his voice tense. "Besides, what can they do? So they follow us to Finley's, that doesn't tell them anything. Whoever they are."

"You're right," she said, and immediately dropped the throttle back. The aircar plummeted, but she kept it horizontal. She saw some thin flakes of ice flutter upward in the slipstream, but Jackie was pretty sure they were from the body, not the rotors. She would have felt the difference.

Carson had seen them too. She was impressed that he relaxed back in his seat as though nothing untoward had happened. A few moments later they fell clear of the clouds and she stopped their descent, proceeding on course. At least he appreciated her flying skills.

Ten minutes later, Jackie cleared the landing with the estate's security system and settled the aircar onto a broad parking area adjacent to the driveway of the Maclaren-Finley estate, in front of the residence. The building was large but hardly palatial. It wasn't the mansion she had been half expecting, but it was big enough. As the aircar's rotors wound down to a stop, Carson popped open his door.

∞ ∞ ∞

Carson climbed out of the car while Roberts double-checked the shutdown sequence. He stood and took a deep breath. *Relax,* he told himself, *just think of him as a professor of geology, and not as one of the Original Eight.* He took another breath and started toward the front door. It opened as he was halfway to the front porch. A man stood at the entrance. He looked to be in his fifties, but if this was Peter Finley—and he certainly resembled the pictures Carson had seen—he would be in his late eighties. No doubt Finley was a beneficiary of the anti-aging drugs that had triggered Kakuloa's original economic boom. The man wore casual clothing, jeans and a worn khaki field shirt. His eyes were bright and alert.

"Doctor Carson, I presume?" the man said, holding out his hand.

"Uh, yes," Carson said, taking the offered hand to shake. "Doctor Peter Finley?" The man's grip was firm.

"The same. Call me Pete." He looked toward the aircar. "You brought a pilot?"

"I recently had trouble with an autocab. And she's a friend of mine." Carson didn't see any point in mentioning their little side excursion on the way here.

"Well, she doesn't have to wait out here." He called to Roberts and beckoned her towards the house. "Come on in, both of you," he said, waving Carson and Roberts inside.

"Thank you, sir, uh, Pete. Thank you for agreeing to see me. It's an honor to meet you. Call me Carson, or Hannibal. This is Jackie Roberts, she's a pilot and the owner of the starship *Sophie*." Carson felt himself reddening. Had he really just gushed like a schoolgirl?

Finley turned to Roberts. "Jackie Roberts? Would that be Jacqueline Roberts? Born on the Eta Carinae Expedition? You look about the right age."

Roberts blushed, surprising Carson. "That would be me. Although I can't say I remember much about it, I was four when we got back. I'm flattered you've heard of me."

"One pioneer to another, eh? Besides, I read all the Carinae planetology reports. Fascinating stuff." Finley turned to Carson, who stood awkwardly, looking from one to the other.

"Relax, Carson," Finley said. "We're both field scientists. I don't bite, despite what you may have heard."

"Well, the Original Eight do have bit of a reputation," Carson said, following as Finley continued inside.

"Yeah, we do, and that term is part of the damn problem. 'Original Eight' indeed. We were a bunch of eager kids stupid enough to volunteer for what we knew could be a one-way trip and lucky enough to hang in for four years until Drake came back in the *Endeavour*. Much less organized than the Carinae Expedition. But you know our story, I'm sure."

Carson did. He hesitated, then said, "They teach it in school. Part of the required history courses here, although not on Earth when I was growing up."

"History courses," Finley shook his head. "Lord, I shudder to think. But you're not here to talk about that," the latter was almost an order rather than a statement or question. "Have a seat." They had entered a living room off the main entrance foyer, and Finley gestured to chairs. "Want a beer? I'm going to have one."

"A beer would be nice, thanks."

Finley looked at Roberts. "Jackie? A beer, or something else?"

"I'm flying. Just water is fine."

Finley nodded approvingly. "Smart lass." He whistled sharply, then said in a raised voice: "Robot, bring us a couple of beers and a water!"

That Finley had a house robot shouldn't have surprised Carson, since they weren't much more complex than the aircar he'd ridden here in, but nobody he knew owned one. They were expensive; most general-purpose robots were used in construction and manufacturing, where their productivity made it worth the cost. Even there they were scarce. Between the continuous influx of immigrants from Earth and the high local birthrate, human labor was readily available, and robots were still just beyond local manufacturing capability. Parts had to be imported from Earth, or time-consumingly built up in a general purpose fabber. Before Carson could stop himself, he blurted out, "You have a house robot?"

"Um, yes," Finley said, as though somewhat embarrassed. "It was a gift."

Just then a machine came gliding in, carrying a tray with the bottles of beer and water on it. It was like no robot Carson had ever seen, except perhaps in ancient low-budget sci-fi vids. A squat grey cylindrical torso with rounded edges was mounted on corrugated tubular legs, also grey. The legs in turn attached to a trapezoidal base, which rolled on flexible treads. The head, for lack of a better term, was a clear plastic flattened spheroid with some kind of machinery and lights inside. The torso also had a panel with lights and switches, and attached to the torso were flexible, corrugated arms that ended in red, claw-like grippers. The whole thing was easily two meters tall.

Holding the tray in one gripper—Carson couldn't quite fathom how that would be stable—it picked up a bottle of water in the other and handed it to Roberts, then did likewise with a bottle of beer to Carson, finally it turned to Finley and repeated the action, handing him a beer. It lowered the tray and then in a very mechanical voice asked, "*Will that be all, Doctor Finley?*"

"Yes, Robot. Thank you."

The robot turned and glided out of the room on its tracked feet, or foot. Carson noticed Roberts watching the robot, then looking at him and Finley. She looked like she was trying to keep from laughing.

"That, uh, that's not a standard robot." Carson said, half asking.

"Hah. No. Naomi built that for me. Something of a joke. There was an ancient TV show, pre-Apollo even, about the first trip to Alpha Centauri. The ship goes wildly off course. *Lost In Space*, it was called. The original had a robot like that, although it was different in the remakes. This one's more capable than it looks, though." Finley shook his head, then added almost apologetically: "My wife has a strange sense of humor."

"How did you, or she, even know about a TV series that old? I mean, I've heard of *Star Trek* of course, but. . . ?"

"Four years of no entertainment other than what was in the *Anderson*'s library. There was some pretty surprising stuff in there. Some joker must have included the original *Lost in Space* because of the Alpha Centauri connection. We all thought it was hysterical." Finley paused a moment, then shook his head. "Well, maybe not Krysansky. I'm not sure he ever quite got American humor."

He grew serious. "But enough of that, Carson. You came here to talk about my little mountain. Apparently, you think it might be a pyramid. Archeologist, eh?"

"Yes. Teaching at Drake University. Several field expeditions, including to Ransom's Planet, Verdigris, and Chara III, I mean, Saint Jacobs. It's the latter where we found the first real pyramid, after the copy on Verdigris."

"Where the hell is St. Jacobs, or Chara?"

Roberts answered. "Chara is a G-type star about twenty-nine light-years from here, on the far side of Sol. Also known as Beta Canum Venaticorum, near Ursa Major."

"What were you doing way the hell out there? Is that even part of T-Space?" He looked from Roberts to Carson, then back.

"Chara III is indeed terraformed," Carson said, "and there's a small colony on it. They named the planet St. Jacobs. But we were following a star map on an ancient talisman like the one I found on Verdigris."

Finley's eyes narrowed. He leaned forward, peering at Carson, studying his face. "Are you shitting me, boy?" he said, his tone almost threatening.

"No sir. I'd appreciate it if you didn't tell anyone about this, but. . . ." Carson unwrapped his omniphone from his wrist, unfolded the screen and tapped out a sequence, bringing up an image of the talisman, a rounded-square stone—Jackie had called the shape a supercircle—with several small cabochon-cut gems embedded in its surface, and with engraved lines connecting some of them. He passed the omni over to Finley. "That's the original talisman," Carson said.

"You're saying this is a star map?"

Roberts and Carson both nodded.

Finley examined the image. "It does look a bit like one." He handed the omni back to Carson. "What does that have to do with a volcanic neck near the *Anderson* landing site?"

"It's not really a volcanic neck, is it, Doctor?" Carson's use of the honorific was deliberate, playing on the man's scientific integrity.

Finley looked up at him sharply. "Three geologists in the original landing team and we all decided it was a volcanic neck. Who are you to say differently?"

Carson held firm. "That's not what you said when you and Sawyer first saw it, was it? Did it really look like an old volcanic neck?"

Finley sighed and sat back in his chair. "She told you about that, eh?" He took a swig from his beer and set the bottle on the side table. "Not like any other one I'd ever seen, no."

Chapter 8: Report from Earth

UDT Homeworld Security, Sawyer's World

"HOW WAS EARTH?" Quentin Ducayne asked the woman sitting across his desk from him, his second in command here. Regina Elliot had just returned on one of the regular passenger runs.

She shrugged. "It's as crazy as ever. Now I know why you delegate me for these visits back. Well, that and to minimize any chance of my interference with your little side projects."

Ducayne leaned forward to object, but Elliot continued, "What *are* Carson and Roberts up to these days, anyway?"

He sat back with a sigh. "See, that's what qualifies you for your position. You know me too well. If you must know—and I suppose you must—right now they're meeting with Peter Finley."

"*The* Peter Finley? What about? And isn't it a little risky letting them talk to one of the Founders about anything?"

Ducayne shrugged. "Technically Carson is a Sawyers World citizen, so he has every right to, despite what I told him about the Official Secrets Act and re-activating his UDT military security clearance. As for what they're talking about. . .you remember that report which had its classification lowered a few weeks ago, the one from Elizabeth Sawyer when the *Endeavour* returned to pick up her and the rest of the *Anderson* crew?"

Elliot looked at him, her eyes narrowing. "The possible alien sighting? What does that have to do with anything?"

"Carson paid her a visit a while back. Her alien matches a sketch he had made of the Kesh. She mentioned that Pete's Peak may not be a natural formation. Remember, she was a geologist, so she would know."

"So Carson is talking to Finley about whether his peak is really a pyramid? Aren't you worried he'll let something slip?"

Ducayne shook his head. "I was at first, then I realized that Sawyer, and Finley, and the rest of the original *Anderson* crew have been sitting on her alien sighting for fifty standard years without a peep. They know how to keep secrets, and more importantly, *why*."

Elliot considered this, then nodded her head. "That's fair. Since we're on the subject of Carson, what's the word from the team we sent to Chara?" A follow-up expedition to the pyramid discovered on Chara III had already been in the works when Carson reported his discovery of another hidden chamber in the similar pyramid on Verdigris, and the evidence that some alien technology had been forcibly removed from that chamber.

"Nothing yet," Ducayne said, "which means nothing urgent enough to expend a message torpedo on." He checked a calendar on his desktop monitor. "According to plan, the *Mandragore* should have left there a few days ago, so it should be back here in about three weeks." Chara, at the far end of known T-Space, was almost twenty-nine light-years away; it was a long trip.

"Anyway, enough about that." Ducayne continued, "What's the news from Earth?"

"I wrote up a report on the political situation while on the voyage here," Elliot said. "You can read it at your leisure, but there aren't any particular surprises. Venezuela under a Velkaryan government is doing about what we thought they would, with the expected results. Velkaryan sentiment is rising in some other countries. The UDT council is turning into a debating club."

Ducayne rubbed his brow. "Fantastic," he said, without enthusiasm. He looked up at her. "Speaking of Velkaryans. . . ?"

She shook her head, anticipating his question. "Nothing specific on Rico. I'm pretty sure they don't have him. As to what happened after the shootout, well, that's a story in itself. You won't believe it."

"Did they recover his body? I thought they hadn't."

"That's the thing. The last anybody saw of him, the local cops had him in a traumapod, still alive."

"The last? What happened?"

Regina sat forward in her seat and related the tale as she knew it, punctuated by Ducayne muttering, "You've got to be kidding me," face-palming, and shaking his head.

Chapter 9: The Chara Pyramid

Finley Estate, Sawyers World

CARSON LOOKED AT Pete Finley expectantly, waiting for him to continue. Finley said nothing, instead taking another sip from his beer bottle.

"You were saying," Carson prodded, "that it wasn't like any volcanic neck you've ever seen. How so?"

"How's your geology? I imagine as an archeologist you have some." He looked over at Roberts. "What about you, Jackie?"

"Basic planetology, why?" she said.

"Okay, a volcanic neck is the hardened magma that fed a volcano, left behind after it goes extinct and the cone erodes away. Sometimes called a volcanic plug. They're not common but not exactly rare either." He paused for a moment to take another drink, collecting his thoughts.

"There actually is a place on Earth where there is something similar, all covered with vegetation like that. The Glasshouse Mountains in Queensland, Australia, are a series of old volcanic necks. I had forgotten about them at the time, one of those things that was probably mentioned in class once, but I'm not a vulcanologist. Naomi and I came across references to them later. In particular, Mount Beerwah looks very similar to the Peak from some angles. But this one was different. I've never seen a plug erode away in such a regular, square pattern. Beerwah has one whole side that has fallen away exposing what looks like basalt columns. It's really trachyte." Finley paused and shook his head. "But I'm rambling."

Carson didn't know or really care what *trachyte* was. He assumed it was some kind of igneous rock. He wanted to know about Pete's Peak, not some mountain in Australia. "So it was the shape that made it unlike any other neck you'd ever seen?" Carson asked.

"That was one odd thing. But like I said, not too different from Mount Beerwah. Anyway, the hardened magma usually extends vertically downward, to the original magma chamber that created the volcano in the first place, or whatever is left of it," Finley explained. "Our geological surveys showed exactly that under the peak, until we lost the signal." He looked at Carson. "I'd say that was proof it's volcanic. Why would anyone build a pyramid like that?"

Carson leaned forward in his chair. "Pete, I assume we're secure here? No eavesdropping?"

Finley looked puzzled. "Certainly not from outside. Naomi would be sure of that. I can't say what *she* might have set up, but I have no secrets from her. Why?"

That was good enough for Carson. Naomi Maclaren had been the engineer on the original landing crew. "All right. Let me tell you about the pyramid we found on Chara III. . . ."

∞ ∞ ∞

Carson proceeded to tell Finley an abridged version of his discovery of the broken talisman on Verdigris, and how the break exposed its internal technetium battery, which had been isotope-dated to 15,000 years old. He omitted any mention of Homeworld Security, saying only that it had reminded him of an artifact he'd found earlier on Ransom's Planet. He let Roberts explain how she had managed to decode the pattern on that one, which led them to the Chara star system.

They hadn't known exactly what they were looking for, but had spotted the pyramid from orbit, nestled on a plateau in the mountains adjacent to the plains of an ancient seabed.

"Strange place for a pyramid," Finley said. "It wasn't just part of the mountain?"

"No, this was clearly different. There was no debris on it, and when we hiked up to it, we saw the carvings on the side. The material it was made of was completely different from the native rock."

"Different how?"

"The mountains were sedimentary, a hard limestone, maybe a dolomite. Sorry, my geology is very rusty." Most of Carson's geology background had been focused on topics helpful for an archeologist.

"Probably upthrust from the old seabed, like the eastern foothills of the Rockies on Earth," Finley said, "but go on."

"The native stone was dark gray. The pyramid looked more like a fine-grained granite. Maybe a feldspar, it was pinkish, but too hard for that."

"Pink, fine-grained granite, you say? Interesting. Polished?" Finley asked.

"Smooth, but no, I wouldn't call it polished, although it might have been at some point. It was worn. I was mainly looking at the engravings on it."

"Sure, of course you would. My volcano doesn't have any engravings."

Carson wasn't buying it. "How could you tell? Yours is covered in soil and vegetation."

"Yes, but I scraped some off. The rock underneath was pinkish gray, I'll give you that, but there are granite intrusions all through that area."

"Where were you when you scraped the dirt off? The carving on the Chara pyramid didn't extend much more than five meters up, above that it was smooth."

Finley frowned, trying to remember. "Twenty to twenty-five meters, I guess. We were about a quarter of the way up, although I slid back a bit. There was too much dirt around the base, covering the talus. Proves nothing."

Carson looked at Finley. Was he just being contrary, or did he really believe there was nothing to be found there? He was the geologist, after all. But Carson wasn't done. "There's more. Pete, you asked what kind of pyramid would have something that looked like a volcanic pipe under it. I'm getting to that."

"Oh?" Finley looked skeptical. "All right then, go on."

"We found a door."

"A door? You went *inside* the pyramid? What did you find?"

Carson wondered how much detail to go into. Should he tell him about what they had nicknamed the *Cosmic Maguffin*, the alien tool which they'd surmised was used to make the carvings, because it functioned like a disintegrator? No, that would just lead down a line of questions and answers he didn't want to get into, and probably Ducayne wouldn't want him to either. He glanced over at Roberts, who shook her head slightly.

"You're the archeologist, you tell him," she said, covering her head shake.

No need-to-know, Carson reminded himself.

"After some stumbling around, we realized that the talisman, which had opened the door, would work on an interior door we found. There was a passage leading down, spiraling around. The place was like a teaching museum, with simple mathematical and astronomical concepts on the upper level, getting progressively more advanced as we went lower, through simple mechanics, physics, chemistry and so on. By the time we reached the lowest level it was up to quantum mechanics. At least that's what Jackie here said. I was out of my depth by that point."

Finley took a minute to digest this. "Well, that's interesting." He paused, then said, "You said it opened the door, and worked on an interior door. What did you mean, 'worked'? It wasn't just a map?"

"No, it was also a kind of key. It had electronics and a power source inside it."

"Right, you mentioned a technetium battery. And it still worked? Amazing. Naomi would love to take a look at that."

While Carson was curious as to what the legendary engineer's reaction might be to the alien technology, he wasn't sure how Ducayne would react to the suggestion that she be allowed to examine it. He gave a noncommittal reply. "I can imagine."

Finley didn't pursue it. "You said the passage went downwards. How far?"

"Hard to say. No more than a couple of hundred meters, probably less. Apparently, the mountain they built it on wasn't completely stable; there were cracks in the lowest floor. We found an opening into a natural cave, with a stream flowing through it."

Finley looked thoughtful. "Sure, sometimes you'll get caves like that in mountainsides. Strange that anyone would build a pyramid on top of one."

Carson shrugged. "I thought so too. Maybe they'd already started building it when they discovered the cave. There weren't a lot of other places nearby they could have built."

"But why build it there at all? Does St. Jacobs have intelligent natives?"

"There's evidence of them previously, yes, but no confirmation if they're still around. There were signs of ancient agriculture, like terraces on the hills near the old shoreline, and stone fences near where we landed."

"Huh. So why would there be one on this planet? The native artifacts we found were hundreds of thousands of years old; they never got as far as agriculture. Do you have a talisman with a star map for Alpha Centauri, too?"

"No, not yet," Carson admitted. "Maybe the fragment I found pointed here, there wasn't enough of the pattern left to tell. But there are more out there. My web search still turns up hits from time to time." Like the one he'd recently received from an anonymous source. He wondered if Jackie had had a chance to follow up on its star chart.

"So even if it is a pyramid—which it isn't—you can't get in without the key."

"Not quite true," Carson said. "We discovered that the talisman we had works on multiple pyramids. There's another one on Verdigris, Delta Pavonis III, but we couldn't get to the lower levels. It's partially buried." That, and someone else had got to it first and used explosives to force an entry. Whoever had done that had been more interested in what was in the *upper* level, but Carson wasn't about to reveal that information. He had something better.

"There is one other thing," Carson said. "The Chara star map was drawn from a particular point of view. That turns out to be somewhere near the star Zeta Reticuli. We got back from there a couple of months ago, before making another side trip."

"Let me guess," Finley said, "there's another pyramid there."

"Well, sort of."

Roberts coughed, perhaps to remind Carson about need-to-know. Oh well, too late for that now. Besides, there had been Dr. Sawyer's report.

"What's that supposed to mean?" Finley said.

"It was pyramid-shaped, but it flew. A spaceship. And we met one of the occupants." Finley's eyes widened, and he started to rise from his chair, his face reddening. Carson continued hastily: "He matched Elizabeth Sawyer's description of what she saw."

Finley sat back in his chair with a thump, the color draining from his face. "You know about that?"

"It has been fifty years since her confidential report. It's still classified, but the level recently dropped. It was brought to my attention. I managed to meet with her, and she confirmed it."

"Did she put you on to me about Pete's Peak? And how did you find out about her report?"

"I'd rather not say."

"*UDT* Security," Finley said, not asking. It was Carson's turn to be surprised. "Oh, don't look so shocked, Carson. Bobbi, my daughter, told me they set up this meeting. Maclaren Arms does business with them. We have our sources too. I'll admit we don't know everything they get up to, or I imagine I'd have heard about your expeditions before this, but we know—or we think we know—that they're mostly on our side too. But the Sawyers World government is officially independent, so they don't get quite the free rein they might on *Union de Terre* colony worlds."

"Uh," Carson really didn't know what to say to this, if anything. Officially, probably nothing.

"Anyway," Finley continued, "There was never any evidence that she actually saw anything. She was stressed out, being in charge of the landing party with no way to return to space. If she saw anything, it may have been a terror bird. They're not uncommon in that area."

"I showed her a sketch of the alien we met. She said it matched what she'd seen," Carson said.

Finley stared at him, his gaze piercing. "Did you show her any other sketches, of characters that *weren't* your alien?"

"Uh, no," Carson admitted.

"So not really proof, then."

Carson immediately got Finley's point. He hadn't asked Sawyer to pick out her alien from a virtual line-up, as it were, just asked "was this the guy?" If he'd been a cop asking about a suspect, any defense attorney would have that thrown out as too leading.

"Anyway, tell me about these aliens," Finley said. "How long have they been watching us, if that's what they're doing, and why did they build the pyramids?" A quizzical look crossed his face, and he added, "They didn't build the ones on *Earth*, did they?"

"No, they didn't. If there's an alien pyramid on Earth somewhere, nobody has ever found it. But the alien Roberts and I met, presumably the same species as what Elizabeth Sawyer saw—"

"If she saw one," Finley interrupted.

"Fine, *if*. Anyway, he said they had nothing to do with building any of the alien pyramids we've found either. Their own technology probably got a jump start from a pyramid on their home planet. The Kesh—that's what they call themselves, according to the one I met—came along ten thousand years after the pyramid-building spacefarers."

"The original pyramid-builders are long gone?"

"It seems so."

"Then why does Homeworld Security care about them? The —what did you call them? Kesh?—the Kesh, I can understand they'd be concerned about. What's the connection?"

"We don't know, and in our one meeting the Kesh weren't very forthcoming. They say we're not ready for a formal first contact with them."

"Ha! They're probably right," Finley said. "Some people have enough trouble with the low-tech aliens we've met so far."

Carson nodded. He'd met a few of that sort, like the Velka-ryans. "Anyway, that's one thing I want to find out, if there is a connection. I've always suspected that there was some spacefarer link between some of the primitive ruins we've found on other planets. If your peak is a spacefarer pyramid—"

"I'm pretty sure it's not."

"*If* it is, it would be interesting to compare what's inside with what we found on Chara III. It might also give us an idea of what technology the Kesh might have that we don't."

Finley nodded. "Okay, I can see that. But what do you want from me? I can't just say, 'go ahead and dig.' Despite the name, it's not really my peak. And it's in the middle of the Anderson Wildlife Preserve. Not that I really give a rat's ass about that."

"The Finley's leopard preserve? I thought you were involved in setting that up."

Finley shook his head *no*, and began to unfasten his shirt.

"What . . . ?" Carson wondered aloud.

Finley stood up and slid the shirt off his right shoulder and pulled his arm from the sleeve. He raised his bare right arm, exposing the side of his chest. Four lines of parallel scars ran down his right side, across the ribs. Roberts gasped.

"Damned leopard did that to me on the hike back from the peak. They'd be a damn sight deeper if Naomi hadn't been handy with a weapon. In fact, I probably wouldn't be standing here."

His scowl turned to a wry grin. "I'd say the damned felinoids can bite me, but they already tried." He put his shirt back on and sat back down, then picked up his beer and chugged it back. "They're not really leopards, of course. They're not even cats, as Ulrika would point out. Anyway, if you want to waste your time digging around an old volcano, I won't stop you."

"Well, thanks, I guess. Do you really think I'd be wasting my time?"

"The story of what you found at Chara and Zeta Reticuli is fascinating. Now, understand that I'm not calling you a liar, but I'm not sure I buy it completely. There are probably details you're leaving out. But I'm not sure what that has to do with what's on this planet. You admitted you don't have a star map pointing to Alpha Centauri, all you've got is a hill that looks vaguely like a pyramid. So does Mount Beerwah, so that proves nothing.

"Come on, Carson. Think like a professor of archeology. What would you tell a student who came to you with a story like that?"

Carson sighed. He could see Finley's point. Maybe he *was* putting more hope than reason into this. It would be one thing if it was just him, a shovel, and his own time, but a proper excavation would take multiple people, resources, government permissions to enter the preserve. He'd need more than a hunch to justify it, and without proof, tales of aliens and flying pyramids weren't going to do him any favors. Especially if it turned out that Finley was right, and it really was just the remains of an extinct volcano. That could be a career-killer.

"Okay, sure, I'd like to do a dig, but I can see that it would be impractical." He stood up and gestured to Jackie with a sideways nod of his head to do likewise. "Thanks for your time, Pete, I do appreciate it."

"Hey, no worries," Finley said, rising himself to escort them out. "It was worth it to hear about what you've been up to. Don't get me wrong, I'm sure there are other spacefarers out there. The terraforming is proof enough of that. I'm just not sure they've built anything here, and, quite frankly, I'm not sure of how most people would react if they found out they had."

Carson nodded. "Yeah, I get that a lot."

"But don't be strangers. I'd like to hear more about some of your adventures." He looked at Roberts. "Yours too, Jackie. I'm glad Carson brought you along. Maybe we can all trade stories over another beer sometime."

"Thanks, I'd like that," Carson said.

"Likewise," said Roberts. "Carson, give me a moment to check out the car."

Finley looked puzzled for a moment, then grinned. "Right, I heard something about you having problems with an autocab."

"That, and it looked like we were being followed part of the way here. Jackie lost them."

"In an aircar? That must have been some fancy flying. But don't worry, security here is good. The Robot would have yelled out '*Danger, Will Robinson!*' if anyone had approached it, but I won't be offended if you check for yourself. I would." He turned back to Carson and shook his hand again. "Cheers, mate." He half saluted, half waved, then turned and closed the door.

"Uh, cheers," Carson said, and at Roberts' reassuring nod, climbed into the aircar.

∞ ∞ ∞

As Jackie piloted the aircar back toward the city, Carson sat staring glumly out the window. *Don't ask about the talisman,* she mentally urged him. She couldn't be certain, but this was Ducayne's aircar, and she'd be very surprised if it didn't have listening devices. If Carson wanted to keep the package he'd received secret from Ducayne, this was *not* a good place to talk about it.

Carson turned to her and began, "Jackie—" but she cut him off.

"Finley seemed pretty sure that it was an old volcano," she said. "You were hoping for something else, weren't you?"

He sighed. "Yes. A pyramid here, if it were built by the same people who built the ones at Chara and Delta Pavonis, would make it difficult to hide the fact of a fifteen-thousand-year-old spacefaring species, whether Ducayne wanted to go public with it or not."

"You want vindication for your theories," Jackie guessed.

"Of course I do. It's one thing to be ridiculed when you're wrong, and I can accept that, but everything we've been through over the past year proves that I was right. And I can't talk about it."

His frustration was obvious, and she couldn't blame him. He'd mentioned what his boss at the university, Matthews, had said about von Dänikenism. She'd heard of von Däniken's "Ancient Astronaut" theories, and agreed with Carson that they were rubbish and nothing at all like the connections he had found between far-flung alien but primitive races.

"So, if it is a volcano, what was with this talk of it being a pyramid?" she asked, trying to steer the conversation away from a sore point, and to get him lecturing rather than asking questions.

"It happens," Carson said. "It wouldn't be the first time a natural geographic feature got mistaken for something artificial. The Bimini Road, for example, which looks like a sunken road from the air. Apparently, Bimini Bay on Kakuloa was named for a similar-looking feature. Sometimes a glacial esker will look like a wall. It's generally pretty obvious once somebody gets down on the ground for a closer look."

"So Pete's Peak . . . ?"

"Pete is a geologist, he would know. He says it's a volcano." Carson turned away again to stare out the window. After a moment, he turned back to her. "By the way, have you had a chance to—"

She reacted quickly, lashing out her right arm to cover his mouth with her hand, and saying: "To look at that data you wanted me to analyze? Sorry, not yet." She glared at him, shaking her head "no", then took her hand from his mouth and held a finger to her lips.

He looked at her quizzically, rubbing his face. She'd hit him harder than she had meant to. "What—?"

She pointed at the dashboard, then at her ear. He got it, and nodded.

"No worries. Whenever," he said, but frowned.

Jackie changed the subject. "What did you think of that robot of Finley's?"

Carson barked out a short laugh and turned back to her. "That was one of the most ridiculous things I've ever seen. You too, from that grin you were trying to hide."

"You're right," she said, "but I recognized it. I'd seen it before. Not his, I mean the original."

"Really? On those long deep space voyages with your parents and nothing else in the ship's library?"

Jackie had forgotten just how much Carson knew about her past, but in this case his guess was wrong. "No, at least not that I recall. It was in the science fiction class I took as part of my starship pilot training."

"Oh, right, to prepare you for the unexpected," he said. Then he grinned. "I guess it worked. I certainly wasn't expecting that robot. And how did it manage to hold onto that tray with those claws?"

Jackie grinned back at him. "There's obviously more there than meets the eye." She pointed to the dashboard again.

"Yes, there very probably is," Carson said, looking thoughtful.

By now they were nearing the spaceport, and Jackie had to focus on her flying.

Chapter 10: Debriefing

Sawyers World, Ducayne's office

"HOW DID YOUR meeting with Finley go?" Ducayne asked when Carson reported in.

Carson shrugged. "Well enough, I suppose" he said. "He seems convinced that what he found really is just a volcano remnant, and I'm inclined to believe him."

"What about Elizabeth Sawyer's comments? Didn't she say he thought it was a pyramid?"

"She said he thought it looked like one. But Finley's the geologist who went out to the site."

"Then we can write it off? That's unfortunate. You had my hopes up for more of whatever's in the Chara pyramid, and what was taken from the one on Verdigris. I guess we'll have to look elsewhere."

"Yeah. Still," Carson said, "part of me is unconvinced. Maybe it's just wishful thinking, but I'd really like to take a look at it myself."

"You think Finley was lying to you?"

"Maybe he's lying to himself. He seemed uncomfortable with the idea of recent spacefaring aliens."

"So am I, but I'm forced to recognize that they existed and they or their successors are still around. Maybe you should go and check it out."

"First I'd like to review the original geology reports of the area. I looked for them when I got back from Finley's, but for some reason they don't seem to be online or in the university library."

Ducayne grinned at this. "You'd almost think somebody was trying to hide something. I'm shocked."

Carson shook his head. Maybe Jackie was right, and Ducayne did have a sense of humor. "Sure you are."

"Couldn't you ask Finley for copies of those reports? If they exist at all, wouldn't he have them?"

"After fifty years? I don't know. Maybe. But if he doesn't, or won't give me copies? Or they're inconclusive?"

"Then you go take a look for yourself. That is what you'd want to do, isn't it?"

"Maybe. But it's in the middle of a wildlife preserve. The area is off-limits."

Ducayne looked thoughtful. "That would be a great cover story if there was something there the local government didn't want investigated. Maybe they know something after all."

"Then why would Elizabeth Sawyer have even brought it up? And Finley seemed willing to support some kind of excavation if it could be arranged. He has no love for the wildlife there, it tried to kill him. He showed us the scars."

"Oh? I hadn't heard that story," Ducayne said. He shifted forward in his seat, leaning toward Carson. "What would it take for you to verify what that thing is? I don't mean a full excavation, just a quick in and out to take a closer look."

"You mean a covert operation? Do you really think it's worth the trouble?"

"You don't?"

That surprised Carson. "Logistics aside," he said, "aren't you worried about the fallout if the operation is discovered? A UDT agency conducting illegal operations on an independent world? What about the Treaty of Alpha Centauri?"

Ducayne looked pained, as though wrestling with a decision. "I'm not suggesting such an operation, just brainstorming. Our governments do have an informal arrangement, as I've mentioned before, but now is not the best time to be pushing on that. There are other things going on, things you don't need to know about. You're right, it's not worth the trouble."

Now Carson was intrigued, but he knew better than to push Ducayne on the matter. But he had begun to think about what would be needed to check the Peak out.

"Okay," he said, "but it would probably just take me and a shovel, depending on how deep the dirt covering is. And someone to watch my back in case of predators." The thoughts came as he talked. "But that area is patrolled; there used to be a problem with poachers. So, some way to get in and out quickly." He was warming to the idea. If there was some way to arrange it, he could decide for himself just what Pete's Peak really was.

"No," Ducayne said. "That's the problem. 'Quickly' implies an aircraft, at least to get you out. Since we're being hypothetical, I suppose you could parachute in. Ever done a HALO jump?"

Carson chuckled. "High altitude, low opening? Remember how you sent me to Tanith? If entering from space doesn't count as high altitude, I don't know what does."

"I suppose you're right. But that would still leave the problem of getting you and your backup out. An aircraft off course with mechanical trouble? It's way too thin. No, just leave it. If it looks worthwhile in future, we'll come up with a cover story, or just cooperate with the local authorities."

Carson shook his head. "Fair enough. It would be embarrassing to go through all that for an extinct volcano."

Ducayne nodded. "It would. Meanwhile, you have plenty of other things to keep you busy."

"I do," Carson said, understanding Ducayne's comment as telling him to just drop it. Not that Carson had any intention of dropping it, but there was something else. "Oh, by the way, somebody might have been trying to follow us on the way to Finley's. There was another aircar trailing us for a while."

"What?" Ducayne frowned. "You should have mentioned that sooner. Maybe we should put an emergency beacon app on your omni."

Carson shrugged it off. "Jackie lost them in the clouds, we never saw them after that."

"Did they follow you long enough to know where you were going?"

Carson thought back. "I can't rule it out. As Jackie said, there's not much on the heading we were on, except for Finley's place. Why would that matter?"

"It might not. But there aren't many reasons you would be going out there. They might guess it had something to do with Pete's Peak."

"And if they did? It's not exactly the jungles of Verdigris. As I said, the reserve is patrolled, watching for poachers. You and I just talked about trying to sneak an excavation team in there. It's not going to happen."

Ducayne sighed. "You're right. It's just something else for me to worry about."

∞ ∞ ∞

Ducayne seemed about to dismiss Carson, then had a second thought. "One other thing," he said.

"Yes?"

He hesitated, then said, "It's confirmed; Rico didn't die in the shoot-out on Earth."

Carson blinked. Rico had caused him so much trouble before ultimately saving all their asses on the Chara expedition. He'd come to like the guy; none of his antagonism had been personal. The last Carson knew, Rico had been on an assignment with Malcolm Brown to retrieve original documents from an old government UFO study, when he got involved with Velkaryans after the same files. He'd been killed delaying them while Brown escaped, although the body had gone missing. "That is good news. Where is he now?"

"That's a very good question."

"You don't know?" Carson said, surprised Ducayne would know one thing without the other.

"The local police found him bleeding out at the Denver Spaceport, the Velkaryans were gone by the time they got there. They put him in a traumapod which immediately put him into a medical coma. And then they lost him."

"They *lost* him? How?"

"We're not completely clear on that. When they got him into a traumapod, it triggered on the DNA tags we gave him, and reported that he was a government agent. The local cops naturally bumped the case up to the Feds, thinking Rico was one of their guys. Sometime after that, Federal agents—or at least, someone with appropriate credentials—showed up and took custody of him, traumapod and all. A while after *that*, another group of credentialed agents also showed up to take custody. As you can imagine, hilarity ensued, for very small values of hilarity.

"The bottom line is," Ducayne continued, "nobody knows where Rico and his traumapod got to, or exactly who picked him up. This was about six weeks ago, when you were on your way to Tanith."

"But that was over a month after he was shot, wouldn't he have recovered by then?"

"Apparently the local cops weren't quite sure how to deal with him, and it was easier to leave him in storage, as it were, than let him out and have someone who may or may not have been either a government agent or a criminal, or both, ranting about his rights. As long as he was in the pod, they could claim medical contingency. I'm speculating; I don't know that for certain. Maybe whoever did retrieve him had a finger in that, too."

"No tracker on the pod?"

"If there was, it was disabled. It certainly hasn't logged itself onto the network as far as anyone knows. I have a couple of our own people on it now, of course. Sooner or later we'll find him."

"Could it have been the Velkaryans?"

"I don't think that's their style. They'd be more likely to just kill him than kidnap him. I'm not sure what use he'd be to them. He certainly doesn't know as much about us as they probably do already. But I can't rule it out."

"Strange." Carson had thought he was getting used to the weird ways of the espionage world he'd fallen into, but it continued to surprise him. "It is good to hear he's not dead. I hope he's not wishing he was."

"I doubt that. Rico is a survivor. Besides, he'd probably sell us out first."

"Maybe. I don't think he has any love for Velkaryans, although I'm not sure why."

"No idea. Anyway, you need to focus on that pyramid, and let me worry about Rico. I do hope we get him back; I have people looking. He has useful skills, and it will be interesting to hear his side. That is, assuming he hasn't reverted to his old tomb-raider ways and is somewhere out on the frontier with a new alias."

"Indeed," Carson said.

Chapter II: Different Plans

UDT Headquarters, Sawyers World

JACKIE ROBERTS WAS on her way to see Ducayne when she ran into Hannibal Carson in the corridor.

"Jackie, just the person I wanted to see," he said.

She frowned. He wouldn't be stupid enough to ask her about the new talisman *here*, would he? Unless he'd decided to go ahead and tell Ducayne already? She gave her head a shake, but smiled and said, "Hi, Hannibal. What's up?"

"Are you available for dinner tonight?"

She hadn't been expecting that. "Dinner?" she asked. "What's the occasion?"

"Do I need one?" Carson said. "When's your birthday?"

"You've forgotten? That's just like you." In fact, as best as she could recall, she had never told him.

"Hah, no," he said. "The first time I asked you that, I distinctly remember you saying, 'In what planet's calendar? The place I was born doesn't even have one, and I don't remember how long its year was.' Although that might have just been your way of saying that it was none of my business."

"You do remember!" She was impressed. Sometimes it seemed that his attention to detail only extended to archeology; it was nice to know that she might be an exception. "Technically, it really wasn't any of your business. Ships' officers aren't supposed to fraternize too much with the passengers." When they'd first met, she had been the first officer aboard the passenger ship *Arabella*; Carson had been heading out on one of his expeditions.

He grinned. "Is that what we were doing? Fraternizing?"

It had become a bit more than that, actually. "Look how it turned out," she said. "I should have followed the rules."

"Then you'd probably be captain on some boring regular passenger liner run, instead of owner-operator of your own ship."

"There's something to be said for boring," she said.

"You keep saying that. And yet you keep stumbling into adventure."

"*Stumbling?* Dragged kicking and screaming, more like. Let's see . . ." she held up her hand and started counting off on her fingers. "Trapped in an alien pyramid." She pushed her left forefinger up with her right thumb. "Shot at with air-to-air missiles." Another finger. "Had my warp drive damaged. Almost blown up by an alien disintegrator. Twice." Two more fingers and her left thumb. "Kidnapped by Velkaryans on that ice moon." She held up her right thumb. "I'm probably forgetting something, but that was just our little trip to Chara III." There had been other incidents, both before and since.

"And you loved every minute of it."

Jackie clenched her teeth and her fists. She wanted to hit him. "I most certainly did not!" Then she relaxed, remembering some of the other times. "Although it did have its moments."

"Ha!"

Jackie cuffed him across the shoulder. "You still haven't said why you're inviting me to dinner."

"Do I need a reason? I'm sure you're as tired of autochef food as I am. The cafeteria on campus isn't much better, and nor is that at Ducayne's headquarters. When was the last time you went out?"

She grinned. He had a point about autochef food, but when she was planetside she didn't limit herself to that. "On Tanith, and on Skead before that, if you don't count the campus pub on Taprobane. So, more recently than you, I imagine. But I'm not turning you down; that was weeks ago. What did you have in mind?"

"Rick's Café."

Had she heard him right? That was one of the most exclusive restaurants in Sawyer City. "*Rick's?* When, next month? I hear it takes that long to get a reservation. I'll probably be off-planet."

"Tonight, if you can. You're not planning on flying in the next twenty-six hours, are you?"

"Not if it meant I'd have to pass up drinks with a dinner at Rick's. But what's this about? Who did you have to kill to get a reservation at Rick's, and why?" A ludicrous thought crossed her mind, and she choked back a laugh.

"What?"

"Just a crazy random thought. You're not going to *propose* to me, are you?"

"*What?* No! But why would that be funny?"

"You don't have to sound so horrified! We did have a thing before you dumped me, but it was funny because it would be so out of character."

"That again? You dumped me."

They'd had this discussion before, and Jackie raised her hand to forestall an argument. "Never mind. Let's just call it an unfortunate series of miscommunications. You *did* rescue me on that ice moon, although I rescued you at Zeta Reticuli, and got myself shot in the process."

"A ricochet, and I was rescuing myself."

"Oh? And just how were you planning to get off-planet without a ship?"

"I— Never mind, you're right, this is silly. But it goes to show that we do make a pretty good team."

"Why, Hannibal Carson, you say the sweetest things." Before he could react, she pulled him to her and kissed him, quickly, on the lips, then pushed him back. *Why did I do that?*

"Wha?" Carson was speechless for a moment, then gave his head a brief shake. "All right, let's start over. Jackie, would you like to join me for dinner tonight?"

"Why yes, Hannibal, I'd love to." She smiled at him to cover her own confusion at her earlier action. "Rick's still has the dress code?"

"Yes. Is that a problem? Your ship's-captain dress uniform would be acceptable."

"No problem." Then she had an idea. "But I think I can do better than that."

"Great. Are you still staying aboard the *Sophie?*"

"I am. Ducayne offered me a dorm, but I prefer to stay with my ship. Short term berth at the spaceport."

"Pick you up there at seven?"

"Roger that. Does that mean you trust autocabs now?"

"More or less. They can't hack them all."

Jackie wasn't so sure about that, but didn't say anything. She might consider bringing along a few discreet tools, though.

∞ ∞ ∞

After Jackie left her meeting with Ducayne—he'd wanted her to do a short courier run—she found herself wondering again what Carson's dinner invitation was about. If it was just dinner, there were plenty of options less expensive than Rick's and fancier than the campus cafeteria. Somebody he wanted her to meet? Surely he would have said something. Discussing the new talisman? They could do that almost anywhere, and certainly somewhere less visible than Rick's. And it wasn't her birthday. Was it *his*? No, she didn't think so.

Well, if Carson wanted upscale and dressy, she could do that. She checked the time. Yes. Even if there wasn't something appropriate in her wardrobe, she'd recently discovered how versatile her ship's fabber was when it came to making clothing. This would be fun. *How long has it been since I last wore a dress? They're not very practical for. . .almost anything. Well, perhaps for one or two things. Do I even want to go there? But what kind of dress?* It was time for a little research.

Chapter 12: Reid

Alpha Centauri, Kakuloa, New Darwin

REID DISEMBARKED FROM the passenger ship *Southern Cross* at the recently reopened New Darwin spaceport on Kakuloa. It would have been simpler to fly straight to Sawyer City, flights were more frequent, but sometimes a circuitous route was best.

The formalities here were minimal. He cleared the port and headed to the local office. Not the official one, of course. That was probably under constant watch, at the very least by a discreet camera. There was no point in making it easy for anyone surveilling the place.

He tapped out a message on his omni. "This is Reid, just in from Earth. On my way." He hit encrypt and sent it. The message would be encrypted, broken into several different packets, and each sent to a different address. From there they'd be routed through various hops, eventually being reassembled and decrypted when they reached the local safehouse. It could probably be intercepted if somebody was looking hard enough, but then if somebody knew enough to look that hard, they were already compromised. It wasn't something he worried about.

He arrived at the safehouse a half-hour later, an apartment above a non-descript restaurant near downtown New Darwin.

"Mr. Reid, welcome to Kakuloa," said the agent who met him. "I'm Dalhousie. Will you be here long?"

Reid appreciated that Dalhousie didn't ask him *why* he was here. In fact, there was no real reason, but it obfuscated his trail, and let him hand-deliver a few messages from headquarters on Earth. Not that Reid himself knew what those messages might be, if in fact any at all. He was just handing over the data device.

"Not long," Reid said. "I'm just touching base. I'll hang out for a day or two and then head to Kreschets Landing. Is there anything exciting going on here?"

Dalhousie snorted. "Your ship landing was probably the high point of the week." At Reid's alarmed look, Dalhousie said: "Relax, I'm exaggerating. Traffic has picked up since the spaceport reopened last year. We get two flights from Earth a week, and two a day from Sawyers. Almost everything from anywhere else though lands at Kreschets, except for private stuff. But you just missed the annual Crab Festival."

"Well, thank goodness for that."

"It's not as bad as it sounds. There's a massive crab cookout on the beach, and everyone gets drunk and parties. It gives us a chance to gripe about how we can't do that on South Island."

New Darwin was situated on one of two large islands that straddled Kakuloa's equator. While human habitation was technically allowed on South Island, activities—especially anything related to the beach—were restricted. Further south, the large continent—imaginatively named Southern Continent in the same naming tradition as the Western Ocean—was completely off limits, being home to several colonies of a species of tree squid related to, but apparently even smarter than, the squids which flourished around the old berry plantations between Kakuloa City and Chandrasekhar Valley.

"Well, I'm sorry I missed it then," Reid lied. "But I'm glad you got an opportunity to spread the good word." Agitating against impositions on human activities because of concessions to intelligent aliens was a routine Velkaryan activity. And in this case, nobody had even proved that the squids were intelligent. Smarter than dolphins, maybe, but Reid didn't think that was saying much.

"Sure," Dalhousie said. "Well, let me know if you need anything, and other than that, I'll stay out of your way."

Chapter 13: Academia

Drake University, Sawyer City

CARSON GLANCED AT the text message on his omni, and grimaced. *"Come to my office—Matthews."*

Dean Matthews was head of the Archeology Department, and Carson's boss. Somehow, meetings with him were rarely pleasant. Carson acknowledged the text and made his way to the office.

"You wanted to see me?" Carson said as he entered.

"I did. Close the door and have a seat."

Uh oh, Carson thought as he sat down.

"I've been going over the department's recent publications," Matthews said.

"Oh, yes?"

"Yes. Tell me, what are you working on right now?"

"You mean, for publication?"

"Exactly that. Lately your average paper count is the lowest in the department, and I must say the quality isn't what I would have expected from you. 'Stone Fences of Chara III'? 'A Unique Tomb of the Late Verdigris Neolithic'? Those were catalog papers a grad student could write. What's the point of you gallivanting all over T-Space if that's all you come up with?"

That hurt, but Carson could see his point. "I can only work with what I find. Those tomb-raiders on Verdigris hijacked our artifacts. At least they left me the recordings."

"Spare me your excuses. Look, Hannibal, I appreciate that your—great-aunt was it?—left money to endow a chair in your name, and I've cut you some slack because of that, but the Board of Regents expects a bit more from our professors than what we've been seeing from you. All this travel takes a lot of time away from your work."

"It doesn't, really," Carson protested. "I do research and work on papers while I'm aboard ship. After all, there's not much else to do."

"Hmm, well, with all that time to work I would expect more output. I hope you're not wasting it on that von Däniken nonsense again. Listen, there's plenty of good archeology to be done here on Sawyers World. We've barely scratched the surface here; we still don't know definitively what happened to the paleolithic aboriginals."

"We don't even know definitively what happened to most of the paleolithic hominins on *Earth*. But I see your point." The dean's comment gave Carson an idea. "You know, the Anderson Wildlife Preserve is adjacent to known aboriginal hunting areas, and probably overlaps them. Maybe it's time someone did an archeological survey of that area."

Matthews blinked at the turn in the conversation. "No doubt, but these things take time to plan, and funding. I won't complain if you want to look into that at some point, but right now you need to get your head out of the clouds and focus on your day to day responsibilities to this university."

Carson knew when to make a tactical withdrawal. "You're right, of course," he agreed. "Which reminds me, I have a class to prepare for. Was that all, sir?"

Matthews harrumphed. "Yes, that was it. You've done some great work in the past, Hannibal. I just don't want you to start resting on your laurels. All right?"

Couldn't you come up with some more clichés to throw in there? Carson thought, but said, rising, "Of course. Thank you."

Chapter 14: Rico Relocated

Elsewhere

"ALL RIGHT, RICO. You can get up now," Rico heard Agent Friday, or whoever he really was, say.

Rico blinked his eyes against the light as the traumapod slid open. He moved to sit up and found it easier than he had expected. However long he'd been lying in the traumapod, it must have been doing something to combat the muscle-wasting he would have expected from all that inactivity. Probably something similar to the zero-gee treatments, but he wasn't aware of the details.

"That's a nice change," he said. "Did you finally decide you had nothing to hold me on?"

"Hardly that, but you're more useful awake than asleep. We've got a nice little room for you."

"Let me guess. Bars on the windows, locked from the outside? Where am I, anyway?"

"Oh, there are no bars on the windows," Friday said. "In fact, there aren't any windows. As for where, you're somewhere safe."

"Safe, huh? From what? And how long have I been out?"

"Quite a while, as a matter of fact. We'll bring you up to speed in a bit. You've recovered nicely from your multiple gun-shot wounds, but you need a few days out of the pod to recover from freezer burn."

"Freezer burn? What the fu—"

"That was a joke. I mean TDS, traumapod deconditioning syndrome. Yes, your muscles aren't too bad, but your circadian rhythms will have been messed up to hell and gone. You'll start to feel it in a bit. Like the worst case of jet lag you can imagine, and then some." Friday gestured to the med-tech, who handed Rico a plastic bottle filled with orange liquid.

"Here, drink this," the tech said.

"What is it?"

"Mostly nutrients and sugar. It will help your GI tract get used to handling food again, and give you a bit of energy."

Rico took a cautious sip from the bottle. It wasn't horrible, although it reminded him of something like orange-flavored chicken broth. He grimaced, then swallowed several large gulps.

"I'm sure I've tasted worse, although I don't remember what. How about a little vodka in this?"

"Not a chance," the med-tech said, then added, "Ethanol is contra-indicated."

"Finish it," Friday ordered, "then we'll show you to your room."

Rico chugged the rest back. Maybe by drinking it quickly he wouldn't have to think about the flavor. He handed the empty bottle back to the tech.

The med-tech set it down and walked over to where a wheelchair was parked in a corner of the room. He pushed it back toward the traumapod and gestured for Rico to get off the traumapod cot.

"Okay, into the wheelchair."

"I can walk," Rico said.

"Probably not very far," the tech said. "Come on, into the chair."

"Just do as he says, Rico," Friday added.

Rico swung his legs off the traumapod bed and, holding on to the safety rail, carefully stood up to move to the chair. He tested his legs. Yeah, he could walk, but he feigned being weaker than he felt and let the med-tech help him into the chair. It never hurt to be underestimated; if there was an escape chance, he'd take it.

That chance came soon. The door to the room slid aside, and the med-tech began to push the wheelchair toward the opening. Friday was behind the med-tech. As the wheelchair passed through the doorway, Rico took subtle glances right and left. The corridor was empty, and his two captors were behind him. He launched himself from the chair, pushing it back into the med-tech, twisting it so that it fell sideways. Rico spared a half-second to see if there were controls to shut the door behind him. There weren't, curse the luck. He picked an arbitrary direction and took off running down the left corridor, ignoring the shouting and cursing behind him.

The corridor came to a tee-junction, and after a quick glance left and right, Rico headed left. There were several doors along the corridor wall, all shut, and as Rico tried each in turn, all locked, or with no obvious way to signal them to open.

There, at the end of the corridor, was that an elevator? The buttons on the wall beside the door suggested that it was. Rico dashed for it and slammed both buttons, not caring which direction he would go. He would figure that out as he went. As he waited for the doors to open, he felt an ache in his leg muscles, and an un-characteristic light-headedness. He was weaker than he'd thought.

He heard a muffled rattle behind the elevator doors, and commotion behind him. He'd wondered how long it would take Friday and the med-tech to get the wheelchair out of the way. The elevator door began to slide open, and Rico dashed into the gap.

Straight into the arms of two burly guards.

∞ ∞ ∞

The guards frog-marched Rico back down the corridor to where Friday and the med-tech were waiting with the wheelchair.

"Thank you, gentlemen," Friday said as they turned Rico and sat him down. As he was seated, the med-tech took each of his forearms in turn and, before Rico could react, fastened broad straps over them to secure them to the chair arms. They weren't going to give him any more escape chances. "What the—?" Rico began.

"For your own safety," Agent Friday said, with a wry smile. "Although I do wonder where you thought you were going."

"Right," Rico said, and relaxed to await whatever was next.

Chapter 15: Dinner

Sawyer City Spaceport

HANNIBAL CARSON DIRECTED the autocab around to the small starship parking area, feeling decidedly uncomfortable, and not just because of the vehicle he was riding in. Most formal ceremonies on campus called for the traditional academic cap and gown, under which one could wear almost anything. Or, in the case of the occasional prankster student, nothing. Aside from the infrequent faculty dinners, he rarely wore a suit and tie. Funny how that ancient bit of men's attire might undergo style changes with fashion but hadn't gone totally obsolete. At least it wasn't a tuxedo; Rick's Place wasn't *that* formal, although a white dinner jacket wouldn't have been out of place.

The cab pulled up on the *Sophie*'s starboard side. The boarding ramp was extended but the airlock door was closed. Carson got out of the cab and walked up the ramp. The small control panel had an extra button from what he remembered. A doorbell? He pushed it.

Jackie's voice came from a speaker as the door slid open. "Come on in."

The inner lock door was open, and as he stepped through it, Jackie called from her cabin. "I'll be right out. You know where everything is, make yourself comfortable."

"All right. No rush." He stepped back to the galley area, then opened the aft cabin door to check his appearance in the mirror there. He barely recognized himself; this was not how he usually looked when aboard ship. He stepped back to the galley as he heard Jackie's cabin door open, and he turned toward her. And froze.

"What do you think?" she asked. "Too flashy?"

He barely recognized her. Her green hair, normally cut in pageboy bangs, swept up from her forehead, which somehow emphasized her green eyes. She wore a short-sleeved long dress with a mandarin collar, a *cheongsam*. Jackie stood taller than he remembered, then he realized she was wearing high heels, which together with the slit-to-the-thigh cheongsam, only emphasized her long legs. The overall style was conservative, although the opening below the collar was non-traditional, but *flashy* applied. The dark blue-black silky fabric was highlighted with deep-sky images of a starry nebula, and here and there individual stars twinkled with an understated flashing. She wore no jewelry; she didn't need to. "Wow," was all he could say.

She smiled. "I'll take that as approval. You don't clean up too bad yourself."

"Thanks. And yes, I approve." He looked her up and down again. "Heels? Can you walk in those?" He couldn't remember a time when she hadn't worn either ship boots or hiking boots.

"Zero-gravity reflexes help, but what helps more is the dynamic stabilization built in. Smart materials. If I need to run, the heels lower."

Carson grinned. "You should have just said *yes*. A magician should never reveal her tricks."

She smiled at that. "Fair enough. I won't tell you what else I have hidden up my sleeves."

He looked at her arms, each in turn. The dress barely covered her shoulders. "What sleeves?"

"Exactly. Shall we go?"

∞ ∞ ∞

"You still haven't told me what the occasion is," Jackie said as the autocab steered itself through the streets of Sawyer City. "We already settled that it's not my birthday. It's not yours, is it?"

"What? No. I'm sorry, I should have mentioned. There'll be a couple of other people there. One of them, David Zhang, was a grad student of mine. I'm not his adviser, but he recently finished his thesis and is celebrating."

"Oh. So this *isn't* a date. I'm just your plus-one." Jackie felt vaguely offended, but told herself she shouldn't be. That was just Carson being Carson. "How does a grad student manage to celebrate at Rick's?"

"I'm sorry, Jackie. I should have said something. But you're not 'just' anything, and I wasn't kidding about how you look. Can I say 'wow' again?"

She smiled to herself. "Thanks, but you didn't answer my question."

"Oh, right. It helps that his uncle owns the place."

"Yes, I'll bet it does. But you said you weren't his advisor, so why the invite?"

"He and I always got along well. He was at the dig on Ransom's Planet where Marten found that talisman. Uh, best not to bring that up; we uncovered a lot of other artifacts, there's no reason he'd remember that one."

"Copy that. Who else is going to be there? His actual adviser, I assume?"

"Unfortunately not. Dr. Iverson is off-planet; he submitted his final thesis approval over the net. David didn't want to wait for him to get back to celebrate, so he invited me, and a guest. I'm pretty sure his girlfriend will be there, probably a few others."

"Other girlfriends?" Jackie said, teasing.

"No. Well, maybe, I don't know. But I meant other students and friends, maybe faculty. I didn't ask for the guest list."

"Of course not. Just curious. And wondering what I'll have to talk about."

"Anything except aliens, pyramids, and maybe Velkaryans. You can mention our trip to Chara III—"

"Right, as long as I leave out all the interesting details."

"Uh, pretty much, yeah. I wrote a paper on the stone fences we found, so if anyone was paying attention they'll know I was there."

"Don't worry. After a year as XO on the *Arabella*, I know how to make small-talk with the guests."

"Oh, that's what that was?"

"Watch it, Carson." She said it with a smile.

Just then the autocab pulled over to the curb, announcing *"Rick's Café. You have reached your destination."*

Chapter 16: Rico's Room

Elsewhere

AS "AGENT FRIDAY" had said, the room had no windows. Aside from that, it was pleasant enough. It could have been a small dorm or even hotel room. Unlike a prison cell, there was privacy in the attached bathroom. Or at least, it had the appearance of privacy. Rico had no doubt he was being monitored at all times. He didn't even know if he was above or below ground. The room reminded Rico of the temporary quarters he'd had at Ducayne's Homeworld Security, although there were enough differences in furnishings—or lack thereof—and layout that he was sure this wasn't part of that.

There being nothing else to do, Rico put his idle time in the room—or cell, as he thought of it—into exercising to rebuild the muscle he had lost while in the pod. He was in the middle of yet another set of push-ups when the door opened, and a large man Rico hadn't seen before entered, followed by his earlier questioner, Agent Friday. The big man looked like a guard; tall, muscular, with a no-nonsense expression, although he too wore civvies, not a uniform. He took up a position just inside the door. Rico stood up, wary.

Friday carried a data pad. He gestured to the bed. "Have a seat, Rico."

"Thanks. I'd offer you one but. . ." Rico waved his arm at the room; there were no other furnishings.

"No worries." Friday touched his pad, and a table and jump seat folded out from the wall. There'd been no obvious seam before that. Rico had seen the like before, but hadn't expected it here. Friday sat and put his data pad on the table.

"So. Do you want to tell me what you were doing on Earth?"

"Not really." *Wait,* were*? So where was he now?*

"That might be the first truthful answer I've had from you, Rico. Let's keep it up, shall we?"

"You know the saying," Rico said, "ask me no questions and I'll tell you no lies."

"If you want to spend the rest of your life in this room, we can play it that way. But I already told you we're the good guys. Why would you lie to me?"

This interrogation technique, and that's what it surely must be, was a new one to Rico. His gaze flicked to the muscle at the door. Good cop, bad cop? But the guard was standing impassively, apparently paying no attention to the proceedings.

"Because I don't know that you *are* the good guys," Rico finally said. "I don't really know who you are."

"I told you who we are, the good guys. Homeworld Defense. I want to know what a known smuggler is doing on Earth and apparently working for either the *UDT*'s Department of Homeworld Security or for someone else who knows how to do government DNA tagging. We especially want to know if it's the latter."

"I'm not a smuggler."

Friday glanced at his data pad. "Known associate of Marrok Hopkins, sometimes known as John Stephens, a convicted dealer in illegal artifacts. Known associate of—"

"So? I kept bad company. I never smuggled anything." Well, not in the sense of illegal contraband across borders for resale, anyway. He'd sneaked weapons into places he shouldn't, and he'd certainly been aboard ships that had carried illegal cargoes, but he hadn't been in charge.

"We'll leave that for now. So, you don't deny working for Homeworld Security?"

"I didn't say that."

"You didn't deny it. What were you doing on Earth?"

"Getting shot at." *Again,* were. *Definitely not in Kansas, Toto.*

"I doubt you went all the way to Earth just to volunteer for target practice, especially not as the target. Why were they shooting at you?"

"You said you were Homeworld Defense, but twice now you've implied that we're not on Earth. Who are you really?"

Friday jerked his head back in surprise. Rico didn't buy it, surely the man must have realized what he'd said. Friday looked at Rico for a moment, then said, "Earth isn't the only planet with a Homeworld Defense. We're part of the Sawyers World government. Now, again, why were they shooting at you? Did you do something to piss them off, like shoot first, or did you have something they wanted?"

Sawyers World? But . . . "What were Sawyers World defense agents doing on Earth? That's a bit out of your territory, isn't it? How would the Terran government feel about that? Or the American government, for that matter?"

"Who said we had anyone on Earth?"

Rico snorted. "What, you found me abandoned on your doorstep with a note saying 'take care of little Rico' taped to the traumapod? That's a bit farfetched."

"Anyone backtracking your travel records would know you came from here."

Rico didn't know what to think anymore. He knew he and Friday were playing a cat and mouse game, but he wasn't sure to what end. Screw it.

"Fine. I was on Earth on *UDT* business. That's all you need to know. Now let me go, call the *UDT*, or charge me with something and *then* call the *UDT*."

Friday looked taken aback, but recovered quickly. "Who at the *UDT* would you like me to call?"

Rico was too smart to fall for that. "Anyone you like. Call the embassy, tell them you have a *UDT* citizen in custody, recovering from gunshot wounds, and ask what to do with me. I'm sure that will go over well." Rico had caught a slight change in Friday's expression at his earlier use of the phrase "need to know". He wondered just what sort of relationship the Sawyers World and *UDT* spook departments had with each other.

The agent seemed to pull himself together. He stood up. "All right, Ricardo. If that's the way you want to play it. Maybe one of these days we will give them a call." He retracted the table and chair into the wall then turned and nodded to the guard. The guard opened the door for Friday then followed him out.

The door closed and Rico heard the latch click locked.

Well, he thought, *that was interesting*. Had that last comment from Friday been bravado, or had he really been pissed off? His use of *Ricardo* had clearly been meant to annoy.

He got up from the bed and walked over to where the table had folded from the wall. As before, the surface was seamless. He rapped on the wall in a few places, but noticed no difference in the sound. He shrugged and went to lie back on the bed. He might be here for a while.

Chapter 17: Rick's Café

Rick's Café, Sawyer City

THEIR HOST AND several of his other guests had just been seated when Carson and Roberts entered the restaurant. The *maître d'hôtel* greeted them and signaled to an Asian-looking man wearing a white dinner jacket with a black bowtie. The man smiled broadly and came over to them

"Hello, you must be Doctor Carson. I'm Rick Zhang, this is my place. And who is this charming lady?" He turned to Roberts.

"Rick, this is Captain Jacqueline Roberts of the *Sophie*, a good friend and my sometime pilot. And please, call me Hannibal."

"Delighted." Rick shook her hand, then bowed to her. "Your cheongsam honors my heritage, Captain, and thus my ancestors. Although I doubt any of them wore one so well."

Jackie bowed in turn. "You honor me. But call me Jackie, I'm not on duty." She looked around the restaurant, styled after the café from the legendary film. "Please, if I may ask, how does someone of Chinese heritage come to open a Moroccan-themed restaurant?"

Rick grinned. He probably got that question more than any other. "A Chinese restaurant would be too cliché. Besides, not only is *Casablanca* one of my favorite films, but I lived in Morocco for several years before leaving Earth. I assure you, the cuisine is authentic, plus a few local variations."

He gestured for them to follow him. "Come, come to the table. My nephew is already seated, and there are still a few guests to arrive."

The nephew, David Zhang, stood as they approached the table. "Doctor Carson, I'm happy you could make it." He began making introductions, starting with the young woman to his left.

"This is my girlfriend, Avril Boutelle, she's finishing up her master's in xenoanthropology."

Carson nodded to her. "Yes, you were in my Archeology 501 class last year, weren't you?"

"That's right."

David continued. "Beside her is Wes Archer, my roommate, studying astrophysics. His friend Andrea Ferguson, biology, I'm not sure how they ended up together. I'm still expecting Captain Gupta, I'm not sure if he's bringing a friend. Folks, this is Doctor Carson."

"Just Hannibal tonight, or Carson. And this is my friend and some-time pilot, Jaqueline Roberts."

"Jackie, please. It's good to meet you all. And congratulations on finishing your thesis, David."

They took their seats, and the young man David had introduced as his roommate leaned toward Jackie.

"Pilot?" Archer asked. "As in starship pilot?"

"That's right. I own a Sapphire-class, the *Sophie*."

"Really? I'm envious. Wait, Roberts? Are you the Jacqueline Roberts who was born on the first Eta Carinae expedition?" he blurted out. His girlfriend, Andrea, elbowed him in the ribs. He looked at her as if to ask "What?" and she glared at him and nodded toward Jackie.

He blushed. "Oh, I'm sorry," he said to her. "That was a rude question. Forget I asked."

Jackie smiled. "No worries. It's not exactly a secret, although few people remember it. Although you're the second person to ask that lately. Yes, I am, but obviously I hardly remember it. I was about four Earth-years old when we returned, although we went out on another expedition later."

"That is so cool, growing up on a starship."

Jackie shrugged. "It seemed perfectly normal to me."

"Weren't you bothered by the lack of kids your age to play with?" Avril Boutelle asked.

"Why would I have been? I didn't know any different. There were a couple of younger kids later in the mission, and an older one who must have been eleven or twelve when the expedition departed Kakuloa. Children adapt to what they grow up with. If it doesn't bother the adults, it doesn't bother the kids."

"As long as things aren't too extreme," Avril said.

"I suppose." The line of conversation was mercifully interrupted as Rick brought the last guest to the table. Both David Zhang and Carson stood up.

"Captain Gupta, it's good to see you." David glanced around the table. "I think you all know Rajesh Gupta; you've been on at least one off-world field trip."

Gupta looked around the table, nodding at each of them, until he got to Roberts. "And who is this?"

"Captain Gupta," Carson said, "may I present Captain Jacqueline Roberts of the starship *Sophie*. Jackie, Gupta here pilots one of the University's own Sapphire class ships, the *Chandrasekhar*. I think the last time we flew together was to Verdigris, that must be well over a year ago now."

Jackie rose to shake Gupta's hand. "A Sapphire?" she said. "Wise choice."

He smiled at her then turned to Carson. "I can understand why you don't want to fly with me any longer."

Carson laughed. "Nothing personal. The schedules just haven't worked out." That, and his recent trips had also had secret agendas.

The conversation lulled then as the waiter came to take their drink orders.

∞ ∞ ∞

Most of the people at the table were nearly finished their main course. The food so far had been excellent, Jackie thought, although much of the conversation somewhat less so. The others were all connected through Drake University, not something she had in common with them.

At an ebb in the discussion, she leaned toward Captain Gupta. "So, Rajesh, were you Carson's pilot when he ran into tomb-raiders on Verdigris?"

He nodded, but before he could speak, Avril Boutelle interrupted.

"Tomb-raiders?" she asked. The phrase had caught her attention. "What happened?"

"It is rather embarrassing really," Gupta said. "Carson had uncovered an unusual tomb that we had earlier spotted on radar from orbit. While we were all either inside or gathered around the entrance, several armed men showed up and took over. It turned out that one of the laborers we had hired in Verdigris City had been working in cahoots with the miscreants, and signaled them when we found something. Frankly I was worried they were just going to shoot us all, and I was wishing I'd stayed with the ship."

"If you had, they might have dealt with you first, when they landed," Carson said. "But generally, these crooks won't kill if everyone cooperates. Artifact smuggling is one thing, murder another."

Other conversations at the table had fallen silent when Gupta had started telling the story, and heads swiveled from Gupta to Carson and back in rapt attention.

"Well, I certainly didn't know that. And Doctor Carson made it a point to inform the scalawags that the artifacts would be worth more if their authenticity was established. He was quite emphatic about them leaving our recordings so he could write a paper. Obviously, they couldn't kill us off and leave him alive, so he may have saved our lives." He looked around the group, then at Carson. "By the way, did you ever publish that paper?"

Carson grinned and caught Jackie's eye. She knew the later part of the story. She and Carson had run into Hopkins and some of his henchmen on Chara III, where—ultimately—Hopkins had met his end. Carson wasn't going to share that story, was he? He winked at her. Perhaps not.

"I did," Carson said. "Months later, and in the most obscure journal I could find."

The others at the table chuckled in appreciation.

"Which raises a point," Carson said, and glanced around the table, briefly catching the eye of each of the grad students. "In fact, Dean Matthews has been after me to increase the quality of my own publications. Keep that in mind. If you plan to go into academia, you'll always be judged by your output." He paused a moment, then added: "But I suppose that's true in any occupation." He looked at Gupta and Roberts. "Maybe not piloting?"

"I cannot speak for Captain Roberts, but I have to regularly file trip reports, maintenance logs, and so on. The university has to justify the expense of owning its own ships. And the astrophysics department wants full copies of all my trip logs whether I'm going somewhere off the beaten path or just routine."

The latter intrigued Jackie. "I can understand the interest in new destinations, but why would they care about flights over well-travelled routes?"

"Someone's research project. As I understand it they're studying whether repeated warp traffic has any lasting effect on the normal curvature of spacetime."

"And does it?" Wes Archer asked, looking from Gupta to Roberts and back.

Jackie shook her head; the idea was ludicrous. "Not that I've noticed," she said, and looked at Gupta. "You?"

"Not so far as I know. Even if our ships did have some effect, I can't imagine it would be measurable. The *Chandra* does have special instruments aboard to collect data. But one trip from here to, say, Delta Pavonis is the same as any other, once you take into account normal stellar drift and planetary orbits. Personally, I think the researcher is wasting his time, but I suppose a negative result will help confirm or disprove someone's hypothesis. All data is useful."

There were sage nods from the students at the table.

"Speaking of Delta Pavonis," Boutelle said, turning to Carson, "you mentioned an unusual tomb on Verdigris. What was unusual about it?"

"The shape. You'll recall that most of the tombs on Verdigris are dome-shaped, like stone igloos."

She nodded. "Yes."

"Well, this one was more like a pyramid."

"Really? Was there anything different about the contents?"

Carson smiled wryly. "We didn't exactly have very long to examine them, but I didn't see anything out of the ordinary before the raiders carted everything off." Technically true. He'd found the talisman after that. "They let me keep a tissue sample from the mummified occupant, but DNA testing didn't show any significant differences from other mummified remains we've found."

"What about the current natives?"

"I thought they were extinct?" Jackie said. She was sure Carson had said something to that effect the last time they were there.

"The tomb-builders are, so far as we know," Boutelle said. "But Verdigris still has intelligent natives who don't build stone structures. They're a related sub-species, we think." She turned to Carson for verification.

"That's right," he said. "There are some genetic and minor anatomical differences between the current population and what remains we've found in and near stone ruins. Something like the differences between Neanderthals and Cro-Magnons in ancient Europe. The current population stays clear of any stone ruins. They're less skittish about human cities, but apparently, they have a long cultural tradition regarding the ancient natives. Avril could probably tell you more about that."

"Some," Avril Boutelle said. "Largely their ancient ranges—about fifteen-thousand years ago—didn't overlap, or at least there's no fossil or archeological evidence to indicate they did. There are a few cultural similarities—as best we can tell with an extinct culture—that suggest at least some contact. Possibly some trade, perhaps slavery. Unfortunately, a lot of the archeological history is gone, looted before anyone got serious about making and enforcing laws against it."

"Why did the tomb-builders die out?"

"Nobody knows for sure," Boutelle said. "The prevailing theory is that the climate changes, shifting grasslands to desert and then to jungle as the icecaps retreated and prevailing wind and ocean currents changed, caused their civilization to collapse by disrupting agriculture. They were never as widespread over the planet as humans were on Earth; the geography doesn't lend itself to massive overland migration.

"However," she continued, "that's less true of the current natives, who seem to have been more spread out. They may be better physiologically suited to migration." Boutelle warmed to the subject. "The jury is still out. The most interesting sites are in the middle of the jungle or under desert sands, and the place hasn't had either the archeological or paleontological study it deserves. The local human culture is more oriented to immediate results, things like biologicals and mining rather than the softer sciences."

"You seem to know quite a bit about the place, Avril," Jackie said.

"I spent some time there studying," Boutelle said, "and I like to keep up."

"She's understating it," David Zhang said. "Avril has a part time gig writing reports on intelligent aliens for some import-export company. I guess they're looking for opportunities."

Boutelle shot him a fierce look. "It's not that big a deal," she said, then turned to Jackie. "It's a spin-off from my studies."

Jackie wondered at her reaction, but just then Rick, the owner, came over to the table. "Whom can I interest in dessert? I have an almond honey and vanilla layer cake with an *amlou* filling. . . ."

It sounded delicious. Jackie decided she would find room for it.

Chapter 18: Proxima

Sawyer City

THE DINNER PARTY broke up, and the couples gathered on the sidewalk outside Rick's Place to grab autocabs. One pulled up in front of Carson and opened its doors, but he stepped back from the curb and waved Captain Gupta ahead of him. "After you, please."

"Thank you." Gupta nodded to Jackie. "Captain Roberts, we should get together and trade stories sometime. I'd like to hear more about the courier business."

"It's not as romantic as you might think, but sure," she said as Gupta climbed into the cab. Another one pulled in behind it, which she and Carson took.

"Still feeling paranoid about autocabs?" she asked him. "I assume that's why you let Gupta take the first one."

"A little," Carson admitted, "and I don't think they'd be dumb enough to kidnap the wrong person. So, how was your dinner?"

"Fantastic. I'm full," she said. "I really didn't need a slice of that cake, but it was worth it. Thank you for inviting me."

Carson smiled. "I was happy to. So, what are your plans for the next few days?" he asked. "Are you staying around?"

Jackie wondered if he was leading up to another invitation, but she already had another commitment. "I don't make any money sitting in port. I'm booked for a short duration courier run. And before you ask, I still haven't had a chance to look at that data. Ducayne's paranoia must be rubbing off on me; I'm not sure what I want to run on *Sophie*'s computers."

Carson nodded in understanding. "It will keep. But a courier run, does that mean you'll be gone for a few weeks?" He sounded disappointed.

Jackie wondered at the reason for his disappointment. Her absence, or the data? "No," she said. "It's a mail run to Grainger Station at Proxima. The usual courier ship is down for maintenance."

"And they need a mail run? Can't they just radio?"

She tried not to roll her eyes. "Let me guess. You think that just because Proxima is part of the Alpha Centauri system it's only a few light hours away?"

"Isn't it?" Carson looked puzzled. "Here to Kakuloa is what, ten light hours?"

"About that, round trip. Right now, Alpha Centauri A and B are about nineteen AU apart. Alpha Centauri C, Proxima, is more than five hundred times that, about ten light *weeks*. They don't want to wait that long for the mail."

"Oh. I hadn't realized."

"Most people don't even think about Proxima. It's a red dwarf, and the only Earth-sized planet it has was never terraformed. The Terraformers don't seem to have cared about red dwarf stars. It's not a very interesting system. Frankly I'm not even sure why there's an outpost there. Anyway, it's less than four hours away in warp and the *Sophie*'s available. So, I'm carrying the mail."

"How long is that gig going to last? And do you do the round trip in a day?"

"No. Add a couple of hours for in-system maneuvers, and I need to land if there are physical packages to drop off or pick up. So, a day there, then returning the next day. Probably two round trips unless the *Lark*, the regular courier ship, needs more maintenance than they expect. Why the sudden interest in my schedule, anyway?"

"Dinner tonight was fun. I thought we might do it again. If you'll settle for something less than Rick's."

Jackie turned to look at Carson, trying to read his expression. Did he want to start dating again? Did *she* want that? She covered her confusion with a joke. "I don't know. A girl has to have her standards."

"And here I was going to offer food bars around a campfire," Carson said, recalling their overland trek to the pyramid on Chara III.

She smiled at him. "Hannibal Carson, the incurable romantic. Why don't I call you when I get back from Proxima and we'll see what we're up for?"

"All right. I don't expect to be going anywhere."

∞ ∞ ∞

Jackie had shopping to do before her trip to Proxima. Supplies for the short voyage didn't amount to much, and the spaceport could supply those. Instead she wanted to pick up a spare omniphone.

She hadn't been kidding about Ducayne's paranoia rubbing off on her, and with the modifications he'd had made to the *Sophie*, he could well have a tap on the ship's computer systems. In general, that wouldn't bother her, since the ship's logs were open to inspection anyway, especially given her courier status. Any privileged communications would be encrypted to levels that even Homeworld Security shouldn't, in theory, be able to break. She had her doubts about that, but it didn't apply to the normal ship operations logs anyway. If she was going to decipher the markings on Carson's newest talisman, she would have to do it off-line.

A simple omniphone had more than enough computing power for what was essentially a simple database lookup and geometry problem. Besides, it would give her something to do during the otherwise boring four hours in warp to Proxima.

Chapter 19: Office Hours

Drake University, Sawyer City

HANNIBAL CARSON SAT at the desk in his campus office, forcing himself to read through the turned-in assignments from one of his undergrad classes. His teaching assistant had already gone through them first, of course, but it was only fair to his students to double-check the TA's work. And to the university, he reminded himself. They were paying his salary, albeit much of that out of research grants and the endowment Ducayne had made in the name of Carson's mythical great-aunt.

There was a knock at the open door, and he looked up to see a young woman standing there. He recognized her as David Zhang's girlfriend from dinner the other evening.

"Ms. Boutelle, isn't it? Come on in. What can I help you with?" She wasn't currently in any of his classes, but there was some overlap between xenoanthropology and exoarcheology.

"Just Avril, Professor Carson." She smiled at him. "Do you have a few minutes?"

"Anything to take a break from grading papers." He gestured her to the spare chair. "And you don't need to call me professor. Just Carson is fine. Or Hannibal. What's up?"

"Well, I'm working on a side project. It's nothing to do with my thesis, just some freelance research I'm doing, and it relates to archeology. Something you said at dinner the other night made me think you might be able to help. I just have a few questions; I wouldn't want to take up your time."

"Oh? What was it I said? And what's your project? David said you wrote occasional reports on intelligent aliens, or something."

"Something like that," Boutelle said. "You mentioned that the tomb you found on Verdigris was unusual, that it was pyramid-shaped. We both know most of the Verdigran stone tombs are domes."

"Yes, that's right. That's what caught my attention. How does that relate to what you're doing?"

"Usually my reports just concern still-existing societies. One of my clients is apparently more interested in structures that any species might have left behind, even on planets where no current intelligent life—well other than humans—is found."

"So, some sort of comparative archeology?" Carson was intrigued. That very sort of comparison was what had got him interested in the possibility of an ancient spacefaring species in the first place. Dean Matthews had called it "von Däniken nonsense", but it had led him to the talisman and then the pyramid on St. Jacobs.

Avril nodded, but Carson had an uneasy feeling. "You said structures. What sort of structures?"

"They asked me to write up a report covering all known pyramids."

If Carson had been drinking coffee he would have choked on it. "Pyramids, you say?" he said quickly to cover his reaction. His suspicions grew. "So, you would be including pyramids on Earth? There are quite a few."

"Um, that's a good question. I'll have to check back with them. But certainly Verdigris and Ransom's Planet, and I know there are others, like at Gliese 68."

"Of course, of course," Carson said, wondering just who Boutelle's client was. Would the Velkaryans try something so obvious? "I think there was a survey paper on that a couple of years ago in *The Journal of Exoarcheology*. Or maybe it was in the proceedings from a conference. I can dig up a copy, but you'll have to give me a day or so. How much of a hurry are you, or your client, in? Who did you say they were?"

"I didn't. They like to keep things confidential because of potential competitive interests."

"Competitive interests?" Carson wondered what sort of legitimate business could have competition for a list of pyramids. "All right, fair enough, I suppose we have those in academia, too."

Avril nodded again. "Yes. You wouldn't think so in fields like anthropology or archeology, but there it is. Anyway, a day or so is fine if you think you can find that paper. Or just send me a link to it. That would be really helpful." She smiled at him. He could see how that smile might get people eager to do favors for her, but he'd had enough pretty female—and the occasional male—students try that on him that he'd built up some resistance to it. In this case, he already knew where to find that paper, but he wanted to talk to Ducayne first.

∞ ∞ ∞

UDT Headquarters, Sawyer City

"You wanted to see me?" Ducayne said to him when Carson arrived. "Was it something about the pyramid?"

Carson grinned wryly. "You could say that. I had an interesting request this morning, from a grad student working in xenoanthropology. Not one of my current students, but she has been in a couple of my classes. She does some freelance reports for clients outside the university. Nothing wrong with that, we encourage it, so long as there's no academic dishonesty."

"Fair enough," Ducayne said. Was that a slight smirk on his face? "And what does this have to do with me, or us?"

"She's doing a report on all known pyramids in T-Space. Well, that's not the way she phrased it, she said on planets with known present or previous intelligent life, but that amounts to the same thing. She asked me if I had any convenient references."

Ducayne was definitely grinning now. "I guess she went to the right person."

"But that's not the point. Or maybe it is. She wouldn't tell me who her client was, but I was wondering if it was some Velkaryan front operation. Or worse, if she's a Velkaryan agent herself."

The grin went away. "Do you have any other reason to think so?"

Carson thought about it. "No, not really. It just seems too coincidental."

Ducayne nodded, and the grin came back. "You have good instincts, Carson. It *is* too coincidental. This student, you didn't mention her name. Was it Avril Boutelle?"

Carson's surprise was brief. He should have known Ducayne would be keeping tabs on that sort of thing. "You're watching her?"

"You could say that. She works for me."

"She what?"

"I asked her to pull that report together. She has done other reports for us. 'Intelligence briefings' is the formal name. Nothing particularly sinister about it, it's just compiling data from available sources. I was going to ask you to do it, but I decided that wasn't the best use of your time. It was resourceful of her to ask, although I might have a word with her about being more subtle next time."

"Oh," said Carson, not knowing what else to say.

"Anyway," Ducayne continued, "if you do have something you could give her to get started, that's great. But don't mention Pete's Peak or the Chara pyramid to her. Need to know and all that, and I want to see if she's resourceful enough to include those in her report. Especially the Chara pyramid, which nobody outside this office should know about."

"All right. I'll do that. But about the Chara pyramid, Finley knows about it, and the Velkaryans probably at least suspect."

"You're right, but I wouldn't expect either of those to make it public knowledge either. I can't say I'm thrilled that Finley knows, but you had your reasons for telling him."

"And he knows how to keep a secret," Carson said.

"He does. Anyway, thanks for coming to me with your suspicions about Ms. Boutelle. As I said, you have good instincts. Trust them. We'll talk again later."

As Carson left, he thought about his mixed feelings. He was glad that Boutelle wasn't working for the Velkaryans, knowingly or otherwise, but he was also annoyed that Ducayne hadn't told him. He finally shrugged the annoyance off, recognizing that there was no good reason Ducayne should have told him. Compartmentalization was more important than social niceties where security was concerned.

Chapter 20: Proxima-b

Starship Sophie, *nearing Proxima Centauri*

JACKIE ROBERTS HADN'T quite finished analyzing the pattern on Carson's talisman. The stellar database that came with the omniphone was in a different format from what was in Sophie's navigation computer. Nobody was going to be using an omniphone to pilot a starship, after all. The information was adequate for her immediate need, she just had to revise her original program for the new data format.

She didn't believe the results from the first run of the program against Carson's talisman. She was just setting it up to run against her copies of the older talisman data when the *Sophie* reached Proxima. She stowed it all away for now.

She dropped the *Sophie* out of warp and hailed the station. "Grainger Station, this is the S-class *Sophie* out of Sawyers World on a courier run. Requesting landing info."

"Sophie? *A courier run? What happened to the* Lark? *We're not expecting you.*"

"The *Lark* is undergoing an overhaul. I was asked to take over the run. Transmitting authorization, stand by." Jackie tapped the control to send the coded signal. It was a little unusual, but she had encountered similar reactions before when making deliveries to certain off-world bases. However, her courier clearance was great for easing the way in. Everyone wants to get their mail.

"*Authorization received. Thanks,* Sophie, *and welcome to Proxima-b. You can land at the pad near the base, transmitting details now.*"

Jackie saw the approach plate, a diagram with detailed landing information, flash up on her navigation console. "Copy that, Grainger. Got it."

"Roger. Zone extends to twenty kilometers, report entering. Proxima out."

Well, that was curt, Jackie thought. On the other hand, she realized, she didn't know what time zone they were in. Maybe she had caught someone at a bad time. It wasn't like they got a lot of traffic.

∞ ∞ ∞

Proxima-b, to give it its original designation, was a heavy planet, with nearly twice the mass of most terraformed worlds, although less than that of Skead, Jackie's adopted home at Tau Ceti. Its atmosphere had been thinned by a constant bombardment from the stellar wind from the red dwarf star it orbited every eleven-and-a-bit standard days. Its own day was twice that, being locked in a 3:2 orbital spin resonance like Mercury. Jackie imagined it would be like living on Earth's moon, only with a much higher gravity and a thin atmosphere. That thin atmosphere and high gravity would make landing a challenge, but that just made it interesting. Contrary to what she sometimes told Carson, she didn't *always* prefer boring.

Approaching the planet, the size of the sun—Proxima Centauri—was uncomfortable. Because the star was much smaller than the G- or F-type stars that terraformed planets orbited, its habitable zone was that much closer. Compared to the fingernail-sized disk that their respective suns seemed from Earth or Sawyers World, Proxima was the size of a golf ball, or larger. It just felt a bit unnatural. She had felt the same way approaching Kapteyn's Star to land on the planet where Tevnar discovered the wrecked Kesh ship. Not that she'd said anything to Carson, of course.

She came straight in, killing much of her approach speed with thrusters before entering the cool, thin, air up-range from the base. The ground below her was largely rocky, with patches of ice and meltwater, and scattered vegetation. It reminded Jackie of arctic tundra, except that the sky glow was more like candle-light and whatever was growing down there was more black or purple than green.

She called in as she approached the base's control zone, and, cleared to land, swept over the pad with a mix of aerodynamic and thruster lift, setting down a hundred meters from the domes of the base. She had already transmitted the electronic mail and other digital updates, but there was cargo and a handful of packages to deliver.

She called up the station again. "Proxima Base, do you have a docking tunnel, or do I need to suit up?" With the addition of a helmet, or at least a respirator, her ship coveralls would double as a temporary space suit, but it would be easier if they had a tunnel.

"*Give us a few minutes,* Sophie, *we'll send the bus. You're a standard Sapphire, correct?*"

"That's affirmative." She watched on a viewscreen as a four-wheeled vehicle, not unlike a bus, trundled out from a docking bay at the side of one of the domes and across the pad toward her. As it reached her ship, the main cab of the bus began to rise on scissor jacks above the wheeled frame, coming to a stop level with the Sophie's airlock door. A smaller portion of the cab then telescoped out to the ship's hull. Jackie felt a slight bump as a flexible, inflatable seal made snug contact around the hatch. The whole procedure was not unlike a mobile jet-way used with some commercial airliners and starships.

There came a knock on the outer airlock door, and another voice over the radio. "*We have a seal. You can open up.*"

Jackie, by now waiting in the airlock, checked the outside pressure and, finding it good, opened up the hatch.

"Hi, I'm Jackie Roberts, captain of the *Sophie*," she greeted the man standing there. "Welcome aboard."

"Well," the man said, "I must say you're a nice change from old Joe Riley on the *Lark*. I'm Antonio Mazzone. Call me Tony. Welcome to Grainger Station."

∞ ∞ ∞

A second bus, this one a cargo vehicle, pulled up and docked with the aft cargo door. Jackie supervised as two men and a woman made quick work of unloading the various packages and, more importantly, food, water and other supplies. The base of course had life-support systems that recycled the air and water, but such systems tended to be lossy unless deliberately—and expensively—designed otherwise. Supplies to stock the autochefs and some highly prized "real" food and drink topped off the necessities. Lab equipment and supplies, data updates, and personal items rounded out the shipment.

"All right," Tony said. "That's done." The cargo bus sealed its hatch and detached from the cargo lock, and began rolling back to the base.

Tony turned to Jackie. "I assume you're staying for a while, not turning around immediately?"

"That's right," Jackie replied. "I was planning to lift in the morning. I can stay aboard ship, though, if space is a problem."

"Oh, no problem at all, we have a guest room. Riley likes to stay over, and we have the occasional visiting scientist. Besides, it's nice to see a new face, someone else to discuss things with over the evening meal."

"Evening?" Proxima was still high in the sky. "What time zone do you keep?" Of course they wouldn't go by local time, not with a day lasting three weeks.

"Sawyer City time. I assume you're on that?"

"At the moment, yes. Normally I try to adjust to my destination anyway."

"But you didn't need to this trip. That's why we keep Sawyer time. Anyway, we have a couple of hours until dinner. While the crew gets these supplies squared away, how about a tour of the base?"

"Sure, I'd like that. Just give me a moment to secure my ship."

∞ ∞ ∞

As the passenger bus rolled back to the base, Jackie watched out the window. The area had mostly been cleared, and except for the coloring could as easily have been on the Moon or, she supposed, Mars. *Or that planet at Kapteyn's Star*, she thought, although the gravity was lighter here than on that last one. There were a few scattered patches of dark purple vegetation around the edges of the compound, where unevenness in the rock provided shelter and, probably, a place for water to collect.

"What kind of plants are those?" she asked, pointing to them. "They don't look like anything I've seen on terrestrial worlds."

"Indeed, they're not. Arguably they're not even plants, at least not as we know them. They do perform photosynthesis, and extract nutrients from the soil and are made up of cells with cell walls, but all that is just analogs of anything descended from Earth life. These are not; the biochemistry is different."

"Really? How different?" Jackie was no biologist, but she knew the basics.

"Well, it is built on the same RNA and DNA bases as Earth life, but, other than that, most of the biochemical pathways are different. The cell walls aren't cellulose; they're a different polysaccharide, and they don't use chlorophyll."

"That would explain why they're not green." Jackie said.

"Exactly."

"Life must have evolved here quite differently from Earth." On all the terraformed planets, life had been transplanted from Earth when those planets were reshaped. This one clearly hadn't been.

Tony hesitated a moment, then said, "You could say that, I suppose. But we think it didn't evolve here."

"What do you mean?"

"The biology here happens to match some we've found on planets around other red dwarf stars."

"Maybe red dwarfs just favor a different kind of biogenesis?"

"A good thought, but we haven't found any fossil traces old enough to suggest life arose here by itself. And before you ask, no, the age is not consistent with it having been transplanted by the Terraformers. Best guess is just over a hundred million standard years, give or take."

"Wait," Jackie said, not sure she was understanding what he seemed to be saying. "Are you implying that there were two waves of, for lack of a better term, Terraformers? One terraforming—or whatever the word would be—worlds around red dwarf stars, and another, forty million years later, doing the same with yellow star planets?"

"I'm not implying that at all. It could have been natural panspermia, primitive life hitchhiking on debris kicked up by an impact. None of the life here is very complicated." The words came almost as if by rote. There was no enthusiasm behind them.

Jackie was about to ask who he was trying to convince, her or himself, but the bus had arrived at the base and Tony was busy with the docking sequence. He seemed almost relieved.

How curious, Jackie said to herself.

Chapter 21: Training Exercise

Ducayne's Office

REGINA ELLIOT WAS in Ducayne's underground office, discussing some administrative items, when the comm on Ducayne's desk warbled.

He glared at it for a moment. Elliot knew that there were only a few people who could call him on that circuit. She rose to leave, but Ducayne waved to her to stay seated. He did, however, pick up the handset so she wouldn't hear the other end of the conversation.

"Good afternoon, Mister Ambassador," Ducayne said into the phone. Regina grinned to herself, Ducayne's facial expression belied his pleasant tone of voice.

"Yes, of course I've seen it," he said after a moment. "No, it wasn't my idea." Ducayne looked at her and rolled his eyes. She put her hand up to her mouth to cover her smirk.

Ducayne listened a moment more, then said, "It shouldn't be a problem. We have a good working relationship with the Sawyers government. Uh, we do, don't we?"

A brief pause, and then he continued.

"No, it will just be a training exercise. A dozen *UDT* Space Force ships warp into the system, halfway between here and Kakuloa I imagine. Then they run a simulated assault on Kakuloa."

They had run this kind of exercise before, she knew, but not in a few years. The exercises had begun following an attempt to hijack an antimatter shipment back in the 2090s. After that, the Space Force had run major drills every few months for a couple of years. Then they'd petered out, with one every few years. As Elliot thought about it, she realized that the last such exercise had been before the current *UDT* ambassador to Sawyers World had been appointed. No wonder he was antsy.

"Yes, the Southern Continent," Ducayne was saying. "I'm sure they'll stay away from the squid reservation, it's a big continent. Or maybe they'll land in the desert across the mountains from Kakuloa City. I don't know."

Another pause as Ducayne listened to the phone.

Ducayne said, "Sir, you know as well as I do that Kakuloa is *UDT* territory."

She wondered if the ambassador really knew that; the appointment was likely as much a political favor as anything based on merit.

"No," Ducayne said patiently, "it's under joint jurisdiction, not just Sawyer's World. As per the treaty."

It was Regina's turn to roll her eyes. The ambassador really should know this.

"Yes, you'll have to break it to them. It's not my place to, although I can feed my counterpart some information through the usual back channels. That's just common courtesy."

Another pause.

"It's not up to me, but if they want to involve Space Guard in a joint exercise, that might be a good idea. That will have to be coordinated, though. The Space Force should know that their participation is part of the exercise."

Well now, Regina said to herself, *where did that come from?* A joint exercise with the Sawyers World Space Guard and the *UDT* Space Force could be interesting, especially if Space Guard were acting as the Red Team.

"No, of course we wouldn't want anyone to get the wrong idea."

No, Regina agreed, *and it had better not be a live fire exercise either.*

"A few weeks. Plenty of time to get messages back and forth."

Ducayne had begun to tap impatiently on his desk. That wasn't a good sign.

"If you like. Yes, I can make that recommendation to my superiors back on Earth."

Regina could almost hear Ducayne's teeth grinding. She knew he loved his independence.

"Thank you, Ambassador. And to you." Ducayne placed the handset back in its cradle, confirmed that the circuit was really off, and muttered a curse.

Then he looked up at Elliot. "If you want my job, now is probably a good time to ask."

She laughed and shook her head. "No thanks."

∞ ∞ ∞

"What was that all about?" Regina asked. "Although I think I can guess."

"You probably can. Space Force, or somebody, wants to do a training exercise. Essentially, stage an invasion. Jump into the system and land *en mass* on some remote area of Kakuloa. Obviously, we need to keep Sawyers World in the loop so they don't freak out when a dozen ships materialize in the system. Ambassador Hadron thinks their Space Guard might be a bit upset anyway, and wants to make it a joint exercise."

"What do you think? And why does Space Force want to do this?"

Ducayne thought for a moment, and then said, "Well, it might actually have been my idea."

"What? You lied to the ambassador? I'm shocked. Shocked, I tell you," she said, not shocked at all.

"I never suggested it in so many words. But my reports lately have been raising the spectre of an armed Velkaryan contingent out here. You know yourself that certain parts of the UDT government are getting nervous about Velkaryan activity on Earth, too. Venezuela was just the first. Several other member states are showing increasing Velkaryan sentiment. They've gotten very good at infiltrating social media and the like."

Elliot nodded. She had brought some of that information back herself. "It's been what, four standard years since Space Force's last exercise? They're probably due for one anyway. A show of force might help keep the Velkaryans in line."

"Then it might be better for Space Force to do it in another system, like Delta Pavonis. Verdigris has been grumbling about seceding from the UDT for a while now, or parts of the planet have, according to reports from our agents there. A visit from the Force might sober them up."

"Really?" Elliot had her doubts. "That could either trigger them to action or force them underground for a few more years, building up their reserves and hiding themselves even better."

"Neither of which is particularly appealing," Ducayne said. "Although I do like the idea of making them jump before they're fully prepared."

"The question is whether our Space Force is fully prepared either."

"That's a good point. In which case, a training exercise in this system might be just what they need."

"What about having the local Space Guard be the red team?" Elliot suggested. "Doing an unopposed landing doesn't teach our forces much. For that matter, there must be some places left on Earth they could do that."

"Oh, sure there are. But there's also a lot more traffic, and it's a very familiar system. They need a touch of the unexpected. I'm sure the ship's crews are fine with it, most of them would have been on multiple patrols and visits to other systems. Helping to discourage piracy, smuggling, and that sort of thing. The landing forces are a different matter. Some of them will have experience, but for many of them it might be their first taste of non-standard gravity and non-standard day lengths."

"A full-scale land *and occupy* drill, then? Do these troops cross-train with Peace Enforcers?"

"Technically they *are* Peace Enforcers," Ducayne said. "Except for a few planets like Sawyers World and Taprobane, we're all happy *UDT* member states or territories. Any landing in force would technically be a police action, not an invasion."

"That could be interesting if we ever actually need to carry out a military invasion," she said. "For unpleasant values of *interesting*."

"There's always the approach of dropping rocks from a great height. That would take the spirit out of those on the ground." Ducayne didn't sound convinced, and Regina understood why not.

"Maybe. It's not a precision approach, and it may just end up pissing them off. Especially if they have ships of their own."

"As long as we're only dealing with humans, at least we know what to expect."

"Who are you worried about this week? The Kesh or Carson's ancient spacefarers? Surely not timoans."

"Oh, I worry about timoans too, but they're way down on my list. Our concern is any spacefaring species, especially the ones who are either keeping themselves secret or we've only found secondhand evidence of."

"So, all of the above, then," Regina said. She knew that Carson—and possibly others—had met Kesh individuals on a very few occasions, and they weren't willing to make formal contact. Of more concern were the species the Kesh referred to as "degkhidesh", or enemy of the Kesh, since they—again, according to the Kesh—had attacked a Kesh world some hundreds of years previously. Of the ancient spacefaring civilization who had built the pyramid-museums, little else was known. They had apparently disappeared fifteen thousand years earlier, but that might be temporary. Worse, there could be other species out there who, like the Kesh, had built on the lessons of those pyramids and were technologically advanced spacefarers in their own right . . . perhaps to be stumbled across by the next traveller beyond the loose borders of known T-Space. Or vice versa.

It used to be assumed that the chances of encountering another spacefaring species were vanishingly remote, or else they would have long ago made contact—the so-called Fermi Paradox—but thanks to the ancient Terraformers, that theory had gone out the window. With who knew how many Earth-like planets out there, all seeded with Earth lifeforms, evolution on multiple worlds at roughly the same level as Earth was almost inevitable.

That wasn't even counting the possibility of civilizations developing on planets where life had developed independently. After all, the Terraformers had to come from *somewhere*, and even within T-Space, life—albeit relatively primitive life—had arisen on some non-terraformed worlds. Of course, not counting a few special exceptions like the Eta Carinae expedition, explored space was a region barely more than fifty light-years across. A flyspeck on the galactic map.

"Yes," Ducayne said wearily. "I worry about all of the above."

Chapter 22: Leaving Kakuloa

Kreschets Landing Spaceport, Kakuloa

REID SAT IN THE spaceport lounge waiting to board the shuttle for Sawyers World. Between take-off, landing, and maneuvering to position, it would be a three-hour flight, all but about thirty seconds of that in normal space. Since most of the rest would either be under high-gee or no-gee, there wouldn't even be any in-flight service. Reid looked at the time. Departure had been delayed for some mundane reason, so it would be another hour before the boarding call. He decided to check out the bar.

The place had seen both better and worse days. Kakuloa had once been the thriving hub of interstellar commerce, between pharmaceuticals like the anti-aging drug harvested from squidberries, the tourist beaches and casinos of nearby Kakuloa City, and the exploration missions to stars beyond Alpha Centauri. Sawyers World had then been the ugly stepsister of the two terraformed planets in the system, until Kakuloa's economy crashed.

The official reason for the crash was that the bottom fell out of the squidberry market when pharmaceutical companies on Earth finally figured out how to synthesize the anti-aging drug. The less-widely talked about reason was the fall off in the high value tourist trade as organized crime moved in to take over the casinos, and the psychoactive properties of squidberries and other native plants fed a growing illicit drug trade. *As if,* Reid mused as he sat nursing his drink, *organized crime could really have gained much foothold given the original libertarian, almost anarchic legal system on Kakuloa.*

As far as Reid was concerned, the real problem had been the movement to treat the tree squids as intelligent natives. The measures needed to keep tree squids out of the plantations without harming them raised the price of the squidberries to the point where the synthetics could undercut them. Declaring the entire Southern Continent off-limits to humans just compounded the problem. There were valuable resources on South Continent. Reid couldn't name any off hand, but it just stood to reason.

He drained the last of his drink and set the glass down on the bar a little more forcefully than he'd intended, earning him a dirty look from the bartender. *You'd think Kakuloans would be friendlier to the Velkaryan cause*, he thought as he got up to return to the boarding area. Many were, mostly the older inhabitants, but with the economy diversifying and growing again, the squids were being seen less as a threat to the planet's livelihood and more as a curiosity. What the fools didn't understand was that tree squids were the reason that Kakuloa still had to import all its flour, cereal, rice and other grass-derived crops. Despite their relative ubiquity on other terraformed planets, grasses had never taken hold on Kakuloa, and it was now prohibited to even attempt to grow them here, just in case they messed up the ecosystem in a way that threatened the poor tree squids.

Reid shook his head. It was something else for the Velkaryans to fix when they came into power, but it was not his immediate concern. The Sawyer shuttle was boarding.

Chapter 23: Leaving Proxima

Departing Grainger Station

DINNER WITH THE Grainger Station team was a pale shadow of what dinner at Rick's Cafe had been, at least as far as the food was concerned. The conversation had been slightly more interesting, but xenobiology wasn't Jackie's forte and planetology not much more so. Besides, Jackie wanted to get back to solving the puzzle of Carson's talisman, and she didn't want to do that until she was aboard ship in deep space.

Breakfast was a step up from her usual autochef fare, at least, since the cargo she had carried had included a crate of fresh eggs and frozen, but deliciously spicy, sausages. And coffee.

She finished stowing what little outgoing mail and cargo the station had and bid the station crew goodbye.

"Are you making the next run?" asked Jennifer Rudloe. She was the woman who had helped unload cargo the day before. "If so, we'll see you in a few days."

"Undetermined at this point," Jackie replied. "I'm on contingency in case the *Lark*'s maintenance isn't finished, so there is that possibility. If not, it was certainly good to meet you, and the others."

"And you. Thanks again."

With that Jackie secured the hatches and began the pre-flight checks while the bus trundled back to the safety of the base.

"Sophie, *Grainger Station here. You're cleared to lift at your discretion. Safe trip.*"

"Copy that, Grainger. Cleared to lift. It'll just be another minute or so."

She had green lights across the board, plenty of fuel, and the area around the ship was clear.

"Grainger Station, *Sophie* is departing. Thanks for your hospitality." She powered up the thrusters, and *Sophie* lifted toward space.

Home was an easy target to line up on. Alpha Centauri A and B were by far the brightest stars in the sky, aside from Proxima itself. Jackie didn't even bother precisely lining up the target, instead just eyeballing the half-way point between the two. She'd warp in that direction for three hours, then fine-tune her approach for the last 2500 AU. That should give her plenty of time correlate Carson's talisman against known stars.

∞ ∞ ∞

Three hours later

There was no question about it. Jackie had checked the code and the data twice. She had compared the new omniphone copy of her program against the three existing talisman patterns for known stars; Chara, Delta Pavonis, and the one that had to be Sol, despite Carson's insistence that there was nothing on Earth that could be a Spacefarer pyramid. They had all returned exactly those locations. Maybe Earth's pyramid—if there had been one and that talisman wasn't meant for something else—had been destroyed or buried after fifteen thousand years of geological forces.

Either way, she couldn't wait to see the look on Carson's face when she told him that the star map on his latest talisman unmistakably pointed to the Alpha Centauri system.

Chapter 24: *Mandragore*

Sawyer's World, UDT Homeworld Security

DUCAYNE'S DESK INTERCOM chimed, then a voice announced: "*The* Mandragore *is in-system, we just received a transmission.*"

"They're back early. Great news, thank you." The *Mandragore* must have departed Chara III—the planet of St. Jacobs—ahead of schedule. They must have important news, and yet not so urgent as to use up one of their higher-speed, antimatter-powered message torpedoes. Or perhaps, they were carrying something too big to fit in one of the compact message carriers. Ducayne hoped that was the case. "What's their ETA?" he asked.

"*About five hours. They sent a burst as soon as they came out of warp. Wait, subtract two hours from that for signal delay. We'll probably get another signal shortly.*"

One of the challenges of warp travel within a planetary system is that a ship could easily outrun its own transmissions. Usually a ship came out of warp in the outer fringes of the system, got its bearings, then made a series of hops to get closer to the target planet without wasting days in normal space. Since Alpha Centauri was a busy system, ships had to keep their jumps in and out of warp short and relatively slow, but they would still average faster than light.

"Keep me posted. And have them bring the ship into the hangar when they land."

Ducayne's Homeworld Security offices were largely underground, but the aging hangar building at the Sawyer City Spaceport under which they lay would keep any prying eyes away from the cargo that *Mandragore* had brought back. He was eager to see that cargo for himself.

Chapter 25: *Sophie's* Return

Sawyer Spaceport

IT WAS LATE AFTERNOON when Jackie piloted the *Sophie* in for a landing at the Sawyer City Spaceport. On the approach, she was surprised to see the doors of the familiar old hangar building open, and a ship being towed into it. Landing the *Sophie* was not a time to be rubbernecking, so she only took a quick look, even though her ship's computers could have handled it themselves. *What's that about?* she wondered. She would ask Ducayne when she got a chance, although he was just as likely to respond with "what ship?" even if it were still plainly visible on the hangar floor.

She parked her ship, secured it, and finished transferring the few packages she had brought from Proxima to the port cargo office. Then she called Carson.

"I'm back in town," she said when he answered. "You want to do dinner with me." It wasn't a question.

"I do? I mean yes, of course I do. Did you have something in mind?"

They agreed to meet at an unpretentious restaurant near campus.

∞ ∞ ∞

Drake's Diner, Sawyer City

"You sounded eager to get together. Was the food at Proxima that bad?" Carson asked when they had ordered.

"Well, it wasn't Rick's, but then neither is this place. But I have some news."

"Oh?"

"Do you know anything about the ship I saw pulling into Ducayne's hangar when I landed?"

"No. Should I? Is that the news?"

"Just curious. And no, it isn't. I had a chance to look at the, ah, star data you gave me."

"Star data?" Carson wasn't immediately sure what she meant.

Instead of answering, Roberts held up her hands with her left and right thumb-tips touching, likewise the tips of her forefingers. She bent fingers and thumbs to form the crude outline of a rounded square. Then she put her hands together under her chin as though that was what she had intended to do all along.

Carson got the significance of the gesture. She meant the star map from the mysterious talisman he'd received. She had his undivided attention.

"Oh, right, that star data," he said, feigning only moderate interest. "Anything interesting?"

"Alpha Centauri."

"What?" he blurted out. A diner at a nearby table looked over at him to see what the fuss was about. Carson coughed noisily, trying to cover his outburst.

"What?" he said again, this time in a lower voice. "Did you say—"

She nodded. "Yes. Alpha Centauri. AKA Rigil Kentaurus or Toliman, Gliese 559, Boss General Catalogue number 19728, and a handful of other catalog designations. In other words, *here.*"

Carson had so many more questions. He went with the obvious. "Which star, A or B?"

"It's not that detailed. Given the distances involved, it would just look like a single star anyway. So, Sawyers or Kakuloa, take your pick. Maybe both."

"I'm not aware of anything even vaguely pyramid-like on Kakuloa," he said, keeping his voice low. "Now I *really* want to take a look at Pete's Peak."

"I thought you were convinced it was a volcanic plug?" Jackie said with a light grin, her green eyes twinkling.

Carson refused to rise to the bait. "An intelligent person is always willing to change his mind in the face of new data." He grinned back.

"So now what? You go check it out?"

"It's not that simple, unfortunately. Remember, it's in the middle of a wildlife preserve."

"Right. Finley's leopard. So, how hard would it be to get permission for an archeological survey? It's not like you want to go hunting."

"The thing is, I don't particularly want to tell anyone why I think it's of archeological interest, at least not yet. And I'm sure Ducayne wouldn't want me to either."

"So, what are you going to do?"

"Maybe I could sneak in." He thought about his earlier discussion with Ducayne. "I could parachute in from the *Sophie*, if you're willing." He looked at her, his eyebrows raised. "I'm sure there were times you've wanted to shove me out an airlock, right?"

She snickered. "I don't have to answer that. But if you're jumping, it would be the aft cargo hatch, not the airlock. It's a moot point, though. I'm pretty sure the airspace over the preserve is restricted. I won't risk my courier license for that."

"Surely it's only restricted to a certain altitude. I'll just jump from higher than that."

"I don't think you've thought it through, Carson. Aside from the risks involved—what are you going to do if you land in a tree? Or are attacked by a leopard?—how are you going to get back out? Walk? That's got to be fifty or sixty kilometers to the nearest civilization, which is Camp Anderson, itself a historic site, and there'll be questions raised about where you came from. That's if you're not eaten by a leopard or a terror bird before you get there."

"It's not that much of a hike. We did it on Chara III, heading to the pyramid. I'll admit I have a few details to work out."

"A few?"

"Come on, Jackie. Organizing field expeditions is part of what I do."

"And how many of those have involved parachute insertions into wild terrain where possession of firearms is considered *prima facie* evidence of poaching?"

Carson sighed and shook his head. "Okay, you have a point. This might have a few added complications."

"*Might?*" she said, her voice rising. "This is your problem, Carson. Going off half-cocked and making it up as you go. If I did that flying a starship, I'd probably be dead by now, along with any passengers."

And that was one of their fundamental differences, Carson realized. Even though she was exaggerating his position, she had a valid point that space travel was necessarily much more exacting than his archeological field trips, at least until it came down to methodical excavation. There were some fundamental opposites in their two personalities. Maybe that was the attraction. Well, that and the fact that Jackie was an attractive, intelligent, and competent woman.

"All right," he said, conceding. "I'll give it some more thought. That was just brainstorming."

"Why don't you just tell Ducayne? Maybe he'll come up with something."

"I'm not quite ready to do that," Carson said. "When we discussed it before, I got the impression he had several other things going on with the Sawyers World government and didn't want to ask for any more favors. This is still hypothetical. For all we know there's something we haven't found somewhere on Kakuloa, or elsewhere on this planet. After all, we've got a talisman that points to Sol with nothing found so far on Earth."

"What about Mars?" Jackie said with a half smile. "There's the Cydonia pyramid."

Carson rolled his eyes. He knew she was joking, but said, "That one's five-sided. And you and I both know it's a natural formation that only looks like a pyramid."

"And Pete's Peak isn't? So, what, you want to prove it's a pyramid before asking to excavate it?"

"You have to admit, that would be a lot more convincing. All it would take is enough digging to find carvings on it. Finley was too high up when he looked."

"How do you suppose he would react if he knew you had a tal—, um, chart that pointed to Alpha Centauri?"

Carson considered that. It had been one of Pete's first questions, and he had chided Carson for not having such an important piece of evidence. Would he believe Carson now? But there was a physical talisman to show him, and his partner, Naomi Maclaren, could validate that it was authentic. Wait, *was* it authentic? The star pattern had proved out, but he hadn't had the technetium battery isotope-dated for age. In fact, he hadn't even checked that it *had* a technetium battery. His enthusiasm was interfering with his archeological rigor. Maybe Jackie had a point. And she was looking at him, waiting for an answer to her question.

"I don't know how Pete would react," he said. "I intend to ask him." *Just as soon as I authenticate the dang thing*, he mentally added.

"What about Ducayne?"

Carson shrugged. "It's not like I'd be telling Pete anything he doesn't already know by now."

"No, just confirming it."

"Maybe. Despite what he said at our meeting, he may have confirmed it for himself fifty years ago, and just hasn't admitted it."

Chapter 26: The Chara Artifact

Sawyer Spaceport

DUCAYNE WATCHED THROUGH the window of his more-public office, a small room on the mezzanine that surrounded the hangar floor. The window overlooked the work area. The ship, a C-class modified to convert much of its cargo area to fuel tankage for range, waited until the hangar doors rolled shut behind it, then its own main hatch opened. Ducayne was on his way down the mezzanine's metal stairway as soon as the hangar doors had closed.

"Find anything interesting?" he asked as Walter Black, his agent in charge of the archeology team on Chara III, came down the boarding ramp.

"We did indeed. Carson's tip about the room he found in the Verdigris pyramid paid off. It took us a while to reach it because there was still some debris from the explosion Hopkins set off, but when we found the panel, it still worked. There was intact equipment on the pedestal he'd described."

"And?"

"We've no idea what it is, of course, but we took careful notes of the connections. We can power it up again."

"You brought it?"

"Of course. I figured you'd send me straight back if I didn't."

"You're probably right," Ducayne said.

"Well, let me tell you it was a pain in the ass maneuvering it down the access shaft we came in by."

"Carson said that on Verdigris, the previous visitors had just blown a hole in the wall."

"Believe me, I was tempted," Black said.

"What about the rest of the pyramid?"

"As their report described. Multiple levels beneath it, engravings on the walls and the exhibits. Mostly simple stuff. Carson's hypothesis of a teaching museum makes some sense. The lowest levels were getting into quantum mechanics but there were fewer practical examples and more diagrams and formulas. The specialists are making inroads on the language; it looks like it was designed to be easy to decipher."

"No new tech?"

"Nothing obvious in the museum area. There may be some interesting tidbits, but mostly it seemed intended to bootstrap a civilization to about mid-twentieth century level."

"Huh." Ducayne considered that. "It does make a weird kind of sense. If the locals didn't wipe themselves out with that, they'd presumably be less of a threat when they eventually developed interstellar travel."

Black nodded his agreement. "That was about the best explanation I could come up with too. It's not like the builders had laid out the plans for atomic bombs, but there was enough information to give someone so inclined a head start on them."

"And if they were warlike, they'd use them. That's one way to eliminate a short-sighted civilization." Ducayne had to wonder if the Pyramid Builders' intent was as altruistic as Carson thought it was.

"Yeah. They wouldn't have much access to fossil fuels."

Ducayne saw Black's point. With the terraformed planets only having had multi-cellular, Earth-like life for about 65 million years, they had never gone through anything like Earth's Carboniferous era, nor had they had hundreds of millions of years to form extensive coal beds and oil formations. There were some such, just as on Earth there were a few younger formations, but nothing that would lend itself to the scale of fossil fuel use that Earth went through for two centuries. Any civilization arising on a terraformed planet would have to bootstrap its technology with wood, methane, alcohol and other biofuels, before moving to wind, solar and ultimately nuclear electric. The timoans of Taprobane had already started in that direction—and apparently on their own; no pyramid had been found there. "Damned crafty, whoever built that thing."

"If they really wanted to encourage a nuclear war, wouldn't they have placed more than one pyramid per planet?" Black said.

"That's an interesting point, but enough of this. Let's see what you brought back."

Black and Ducayne walked back to the cargo area.

"We crated it up for shipping, of course," Black was saying. "I can show you pictures and the scans we took." The crate was about two meters long by a meter high and wide. It could have been a large coffin.

"I'll want to look at those, but since we're here. . ." Ducayne gestured at the container.

Black shrugged and helped Ducayne with the tie-down straps, then undid the latches. "It's not really much to look at," he said, and raised the lid.

He was right. Nestled in the foam padding, the device could have been any large piece of control equipment. It had a rectangular boxy shape, made of plastic or enameled metal, it wasn't obvious which at first glance. On one side was a panel with indicators or switches.

"We laid it on its back, the connectors are along this edge," Black pointed. "It's fairly heavy. I'd suggest leaving it in the container until we get it down to the labs."

Ducayne nodded. "Interesting. There are some superficial similarities in size and shape, but it's nothing like the other one. No reason it should be, of course."

"Other one? What other one?"

"The other alien artifact. One was brought back from a wrecked ship on a planet orbiting Kapteyn's Star. From the reports it looked like it had been added after the fact."

Black was suddenly full of questions. "Whose ship? What was the artifact? And where's Kapteyn's Star?"

"The star is a red dwarf a few light-years away," Ducayne said, "and we have no idea regarding either the ship or the artifact. This ship almost certainly wasn't human, and the artifact is unlikely to be whatever this is; it looks quite different."

"I suppose if it were built by a different culture, it could still serve the same purpose," Black said. "But for all I know this is just a control console and all the interesting stuff is still in the pyramid."

"Did you find any other passages, or signs of same?"

"Nothing definitive. The team I left there is still looking. The previous ship brought in some deep x-ray gear."

Ducayne nodded. That had been something Carson had suggested. "Either way," he said, "whoever ransacked the pyramid on Verdigris thought the console was worth taking. Anyway, get it to the lab. I have to leave now for an off-site meeting, but I'll want a full briefing later."

"Will do."

Chapter 27: Finley Revisited

Maclaren Industrial Research Corporation

CARSON'S MEETING WITH Finley was set up in an office at one of Naomi MacLaren's companies in town. That was easier for him to get to.

"Thank you for seeing me again, Dr. Finley," Carson said, "and especially for letting me meet with you here."

"You said you had new evidence, and something Naomi might want to see? You just better not be wasting our time."

"I have, and I think you'll agree I'm not. Where is she, by the way?"

"She has things to do. She's in the building. I'll let her know if it's worth her time. So, what have you got?"

"A little while back, someone inherited a collection of alien artifacts, many of them apparently illegally gathered. It happens, that's one of the hazards of my business. Anyway, the person decided to do the right thing and sent the collection to various museums and university archeology departments."

"Okay, so what does that have to do with my volcanic plug?"

"When we last met, you asked me if I had a talisman with a star chart that pointed to Alpha Centauri." Carson reached into his pocket and pulled out a specimen bag, then carefully slid the talisman out into his hand and held it up. "I do now."

Finley's eyes widened, then narrowed. "That's rather convenient."

"It was actually in my possession when you asked the first time. I just hadn't examined it closely, or correlated the pattern with actual stars. It would have been more convenient if I had. But I'm not asking you to take my word for it." He handed the talisman to Finley. "I've had the technetium inside sampled and tested — that's the tiny hole drilled into the back — you're welcome to check it out yourself, although I'll have to insist that the talisman doesn't leave my sight."

Finley examined the talisman, turning it over in his hands, feeling the surface, tapping his fingernail against it. He tapped the omni on his wrist. "Naomi, get in here. You'll want to see this."

He tapped his omni again and held the talisman up to it. As he turned it around so the small hole faced it, Carson heard the rising squeal of a radiation alert, which faded again when Finley moved the talisman away.

At that moment the door opened and a woman entered, of medium height and tanned skin, with silvering hair. She looked to be perhaps fifty or sixty, but if that was Naomi Maclaren, she had to be in her eighties. Another benefactor of squidberry extract.

"G'day," she said. "I reckon you must be Hannibal Carson. I've heard a bit about you." She looked to Finley. "Right then, what's he brought us?"

Finley tossed the talisman to her, causing Carson to wince at the cavalier handling of the artifact, but she caught it deftly.

"He says it's a talisman that points here, to Alpha Centauri. Technetium battery inside. It *is* slightly radioactive, I just checked."

Maclaren turned it over in her hands. "It is a supercircle, I'll give 'em that." She took her omni out of a pocket, held the talisman up and photographed the pattern of stones and lines. She handed the talisman back to Carson. "Here, mate, hold onto that," she said, and turned back to her omni.

A moment later she looked up from it. "He's right, it does seem to point to Alpha Centauri. Story is consistent, at least."

"Wait," Carson said, astonished that MacLaren just happened to have a program on her omni that could decipher the star pattern. "How did you do that?"

"Don't look so boggled, mate," she said, grinning at his expression. "Pete told me the story. When he said you were coming here with new evidence, I figured I'd rig up a program like your Jackie Roberts did. Writing the program was easy. The hard part was figuring out what the colors represented, and she'd already done that. She sounds like a clever girl; you should hang on to her."

"I, but. . . Yes, she's very intelligent," Carson said, not knowing quite how to react to that.

MacLaren frowned at him. "Or are you not as smart as I thought? Anyway, that's none of my business. This talisman is, or at least you've made it so. A technetium battery, eh? Have you dated it?"

"Yes, of course." Carson brought up the data on his own omni. "It's 14,723 years old, give or take two-fifty."

"Two-fifty? That's pretty sloppy measurement. I assume you mean standard years?"

"Yes, standard years. The problem is we don't know exactly where it's been for most of that time, so we can't adjust for cosmic ray or neutrino flux." He slipped his omni from his wrist and passed it to her. "Here are the details."

She scanned the data briefly. "Hmm. Okay. Mind if I take a copy of this?"

"No, go ahead."

She tapped his omni to hers and handed his back. "Thanks. Now, mind if I run the analysis myself?"

Carson had half-expected this. "No, but I'd rather not let the artifact out of my possession. How long would it take?"

"Just a few minutes. Come on, follow me down to the lab."

"A few—? The university lab takes days," Carson said, hurrying to catch up as she left the office. Pete Finley was right behind him.

"They're either understaffed or have woefully out-of-date equipment," she said.

"Probably both," he admitted.

The two men followed her down the hall to another office, this one with a security panel by the door. Maclaren waved her hand across it, and the door slid open. Carson didn't see what the panel had reacted to; her omni was in her pocket again, and she wore no badge or anything on her wrist. Another of her high-tech toys, no doubt.

She stopped before a bench with a large piece of equipment on it. The device had a chamber built into it, with a clear plastic door, and a panel with several buttons and a screen beside it. She touched a button and the chamber door slid up.

"Go ahead and place your talisman in that chamber. How did you sample the technetium?"

"We drilled a small hole in the back, away from anything else that looked like circuitry. We did the same with the Chara talisman, so it should still function."

"Okay, center the hole face up." She touched another button, and a bright green dot, as from a targeting laser, appeared on the surface of the talisman. "Put the hole where the laser beam is pointing. I'll focus it in."

"Wait, how does this work, exactly? I don't want any more damage done."

"We'll do less damage than you've already done. The green is just for coarse targeting. The real laser fires a nanosecond burst which will boil off less than a picogram of the material to be analyzed. Then we use a combination of optical and mass spectrography to analyze the atoms, and the built-in computer does the math."

"Wow," Carson said, duly impressed. "I would love to have something like this for our department. What does one cost?"

MacLaren had closed the chamber door and was lining the crosshairs up on a magnified image on the built-in screen. She turned to him and smiled. "Sorry, mate, this one's a prototype. As the saying goes, if you have to ask. . . ."

"Then I can't afford it. Sigh."

"Afraid so. But we hope to have them in production before long. We'll see about a stripped-down version for the educational market."

"Now I'm curious. Just what is the market for something like this anyway?"

"Ah, now *that's* proprietary information, and I'm not going to say. You'll have to use your imagination." She had continued to adjust the equipment as she talked. The crosshairs were now centered on the bottom of the hole he had drilled.

"Fair enough," Carson said. "And it looks like you're ready."

"Right. Just a moment while the caps charge." A red light lit up on the panel, and the green targeting laser turned off. The sample chamber lit up with a red light, and Carson heard a latch engage on the chamber door, and the faint whine of a fan spinning up. "Okay, here we go. Here, it's your sample, you can do the honors." She pointed to a large button on the panel. "Just push that and release it."

Carson reached out a finger, hesitated for a moment, and pushed the button. The was a brief, almost unnoticeable flash from the chamber and a muffled popping sound, and the fan noise picked up.

"Uh, that's going to have vaporized technetium in it," Carson said. "That's a beta emitter; not good to breathe." But surely Maclaren knew that.

"No worries," Maclaren said. "It's got a multistage cryogenic filter. Everything is trapped."

There was text scrolling up on the display panel now. After a few moments, the whine of the fans wound down, the red light in the chamber turned off, and the door unlatched. Maclaren studied the numbers on the display, muttering. "Since it's still a prototype, the user interface needs work. There's a lot of diagnostic data a regular user wouldn't need to worry about. Anyway," she said, pointing to a number on the screen, "there's your sample age. 14,738 years, a little different from what your lab got but well within the error range. You raised a good point about the location, though. I'll have to have my guys build in some accounting for that."

She opened the chamber door, withdrew the talisman, and handed it back to Carson. "So," she said, looking from Carson to Finley and back, "what you have there is something that until a few days ago I would have said couldn't exist. A sample of an isotope that is only found in nuclear reactors or the aftermath of a recent supernova, and thousands of years older than any nuclear reactors we know about. Let's go back to the office and you can tell us more about these aliens."

∞ ∞ ∞

"There's not really much more to tell that I haven't already told Peter," Carson said when they were back in the office. "We assume that whoever made the talismans built the pyramids we've found on different planets, and may have had some influence on similar-shaped structures built by natives."

"What about these—Kesh, you called them?—are they what Elizabeth saw that day back in camp?"

"That seems a good bet. She said the sketch looked like what she saw."

"But the Kesh had nothing to do with the pyramids?"

"That is less clear. The one I talked to said no, and the writing we found in the one pyramid doesn't resemble any Kesh writing that I saw. My working hypothesis is that the Kesh discovered a pyramid on their home planet maybe seven or eight thousand years ago, after the original Pyramid Builders had gone, and used that to bootstrap their civilization. That's probably the only reason they developed space flight before we did."

"But they've had it for thousands of years now. Why aren't all the terraformed planets now Kesh colonies? Why weren't they already here when we landed fifty years ago?"

Carson coughed gently, and Pete said, "Apparently at least one of them was, right? Although the other part is a good question."

"One I don't have good answers for," Carson said. And what answers he did have, he wasn't quite ready to share, at least not before getting a much better feel for how people would react to it. He wasn't about to tell what little he knew of the Kesh civil war or the mysterious degkhidesh at this point, especially since most of that was only what the Kesh calling himself Ketzshanass had told him, and might not be true. "It is possible," he continued, "that as we get further out we will discover Kesh-settled worlds. We don't know where their home planet is, and it's likely they expanded in directions away from what we know as T-Space."

"You mentioned Zeta Reticuli," Pete said.

"Which the one Kesh I spoke with would neither confirm nor deny was his home system. That may just be the closest they ever got to Sol in their settlements, although obviously they explored further. Perhaps when they discovered Terrans, or Taprobanis for that matter, they decided to pull back and leave a buffer zone. We just don't know."

Maclaren nodded. "It makes a kind of sense. Mind you, it also makes a kind of sense to just wipe out any potentially dangerous competition, for which we can be thankful that they didn't do. No bloody Velkaryan-equivalents in that lot, I guess."

"There's one other possibility," Carson said. It was something he had discussed before, with those in the know.

"Oh, what's that?"

"Consider the original Terraformers. There is no question that the life we've found on the terraformed planets descended from life on Earth, and that Earth life predates that by billions of years. We keep saying that there's no evidence of just who the Terraformers were, but that isn't quite true."

"What do you mean?"

"Well, *we're* pretty sure they didn't come from Earth, despite some people's wild theories about intelligent, space-faring dinosaurs, because we have found absolutely no evidence of a pre-human, advanced civilization either on Earth or anywhere in the Solar System, and we've been living there all of our history. But imagine how a visitor from another star system would feel when they discover a planet whose life forms clearly arose there, and yet are related to the ancestors of life forms on every other planet where you've found them so far." Carson paused, then added, "It's misleading evidence, but still, Occam's Razor is going to tell you that that's where the Terraformers came from, and so is probably a planet you don't want to mess around with."

Maclaren turned to Finley. "He's right, Pete. Remember how we all felt when we first realized that Kakuloa had been terraformed? I think we were all looking over our shoulders just waiting for the Terraformers to come back."

Pete nodded. "Yeah. Sometimes it still gives me the willies when I stop and think about it. I guess it also means any civilization arising on a terraformed world would have pretty peculiar ideas about biology and geology. Heh. What do you think, Carson? Where did the Terraformers come from?"

"I have no idea, other than 'probably not Earth', and I'm not sure after all this time that it's an answerable question, so I try not to think about it. I've certainly heard my share of wild theories, everything from said intelligent dinosaurs to time-travelling humans from our own future. I suspect the real answer is more mundane, but that we just haven't discovered the critical clue that will explain it yet. That's one reason the spacefaring pyramid builders intrigue me."

"But if they're only fifteen-thousand years old, there's no reason they would know any more than we would. That's still off by a factor of over four thousand times."

"Right," Carson agreed, "but what if they discovered the clue that we haven't, yet?"

"Huh," Finley said. "What if, indeed. Okay, Carson, you've got us interested, and I'll stipulate that your talisman is genuine and points here. Now what?"

∞ ∞ ∞

"Now? I'd like to go and settle once and for all whether your peak really is a volcanic plug, or a pyramid."

"And I told you before, if it were up to me, I'd say go and dig to your heart's content. But it's not up to me."

"I don't need to do a full excavation. I just need to dig through the surface covering at a level close enough to the ground as to uncover engravings, if there are any. That would prove what it is, and make it easier to justify a real dig."

"Again, it's not my Peak, or my wildlife preserve. So, what do you want me to do?"

"Pete, stop teasing the poor lad," Maclaren said, slapping his knee. "We have connections, maybe we can help." She looked at Carson. "You must have given it some thought. What did you come up with?"

Carson had, but there was no way he was going to bring up his original idea of a high-altitude parachute jump into the area. As Jackie had pointed out, that didn't help him get out.

"Well," he said, "one of the less outlandish ideas was under the cover of some kind of biological or ecological survey of the preserve. I don't know if or when that was ever done, but it seems a logical thing to carry out."

Maclaren nodded slowly. "That could work, but why would an archeologist be going along? I'm assuming you want to be part of it."

"Of course I do. As it happens, the area between the Peak and the *Anderson* landing site is of archeological interest." He nodded toward Pete. "Your team found obsidian spear-points and the like associated with a volcanic ash layer. We've found similar artifacts, spear-points and arrowheads, throughout the area. The university has a fair collection. It was probably a hunting area, a hundred thousand years ago."

"So, you're going to be collecting arrowheads?" Finley said. "That sounds a bit thin."

"We've never found any sign of a village or campsite near there, and nobody's been looking since the leopard range was declared off-limits. It would be only natural to try and piggyback on the ecological survey."

"Aren't you worried about attracting illegal artifact hunters? Tomb raiders?" Maclaren asked.

"On this planet? Sawyers World is a bit too civilized for them, and the only artifacts are paleolithic stone tools. Collectors tend to be more interested in art objects, neolithic level stuff like that found on Verdigris or Ransom's Planet. The illicit dealers are only interested in what the collectors will pay for."

"Right. You're the expert," she said.

"Besides, we wouldn't exactly be advertising it. The pyramid, if it is one, should be kept quiet."

"We can agree on that," Finley said.

Maclaren nodded in agreement. "A biological survey might be a good cover," she said. "How well do you know Ellie Greystone?"

Carson was momentarily confused. "Do you mean Doctor Eleanor Greystone, the head of the university biology department?" he asked. He knew who she was, of course. "Mostly by reputation, although we've said hello to each other at faculty receptions and the like. Why?"

"I know her," Maclaren said. "Not well, but she's a friend of Ulrika Klaar. She has connections in the Office of Land Management. Tell her you'd like to set up a joint biological/archeological survey and if she has questions to talk to me or Pete, or to Ulrika."

"Are you going to tell Klaar about this?" Carson asked. She had been a biologist on the first landing team, another of the Original Eight. He wasn't enthused about how the information was spreading, and knew Ducayne wouldn't like it at all.

"The *Anderson* team has never had many secrets from each other," Pete said. "She was married to Fred Tyrell, the other geologist on the crew besides Sawyer, and he knew as much about the geology as Sawyer or I did. Maybe more. So, yes, we are. At least if you want to proceed with this."

Carson sighed. If it would get him his look at the peak. "Okay." He wondered how he was going to break the news to Ducayne.

Chapter 28: Reid's Return

Velkaryan HQ, Sawyers World

AS WAS STANDARD procedure, Reid waited a day before reporting to Deitrich at the Church of Divine Stellar Providence in Sawyer City. It might have been a futile gesture toward operational security, but at least things like surveillance cameras, automated facial recognition and correlation between databases weren't nearly as widespread, or as tolerated, here on Sawyers World as they were anywhere on Earth.

Deitrich looked over Reid's orders and grunted an acknowledgement. "You took your time getting here, but that's to be expected," he said. "There have been a couple of new developments related to your assignment."

"Oh?" Reid said. "Such as?"

"Our sources say that the Sawyers Office of Land Management is organizing some kind of ecological survey of the Pete's Peak wildlife area, and since arrowheads and the like have been found nearby, there has been a request for an archeologist to accompany them."

"Let me guess. Carson?"

"There was no name given, but we assume so. Now, how much actual digging he can do there is a question, but all he has to do is prove that it is a pyramid, rather than a volcanic neck. Then the can of worms is open, and he can push for a full dig."

That made sense, but, "Surely he knows what he's likely to find if he does," Reid said. "Evidence of technologically advanced aliens. Why would he want to make that public, and perhaps cause a panic?"

"You've been on Earth too long. The outworlders, at least those who didn't just emigrate, aren't likely to panic. They live with interstellar travel and aliens, albeit primitive aliens, every day. Most people on Earth don't really think about it, unless they're in some related business," Deitrich said. "Anyway, Carson has been pushing this idea for years. He noticed too many similarities between primitive cultures on different planets. It's the sort of thing he'd want made public, to vindicate himself. But it's also possible the discovery would be kept secret."

"Because Carson is working with Homeworld Security?"

Deitrich nodded. "Almost certainly. He still teaches at the university, but he probably keeps that job as a cover."

"Does the Sawyers World government know about his involvement? That has to be breaking some kind of laws or regulations."

"Only if the *UDT* is paying him. Maybe they aren't, at least not directly. You know how academics can get."

Reid didn't, exactly, but he got Deitrich's meaning. "But they must have some inkling of what he thinks about this Pete's Peak. Especially since that area has so-conveniently been off-limits for decades."

"Most likely, yes, somebody in the Sawyers World government knows, or suspects. As to why they're allowing an archeologist to go along on this survey, it comes down to just a few possibilities. Either they know he won't find anything, or they're not sure, and want to see what he does find. Or perhaps they know he will find something and are convinced they can keep a lid on it, or they do want it to be made public. I don't see what they'd stand to gain in the latter case, so I'm discounting it."

"If they do know that it's a pyramid, then they haven't found a way in. They can't possibly know what's inside."

"Neither do we," Deitrich pointed out. "We know what *we* hope to find, but there are no guarantees. It might even be that they know there is *nothing* inside, but I'm going to go with assuming that they're not even sure what it is."

Reid concurred. "Either way," he said, "my job is to watch Carson and make sure we get into the pyramid, if it is one, before he or anyone else does."

"Quite so. If there's anything you need from my office, let me know. Oh, there was one other thing, not related to Carson."

"Yes? What?"

"We're hearing rumbles about some kind of joint war-games exercise between the *UDT* Space Force and the Sawyers World Space Guard. It's the kind of thing that Space Force used to do regularly some years back, but they haven't in a while. We plan to monitor them, of course, but let me know if you hear anything about them."

"Will do. Do you know when?" Reid wanted to sit in on the monitoring, if possible, and not just to see how the games went. Monitoring the motions of multiple ships across multiple light-hours was a technical challenge in itself, and Reid was curious to see how they would manage that.

"No. Sometime in the near future, but that could mean almost anything."

"Ah. Well, I'd be interested in observing that if I may, if it doesn't conflict with my primary mission."

Deitrich nodded. "I'll keep that in mind."

Chapter 29: Matthews

Drake University, Sawyer City

CARSON TAPPED ON Dean Matthews' open office door. "Do you have a moment?"

Matthews looked up from his desk. "Dr. Carson, certainly, come on in. What's on your mind?"

"Well, it's about the paleolithic aboriginals, the discussion we had a week or so back?"

"That wasn't all we were talking about, but yes, what of it?"

"Well, I happened to run into Dr. Greystone, head of the Biology Department—"

"I know Ellie Greystone."

"Sorry, of course you do. Anyway, we were chatting briefly, and she mentioned a rumor that the Office of Land Management is putting together an ecological survey of the range north-west of Camp Anderson, a few dozen kilometers from where the original arrowhead finds were made. I'd like to see if I can tag along and participate from an archeological perspective."

"Oh? Do you really expect they'll find anything? That area has been fairly thoroughly surveyed. Do you think there's anything there?"

You have no idea, Carson thought. "It's possible. As I said last week, the area hasn't had a thorough archeological survey because it's a wildlife preserve. It might just be more arrowheads, but that would add to the established range of the aboriginals."

"I wouldn't mind taking a look myself," Matthews said, looking thoughtful. "When would this be?"

"That's the thing. I only just heard about it. I believe it's just a few weeks from now." That was really a hope, not a belief, since he had only discussed it with Finley and Greystone the day before.

The dean frowned. "What about your classes?" He shook his head. "No, I don't think so. That's very short notice, and I need you to keep up with your teaching load as well as get some more publications out. Maybe after the semester ends."

Crap. Probably he could get the expedition scheduled later, since it was largely a cover story anyway, but Carson wanted to get out there as soon as he could. The more people who knew about it, the greater the chance of someone else getting there first. He pushed it. "But the survey may be over by then. This is a unique opportunity."

Matthews nodded. "You're right, it is a valuable opportunity."

Yes!

Matthews continued before Carson could say anything. "The department should be represented. I suppose I could go in your stead. I don't want my field work to get too rusty."

No! Carson wondered if the dean just wanted to be in on any interesting archeological finds made. But there was no way Carson was going to miss out on finding what might be another pyramid, although that was not a find that Ducayne would want publicized. Having Matthew along, with or especially without Carson, was the last thing he needed.

Carson thought quickly. "Of course," he said. "I'm sure you'd be welcome to go along, if permission can be arranged. That might be tricky, even for me. This area hasn't been surveyed; it's part of the Anderson Wildlife Preserve, the domain of Finley's leopard. I believe one of the things the ecologists want to do is take a census of the leopard population, balance that against the prey species, and get an idea how well they're doing." Matthews expression had changed, now looking more cautious than eager.

Carson drove it home. "Funny thing about those leopards. I've heard their usual prey numbers are falling and the leopards are changing their hunting patterns. Apparently, they'll eat almost anything if their preferred prey isn't available."

"I see. But I assume the expedition will have guides, rangers?"

"Well, that's the thing. Finley's leopard is considered an endangered species, so the guides will only have non-lethal weapons. Frankly I'm not sure how well they'd deter a hungry

Finley's leopard. Although, they're probably no worse than some of the predators I've encountered on other planets; I'm sure the stories are exaggerated. If I were going, they'd probably make me leave my own sidearm behind."

"Of course," Matthews said, looking uneasy. "Well, I'm sure it would be fine with a trained team."

"Oh, no doubt," Carson said airily.

"When did you say this expedition is, again?"

"Just a couple of weeks from now, I only heard about it recently. I'll have to check on the exact dates."

"Oh. A couple of weeks? That may not work for me after all." Matthews made a show of checking the calendar on his omni. "Hmm," he muttered. "Regents' meeting, departmental reviews, damn." He looked back up at Carson. "I don't think that works with my calendar. Damned shame."

"Oh," Carson forced disappointment into his voice. "So, the department won't be represented? Maybe Jorgensen?"

"Not his area of expertise, you know that."

Carson did know that, which was why he'd suggested that name. "Oh, you're right. I think I could accommodate my class schedule, but maybe we should just forgo this one."

Matthews eyed Carson. Did he suspect? "I'll tell you what. Because this is a unique opportunity, and such short notice, you can take three days. But make sure all your academic duties here are covered."

"Three days won't let me cover much ground." Actually, it should be more than enough for a quick look, but he wanted to let Matthews think he was winning this one.

"You'll just have to do the best you can. If you do find anything, we can look at organizing something longer after the semester is over."

Carson sighed and let his shoulders slump. "Oh, well, of course. Thank you."

"And listen, Carson. Keep me posted on what you find, and let me know if the schedule changes. Perhaps I can work it in."

"Certainly. I can take that as approval to go, then?"

"So long as it doesn't interfere with your teaching and other research duties, yes. But just three days."

"Thank you. I'll keep you informed." Carson started to leave, then turned back briefly and, grinning, said, "So long as I don't get eaten by a leopard."

Matthews just shook his head. "Try not to."

Carson left the office, wondering just how much Matthews would miss him if a leopard *did* eat him.

Chapter 30: Ducayne

Ducayne's office

"I DON'T KNOW HOW you managed it," Ducayne said before Carson had a chance to explain anything, "but there is going to be an ecological survey, and soon."

"About that—" Carson managed to get out before Ducayne cut him off.

"My sources say that both Pete Finley and Dr. Ellie Greystone were involved, so whatever you said to them, it worked. It also means they want you along, 'to determine if the area contains anything of archeological significance' as the official proposal puts it. There is one catch, though."

"A catch? What?" Carson said, deciding not to say anything just yet about the talisman.

"More of a who. Alex Finley will be going with you to check out the structure."

"Finley?" Carson could guess whose idea that was. "Any relation to Peter?"

"His grandson."

"So I'm going to have to babysit some kid—"

"He's twenty-two, not a kid. And he's got field experience, I checked. I'll give the Original Eight this, they raised their kids, and their grandkids, to be just as capable of surviving on a wild planet as they were." Ducayne paused, then added as an aside, "If they were more interested in politics, I might worry about them thinking of setting up a hereditary aristocracy."

Carson ignored the latter; Ducayne had strange priorities. "Okay, so long as he can take care of himself. I'm almost surprised Pete himself didn't want to come along."

"He did, but he knows that would attract too much attention. The downside of being a public figure," Ducayne said. "Anyway, I'll send you the other details. Was there something else you wanted to see me about?"

"No, I suppose not."

"All right then. Thanks for coming by."

With that, Ducayne ushered Carson from his office.

Chapter 31: Expedition

Sawyers World, 60 km from Camp Anderson

A TRIO OF AIRCARS flew over the grassy terrain northwest of Camp Anderson. Carson and Alex Finley were in the lead car, with Finley doing the piloting. Despite Carson's earlier misgivings, he had taken a liking to the young man, who came across as both friendly and competent. That was more than could be said for some of the heirs to wealth and influence that Carson had encountered on Earth.

"There's an open field about five kilometers from the peak," Finley said. "My grandparents first landed there when they came to check it out. At least, it was an open field fifty years ago; it's probably overgrown a bit since then, but we don't have to worry about runway length."

Carson had reviewed the relevant mission reports. Naomi Maclaren and Pete Finley had flown to the site in the *Anderson* expedition's fixed-wing electroplane. This "ecological survey" expedition was in aircars that could set down vertically and were enough for their needs. If serious digging were required, they'd need a helicopter to bring in gear.

"That will be fine for now," Carson said. "We might want to find somewhere closer if there's any heavy excavation involved, to get the equipment in."

"We can work that out as needed. But we're going to keep the explosive ground clearing to a minimum." Alex had heard about Carson's impromptu fuel-air bomb to clear a landing spot for the *Sophie* near the Verdigris pyramid.

"Spoilsport," Carson said, and grinned.

∞ ∞ ∞

The aircars were challenged as they approached the boundary of the wildlife preserve.

"*Warning, aircar X2Z-375,*" a robotic voice came over the radio, the automated system picking up the cars registration code. "*You are approaching Anderson Wildlife Preserve, a prohibited area. Unauthorized entry is subject to fine. Unauthorized landing or disturbing of the wildlife is subject to penalties up to and including confiscation of your vehicle and jail time.*"

"I thought we had clearance," Carson said, looking at Finley.

"We do. One moment." Finley tapped out a command on the car's dash panel and hit SEND.

A moment later, the same robotic voice came back with "*Authorization code received and acknowledged. X2Z-375 and two accompanying vehicles approved for entry to the reserve. Enjoy your stay.*"

Finley confirmed with the others that they too had been cleared, and continued on course.

"Can we overfly the pyramid first? I'd like to see it from the air."

"Sure, although we don't know for sure that it is a pyramid." Finley angled the aircar towards the peak rising above the trees in the distance.

"We'll find out soon enough."

A few minutes later they were above Pete's Peak, which still looked like the overgrown hill it had seemed from aerial photographs. The sides were steep and flat, with scrubby vegetation and the occasional small tree growing out of the dirt on its sides.

"Doesn't look like much to me," Alex said. "A little too regular to be a volcanic neck, perhaps."

To Carson's eye, there was more to it. He could see the resemblance that Pete Finley had noted with unexcavated pyramids in the Yucatan, but unlike the stepped structures there, this one had smooth sides. "See how sparse the vegetation is on the sides?" Carson said, "How small the trees are?"

"Yes, what of it?"

"That means the soil layer is thin. There's not enough for them to build up a deep root structure. Anything growing too tall will tend to uproot itself, although on that slope they won't get much water anyway."

Alex considered that. "You could still get that over volcanic rock, couldn't you?"

"Perhaps," Carson said, "but that's more likely to have cracks that roots could find their way into. It's suggestive, not conclusive."

"If you say so. What now?"

"Let's find our landing site. I want to check this out from ground level."

"Roger that."

∞ ∞ ∞

As they approached the landing site about ten minutes later, Carson studied it from the air. It was more overgrown that he expected, no doubt the result of another thirty-some years—fifty Earth-standard years—of growth since the first expedition here. But there was something else about it. The clearing's boundaries, at least on the side nearest the peak, seemed unusually straight. He might want to follow up on that.

The three aircars set down in the cleared area, and the crew began to unload gear. "I'm going to take a walk around," Carson told Alex. "I'm curious about this clearing."

"Don't wander into the woods. I'd hate to lose you before we get started."

Carson grinned. "So would I."

He started by pacing the full length of the clearing, from the northwest, where it just sort of faded out into ever taller vegetation and brush, to the southeast, where the demarcation between clearing and forest was more distinct. Beneath the grassy vegetation, the soil of the clearing seemed harder toward the southeast side, more compact. It didn't seem to make any difference to the grass, but there were fewer small bushes. At the edge of the clearing, a thin margin of saplings and younger trees quickly gave way to taller, thicker, and obviously older ones.

That was strange. He would have expected a gradual transition all around, as it was on the northwest side. Clearings like this were often the result of a natural progression, from a small lake or pond which filled in or drained to become a bog, then a meadow, then a clearing with a few bushes or small trees as it was now, eventually becoming just another part of the forest. That process worked from the edges inward, but here it seemed very distinct. A change in the soil might do it, or if part of the field had been artificially cleared. But that was impossible. This couldn't be more than one or two hundred standard years old, and the natives whose stone artifacts had been found had been gone for a thousand times that—and had likely never had agriculture.

There was something else that might have done it, Carson realized, but he would need more evidence. He headed back to help finish setting up the camp.

∞ ∞ ∞

"Find anything interesting?" Alex Finley asked him when he returned.

"I think there's something funny about this clearing," Carson said. "At least the southeast half of it. But right now it's more just a feeling than anything specific. Anyway, I don't think it has anything to do with our paleolithic hunter-gatherers. Anything from them is going to be under the surface a ways."

"Want to do a survey with the ground-penetrating radar?"

"I just might, at that, but it will keep for now." He wasn't sure if anything would show up if it was what he thought, but if anything did, he wasn't sure he wanted this team, however well security screened, to be aware of it. Fifteen-thousand-year-old pyramids were one thing, but signs that a Kesh pyramid ship had landed within the last century or two were another.

∞ ∞ ∞

Next day

RIGHT AFTER BREAKFAST the five-person bio-survey team began laying out the grid they would use to quantify and locate their findings—the official reason for this expedition. Meanwhile, Carson, Alex Finley, and their nominal guide, Steve Dundee, set off for Pete's Peak. It was a five-kilometer straight-line trek through the forest.

"You know," Finley said, "when Naomi and Pete made their trip, they followed a homing signal from a beacon they dropped on the way in. We have navsats now, so we should have an easier time of it." He stopped and made a point of looking around at the trees. "Somehow I'm not convinced."

"No kidding," Dundee said. "Satellite photos are only going to show the treetops, and there's no call for radar maps, not with the place off-limits to the general public."

"Oh, I know," Finley said. "I'm more amused than anything else."

"It could be worse," Carson said. "You should try hacking through the jungle on Verdigris. This place doesn't even have ribbon snakes."

"Ribbon snakes?" Finley asked.

"A kind of flying snake," Dundee said before Carson could answer. "They glide out of treetops. The green ones, jade ribbon snakes, have one of the most toxic venoms known. Nothing like that around here, although keep away from any red snakes."

"You've been to Verdigris?" Carson asked Dundee.

"Yeah, did a stint with a biologicals company there. Came back when I decided I didn't like the place. Jungle aside, I missed the stars."

Carson understood. The almost ever-present skyweed made starry nights rare on Verdigris.

The trio maintained a brisk pace, with Dundee moving ahead of the other two then falling back to let them pass, checking both ahead and behind for any signs of predators. After a while, Carson began to find this irritating.

"Is all that back and forth really necessary? It kind of feels like you're herding us. I've been in wilder terrain than this."

"Sorry you feel that way. It's partly for your protection, but it's also to protect the animals. I know you've been on frontier worlds, but they probably didn't have any rules about just shooting an animal causing you trouble. This place is unique. Even though much of the planet is far more settled than some of your frontier worlds, this preserve is relatively untouched, so the animals haven't learned to avoid humans. And because it's a preserve, you're not allowed to shoot them."

"What about the weapon you're carrying?" Carson had been forced to leave his personal sidearm back at the camp, something he was not happy about.

"It's a last resort, and it shoots shock darts. Mostly I know what to watch for and can avoid it or scare it off."

Carson knew he had a point. Someone unfamiliar with an area wouldn't know what was normal and what might be dangerous, and would have a natural tendency to either under- or over-react. "How much of a problem is it really, though?" he asked.

Dundee shrugged. "There have been a few incidents over the years. The leopards have been known to attack humans, and you'll get the occasional terror bird too. They're actually more aggressive than the leopards."

"I thought terror birds stuck to open ranges?" Finley said.

"Mostly, yeah, but they've been seen in forested areas too, probably in pursuit of prey. Anyway, that's just the big predators. There are some smaller, venomous animals to worry about too, like redsnakes. For that matter, the tusks and hooves on an uglibeast can mess you up pretty badly if it takes a dislike to you."

Carson could imagine. An uglibeast was something like a wild boar, but uglier and with bigger teeth. On the other hand, they did make good eating. "How does a shock dart do against an uglibeast? They can be pretty big, can't they?"

"Up to two hundred kilos or so, yes. Still, a dart packs a punch; it will put even an uglibeast down for a minute or two. Best to avoid such animals though."

"Got it," Carson said, then deadpanned: "Leopards, and terror birds, and uglibeasts, oh my."

Dundee grinned. "That's the spirit. Just stay on the yellow brick road."

Carson looked at the low undergrowth on the forest floor, small bushes and ferns, punctuated here and there with pink, tri-petaled flowers, and wondered if there might indeed be some kind of road beneath the dirt. There hadn't been anything like that near the pyramid on St. Jacobs, and if there had been at the Verdigris pyramid, it had been hidden under meters of sand and soil. *I'll settle for a grey-pink pyramid*, he thought.

Chapter 32: Rico Revisited

Somewhere in Sawyer City

RICO HAD NO IDEA how many days had passed since he'd been moved to the room. With no windows, the only way he could keep track of time was by the meals he was served. He could turn the lights on and off whenever he wanted, so that didn't help. The meals came through a small hatch in the wall beside the door. Each consisted of a generic hand-meal and some kind of protein drink. There was no differentiation between breakfast or dinner, and Rico had no idea if the meals were delivered regularly or not.

He had tried to rig up a crude water clock, letting the faucet in the bathroom sink drip slowly into the plastic tumbler he drank out of, and counting the number of times it filled and he'd emptied it. He gave up on that after he fell asleep and woke up to find the cup overflowing.

He was up to his eleventh meal, and slowly going crazy with boredom, when he got another visit from "Agent Friday".

"Are you ready to talk?" Friday said.

"I may have forgotten how," Rico replied dryly. "Have you called the *UDT*?"

"What's Project Blue Book?"

Rico's eyes widened in surprise before he could suppress his reaction. Had Friday known about it from the beginning, or had he talked to Ducayne's outfit? And if the latter, why would they have told him anything?

"I dunno. Some kind of coloring book? Or something pornographic like a blue movie?" He didn't know where he'd heard that last term, it certainly wasn't current slang, but wherever he'd heard it the phrase had stuck.

"What is the *UDT*'s interest in flying saucers?"

"Same as their interest in flying cups? I have no idea what you're talking about."

"Rico, this would go a lot faster if you'd just tell us the truth. You do know that lying to a government agent is a crime, right?"

"So is impersonating a government agent. You talk a lot, but you haven't given me any proof that you are who you say you are. This room I'm in could be anywhere."

Friday glared at Rico. Rico got the idea that the agent would be much happier if Rico were still in the traumapod, wired up to whatever lie detector and shock apparatus they'd used before. That he wasn't so wired up now was interesting. If all this was being recorded, as Rico assumed it was, then perhaps they didn't want any evidence of mistreating him. Which could mean they were planning to let him go. Eventually. Either that, or this was the "good cop" phase, and things were going to start getting nasty. Whatever. Rico had been put through hell by characters a lot worse than this joker.

As if Friday knew what Rico was thinking, he said, "If we were really bad guys, Rico, we'd be raking you over the coals, perhaps literally, to get what we wanted. You already know the lie-detecting gear we have."

"You're going to have to work on your threats. That was about as lame as they come."

Friday glanced at the guard by the door and made a slight nod. The speed at which the big man moved caught Rico unaware, and he found himself hoisted by his shirt front and slammed against the wall. The guard held him there, a half-meter off the floor. Rico started to react, trying to kick the guard in the crotch, but the man tossed Rico aside and stepped back. Rico fell to the floor.

"Is that what you had in mind?" Friday said as Rico picked himself up. The guard had resumed his position by the door. He hadn't uttered a word.

"Uh, I guess that was a good start." Rico sat back down on the bed, rethinking any plans he might have had of rushing the guard.

"You need to be more careful," Friday said. "Wet bathroom floors can be slippery. I'd hate for you to have a nasty fall and injure yourself."

Rico considered that. The threat was thinly veiled, but it also suggested that perhaps everything *wasn't* being constantly recorded.

"Right," Rico said. "Lucky for me I'm not particularly accident prone." As he said that, he remembered the number of times he'd woken up in a traumapod over the past year, and smiled ruefully.

"Something funny?" the agent asked.

"Inside joke."

"Want to tell me about it?"

"Not really."

"Anything to say about what you were doing on Earth?" As Friday asked that, he raised a finger and beckoned the guard over.

Here it comes, thought Rico. "I told you before. *UDT* business, and you don't need to know any more than that." He steeled himself against the inevitable blows. They didn't come.

"All right, Rico. Here's the deal. If I prove to you we are who I say we are, will you start cooperating?"

Rico wondered what the catch was, but said "I'm always happy to cooperate with law enforcement and other government authorities."

Friday raised a skeptical eyebrow, then gave his head a slight shake. "All right." He looked toward the guard and stood up. Rico braced himself.

"I'll be back," Friday said. "I need to make some arrangements."

"Set up a masquerade, you mean?" Rico said, relaxing.

"Don't flatter yourself. You're not worth the effort. I'll be back."

With that, he and the guard left Rico alone again.

Chapter 33: Trek

Anderson Wildlife Preserve

CARSON AND THE others hiked on for about an hour. In several places, they'd noticed strange scars on widely separated tree trunks, like a healed-over slash.

"That might be from the trail my grandfather blazed," Alex Finley said when Carson commented on them. "He's told me the story. Said he used his geologist's pick to mark some of the trees to make it easier to find their way back."

"I'm surprised they still show after all this time," Dundee said.

"Some of them probably don't," Carson said. "It depends on the tree, and how deep the mark was, and things like precipitation and growth rates and such." At his companions' puzzled expressions, he shrugged and added, "It's one of the things archeologists look for when trying to date a site, or for how long a place might have been occupied. It's not very quantitative, but it gives a general feel."

"Well, learn something new every day," Dundee said, before checking his omni and continuing forward.

It was a few minutes later that Carson noticed a subtle change in the character of the forest. The trees seemed not so tall as they had before, and the space between them was larger. They were the same species as elsewhere in the forest, so something else must have changed.

"I think we're getting close," he said, and looked at his omni to check. "Maybe another hundred meters."

Dundee scanned the area all around them before looking at his own omni. "Agreed. Let's go."

The ground began to slope upward in the last dozen meters, probably build up from material that had eroded down the slope of the peak, which rose sharply at a forty-five-degree angle just beyond.

Carson looked up at it, taking it all in. The slope was flat, with scattered scrub brush and the occasional tree growing out of it. While he could see no obvious exposed stone, the flatness and regularity of the surface, despite the covering of vegetation, convinced him that this was no natural feature. It was a pyramid, and from the looks of it, someone—or some*thing*—had deliberately tried to, if not bury it, at least disguise it. He wondered who, and why.

Chapter 34: Space Guard

Somewhere in Sawyer City

IT HADN'T BEEN very long, perhaps an hour, when the door to Rico's cell opened again. Friday and the guard were back.

"On your feet, Rico," Friday said. "Hands behind your back."

"What's this?" Rico asked as he complied. The guard stepped behind him and cuffed Rico's hands together, then bent and shackled his ankles with a short chain.

"Insurance. In case you change your mind about cooperating. We're going to go for a little walk. You missed a lot when we brought you here."

Finally, Rico thought, *some answers*. "Lead on, then."

∞ ∞ ∞

Agent Friday led Rico, with the guard following, along the corridor that he had been wheeled down several days earlier. They passed the door to the medical bay, or whatever they called the room where the traumapod had been, and kept going past that to a wider area in the hall, where there were elevator doors.

The elevator arrived, and Friday gestured for Rico to enter. "Stay facing the back wall, please," he said, then he and the guard followed him in.

Rico glanced around at the rear wall and as much of the elevator he could see without turning. It was obvious that Friday didn't want him to know what floor they got on at, and maybe not which what floor they'd get off at, or anything in between if the elevator stopped anywhere else. Rico could appreciate that. *At least they didn't put a bag over my head.*

He could tell from the acceleration that the elevator was going up, not down, but there was no chime or other audible indicator of how many floors they passed. There weren't many tall buildings in Sawyer City, if that's where they really were, but the elevator could have just been slow. Either way, Rico counted about forty-three seconds from the time the elevator started until it stopped. He had no idea what he could do with that information, but it was something.

The doors opened and Friday and the guard each took one of Rico's elbows and backed him out. There were no floor indicators on the outside of the elevator here, either, just the call buttons. They turned him around.

Rico looked out over an open, modular area that could have been any government or commercial office. There were windows across the room. He was on perhaps the fourth or fifth floor, and there were other buildings outside. It could well be Sawyer City, but he didn't immediately recognize anything which would tell him just where.

The personnel at the desks, and a few standing or walking, were dressed in a mix of civvies and uniforms. A couple of them glanced over in his direction and then returned to their work. The uniforms weren't police. They might have been Space Guard, but Rico wasn't certain, and didn't get a close look at them.

"This way," Friday said, tugging on his elbow.

There was little in the way of decoration on any of the few interior walls. Some generic scenic photographs, of which Rico recognized a few scenes from Sawyers World and Kakuloa, and a few deep sky images, some showing ships or asteroids. One paneled wall held a large plaque, the seal of the Alpha Centauri Treaty Organization, not of the Sawyers World government. Now that was interesting.

Friday guided Rico to a small conference room and waved him inside. He muttered something to the guard, who remained outside while Friday followed Rico in and closed the door.

"Have a seat." the agent gestured to the chairs around the table dominating the room. One wall was glass, but with Venetian blinds lowered and mostly closed. There was a large wall screen behind one end of the table. Rico chose a seat where he could see the door and, to some extent, through the glass wall. Friday sat across from him, but also in a position where he could see the door.

"Well, anything to say?" Friday asked.

"I'll give you this. If you're not who you say you are, you've gone to elaborate lengths to convince me otherwise. I could still be on a sound stage somewhere."

"Oh, for the love of—"

"But I don't think I am," Rico continued. "So tell me, what does ACTO have to do with Sawyers World Homeworld Defense?"

"You saw the seal? Good. How much do you know about the Treaty of Alpha Centauri?"

Rico didn't see any harm in telling what little he knew. "Same as most, I guess. Established between the original settlers and Earth, it grants autonomy to Sawyers World and joint authority over Kakuloa. I guess it has something to do with law enforcement on Kakuloa and in space in the Alpha Centauri system. Not really something I ever thought much about. Why?"

"Close enough. Yes, Sawyers World is autonomous but with an invited *UDT* presence. Space Guard is officially a branch of the Sawyers World military—hell, it's *most* of the Sawyers World military—but cooperates with the *UDT* Space Force on in-system operations, like catching smugglers and terrorists."

"It sounds complicated," Rico said, quite honestly.

"You have no idea."

"So why do you, whether you're ACTO or Space Guard or whoever you are, care about me and what I was doing on Earth? I'm not a smuggler or a terrorist."

"Well, here's the thing," Friday said. "We don't know that. All we know is you were involved in a shoot-out with Velkaryans— yes, we know about the Velkaryans—and that you are, or were, or associated with, a known smuggler. So, known smuggler connections, and involved in shoot-outs in public places. Maybe you're both a smuggler *and* a terrorist."

"But—"

"Anyway," the agent continued, ignoring the interruption, "since you were apparently shooting *at* the Velkaryans rather than *with* them, that's a point in your favor. We're concerned about the Velkaryans; we need to know if we need to be concerned about you."

"Oh, is that all?" Rico looked at him and smiled broadly. "The answer is *no*. Can I go now?"

"Just 'no'? And you expect us to take your word on that?"

"I told you, call the *UDT* and ask them yourself."

"You promised to be cooperative."

"I didn't say I would reveal classified information." *Oh, shit, I shouldn't have said that*, Rico realized.

"Your assignment on Earth was classified? By whom?"

"I didn't say that."

The agent waited, staring at Rico, as if wondering if Rico would say more. Then he said, "Tell you what, Rico. I'll tell you a few things that we do know and you can correct me if I'm wrong."

Rico thought about that, then remembered the phrasing. "I can neither confirm nor deny—"

"Cut the bullshit, Rico. I won't ask you anything like that."

Rico didn't believe him, but was curious as to how much Friday thought he knew. "Okay, I'm listening."

Chapter 35: Pete's Peak

Pete's Peak

"I'M NO GEOLOGIST," Steve Dundee said, looking up at steep sloping side they were facing, "but that doesn't look like any volcanic plug I ever saw."

"Seen many, have you?" Alex Finley asked. Carson thought Finley sounded a bit defensive, possibly because his grandfather was the one who had declared it a volcanic plug or neck, at least publicly.

"Well, no," Dundee admitted, "just pictures. But wouldn't it be steeper and more irregular?"

"That's what we're here to find out," Carson said. "In Peter Finley's defense, their scans did show some kind of solid mass descending straight downward, as you'd expect from an extinct volcano."

"All right. Where do we start?"

"I want to do a complete walk around it first, to see if there's anything obvious on any of the sides," Carson said. "I don't think Maclaren and Finley did when they were here. Alex?"

The younger Finley shook his head. "No, from what I remember of what he's told me, they just walked around until they found somewhere clear to climb up. It was getting near nightfall, so they didn't want to waste any time."

Carson checked his omni. It was not yet noon. "We have plenty of time, so that's not an issue." Still looking at his omni, he set a marker at their current location. "If we find something interesting before we get back to this point, we'll investigate. Otherwise this seems as good a point as any to dig for a bit. Does that work for you, Steve?"

Dundee nodded. "For now, sure."

"Sounds good," added Finley. "Let's go."

They led off to their left, keeping the Peak's slope on their right, walking where the ground began to slope upward but was not so steep as to make it difficult to walk.

"You've seen other pyramids, both on Earth and elsewhere," Finley said to Carson. "Were they like this?"

It was an astute question, Carson thought. "There's a lot of variation," he said. "For one, there's the actual style of the individual pyramid, depending on which culture built it. Mayan step pyramids are quite different from Egyptian pyramids, for example. The big blocks of the Egyptian pyramids look like steps, but they were originally covered with limestone casing stones to make the sides smooth. There's still some of those left near the top of the Khafre pyramid, but most either fell off over the centuries or were carried off for building material. The much smaller pyramid I found on Verdigris—" he referred to the one where he'd found the talisman, and was raided by artifact smugglers, not the Space-farer-built structure that someone else, probably the Velkaryans, had found near New Toronto before him "—was a variation on the local dome-shaped tombs. It was pyramidal, but the tomb opening was similar."

"None of them were covered like this?"

"Well, a lot of what I've seen first-hand, especially in the Yucatan, had already been excavated. Early sketches of them show quite a bit of dirt and vegetation covering them, but the wide steps and surrounding jungle made it easier for leaf debris and plants to accumulate. The Egyptian pyramids are in the middle of a desert, so aside from where sand has drifted over the base; they're pretty bare. The one on Verdigris was moss-covered, just like pretty much anything else on that planet."

"It's really that bad?" Finley asked.

"No, not really. I'm exaggerating, but the place didn't get the name Verdigris for no reason. Not that it's all like that, it has polar caps and even a desert or two. Have you never been off-planet?"

"Only to Kakuloa, and to Earth once. I hated that last, it's way too crowded. But never further out, not yet. I'd like to."

Carson nodded. He understood that outward urge, and the feeling of Earth being too crowded. He'd left as soon as he'd had the chance. "It's worth doing. But you're only what, twenty or so standard years old? Lots of time."

"Twenty-two, but sure. I'm not sure my father entirely gets it. He was the baby of the family, my aunts are older, so maybe that has something to do with it. But his parents, Pete and Naomi, they understand."

Carson nodded. His own parents hadn't entirely understood his desire to leave Earth either. He could only imagine what it was like growing up with grandparents who were part of the first interstellar expedition, and how protective they might have been of their children growing up on a wild planet. He was curious about Alex's mother's side of the family, but was too polite to ask.

"You could always enroll in an extraterrestrial archeology class at the university," he said. "Most of the field trips are off-world." *I sound like Dean Matthews shilling for the department*, Carson realized. "Or planetology, or any of several other fields. Heck, the economics department probably has something on interstellar trade."

"Ha. I'll keep that in mind." As Alex said this, the trio reached the first corner of the structure.

Dundee went ahead and wide of the corner, just in case something was lurking out of sight, then signaled for them to come forward. As they rounded it, Carson looked along each side, as far as he could get a clear line of sight through the vegetation. The corner, ignoring the slopes of the sides, was a perfect right angle. By now, Carson was no longer surprised.

Chapter 36: Rico's Revelation

Space Guard HQ, Sawyer City

RICO WATCHED AGENT Friday scroll through something on his data pad. After he had inadvertently admitted to knowing classified information, Rico was determined not to give away anything further, but without actually lying.

The agent looked up from his pad. "You went to Earth on the passenger ship *Southern Sky.*"

Rico thought for a moment. "No, I didn't."

"What?" Friday looked at his data pad. "Okay, you went to *Earth's moon* on *Southern Sky*, then took a shuttle to Earth."

"That's right." This was all public records stuff, there was no point in denying it.

"You landed at the Denver Spaceport, then checked in at the Weston Hotel downtown."

"Correct."

"Did you meet anyone there?"

"There were lots of people there. The doorman, the clerk at the registration desk, the—"

Friday raised his hand to cut Rico off. "Enough. Why did you go to St. Louis?"

Why-questions were a can of worms, Rico knew. It was best to side-step them if he could. "I can neither confirm nor deny that I went to St. Louis."

Friday took a deep breath and let it out slowly. Rico saw the muscles in his jaw working, and tried to hide a grin.

The agent started again. "You took the St. Louis-bound maglev from Denver."

"I did."

"You disembarked in Kansas City and let a rental car drive you the rest of the way. Why? Were you being followed?"

"I don't know." That was the literal truth. He didn't *know* he was being followed, he merely suspected it.

"Did you *think* you were being followed?"

Well, it had been worth a try. "Yes."

"Thank you. Was that so hard?" Friday glanced at his data pad again. "Did you go to St. Louis to meet with someone?"

"Yes." There was no point in denying that.

"A Velkaryan?"

That hadn't been Rico's original intent. The man he went to meet was an old associate of Hopkins from the artifact trade days. But the man who actually met him had turned out to be the Velkaryan, Reid.

"Not exactly," Rico said.

"Well, what, exactly?"

"The person who met me wasn't the person I was supposed to meet. He turned out to be a Velkaryan, although I didn't know it at the time."

"Were you delivering something?"

"No."

"No?" The answer seemed to surprise Friday.

"No. I was not delivering anything," Rico said. "Why, what did you think I was delivering?"

The agent scowled. "Never mind. Were you there to pick something up?"

"Not as such." That would have come later.

Friday studied Rico for a few moments, then shrugged and swiped the page on his data pad.

"Did you visit the Steel Mesa underground storage facility in Pennsylvania?"

So, they knew that much. "Uh, yes I did."

"More than once?"

"Yes. It's an interesting place."

"I'll bet. Did you remove anything from there?"

"Only what I walked in with."

Again, Friday studied Rico, and glanced at his data pad. Rico wondered if there was some kind of lie detection equipment built into the conference room, but again he had answered with the literal truth.

"Were you aware that a Steel Mesa delivery van en route from the facility to Denver went missing a few days after you visited?"

"No, I wasn't." *So that's how they did it.* "What was in it?"

"Records. They later found the van sunken in a reservoir. The records were missing."

Rico hadn't known the details of how the Velkaryans had planned to hijack the shipment, he'd just been pretty sure that they would. Which is why he'd arranged another way to get the specific files that Brown had asked for.

"Oh," was all he said.

"They also found the driver. Dead. His neural implant had shorted out from an electromagnetic pulse, probably when someone stopped the truck the same way."

"*Ouch*, shit. I'm sorry for the guy, but what does that have to do with me?" *And why did the dumb-ass have a neural implant anyway? Rico never would.*

"That's what I'd like to know."

Rico just shook his head and shrugged. "Sorry."

"There was another delivery to Denver from the storage facility. Just a single box."

"People get things from storage all the time. Only one?"

"Only one which arrived just before your shootout at the Denver Spaceport, and the hasty departure of the ship *Dragonfly* right off the ramp behind the charter agency where you and the Velkaryans were trading fire."

Rico remembered that. The ship, with Brown and the files aboard, had been climbing out as he went down. He looked at Agent Friday blandly. "Was that a question?"

Friday shook his head. "Never mind." He rose to leave, then sat back down. "One more question. What do you know about Zeta Reticuli?"

Rico didn't know much, but did know that Brown had been particularly interested in something about that star, although Rico had no idea what. Not that he was about to tell Friday even that. Time to try a bluff.

"Zeta Reticuli?" he asked. "Is that some kind of pasta dish, like macaroni or rigatoni?"

Friday shook his head again, as if in resignation. He stood up. "Wait here, I'll be back." He walked to the door, rapped on it, then opened it. Rico could see the big guard still standing outside, then Friday left and the door closed.

Rico stood up and, impeded by his shackles, shuffled over to the blinds and peered through the gap between the slats. It still looked like a government office. He didn't see where Friday had gone. He wondered how far he'd get if he tried to make another break for it. Probably not even to the elevator, between his leg chains, the guard at the door, and the number of capable-looking individuals in the office outside. He shuffled back and sat down again.

A minute or two later the door opened again. Rico looked up, and gasped in surprise. Entering the room, with Friday behind him, was someone Rico hadn't expected to see again for a long time, if at all. His *UDT* boss, Quentin Ducayne.

"Hello, Rico," Ducayne said. "I'm glad to see you're still in one piece."

Chapter 37: At the Pyramid

Pete's Peak

THE TRIO ROUNDED the third corner of what Carson was now convinced was a pyramid, even if it was covered with dirt and vegetation. So far, they had seen nothing to distinguish any area along the side from any other. No unusual depressions in the ground, no bare areas where the soil covering had worn away, nothing.

Dundee was leading, still looking out for animals. Carson followed at a distance of about ten meters, and just behind him was Finley.

"Well, I think this was a waste of time," Finley said over Carson's shoulder. "We should have just started digging where we first found it."

"We could have," agreed Carson, "but wouldn't you feel silly if we'd done that and then later found a doorway on the opposite side?"

"And if it does turn out to be just a volcanic plug?"

"Seriously? I think we'd have to reexamine all our assumptions about geology. I've never heard of a square volcano."

"Well, it's the neck, not the whole volcano," Finley said, "but you have a point. On the other hand, these terraformed planets have caused us to rethink a few things about geology anyway."

"Somehow I don't think the Terraformers would have gone out of their way to make a square-necked volcano. Even if they had, I doubt there'd be any sign of it after sixty-five million years."

"I guess we'll find out soon enough. How much further to the last corner?"

Carson checked his omni. "About forty meters."

"Where was the doorway on your other pyramid?"

"In the center of one side. I figure that gives us a one-in-four chance of finding it first try, if we start digging at the center of a side."

"What side was it on? North, south, or what?"

Carson stopped so abruptly that Finley almost bumped into him.

"What?" Finley said.

"That's a damned good question. I don't know that there was any significance to it, but maybe there was."

"So? Which side?"

"I don't remember. Give me a minute." He couldn't believe he'd overlooked something as obvious as that. He was an archeologist; it was his job to notice such details. He thought back to when they'd first come across the St. Jacobs pyramid. They'd been coming up a mountain, and around a ridge to the plateau where it sat. The sun, the star Chara, was behind and to their left. It was afternoon, so it was south-west. That would put the door on the east side. Was that also true of the Verdigris pyramid? Carson thought back.

On Verdigris, they'd made their way through the jungle from where the *Sophie* had landed, and come across the excavation leading to the side of the pyramid. They had turned one corner after coming at it from the south side.

"The east side," he said, remembering. He looked at his omni again, confirming that they were on the east side of this pyramid, and the center was . . . "Let's backtrack about twenty meters."

Dundee had stopped when they did, still ten meters ahead. Carson called to him. "Steve, come back this way. I have a hunch, something Alex said."

They backtracked the twenty meters to the center of the south side. It didn't look any different from what they'd seen on every other side, but as far as Carson was concerned, that just meant there was no reason *not* to try digging here. He shucked off his backpack and unstrapped the field shovel attached to it.

"Okay, I'm going to go a short way up to where the slope becomes distinct. The soil will be thinner there. I might as well see what there is to see."

"All right. What do you want me to do?"

"Take a few pictures for context. If I find anything, we'll break out the measuring gear and make it more formal. Other than that," Carson paused and grinned, "catch me if I fall."

"I'll let Steve do that. I'll be taking pictures." Finley said and grinned back.

"Right."

Carson ventured up the slope, grabbing at bushes and digging in with the shovel to help him make progress. Within a few meters, the steepening talus at the base of the wall gave way to the flat sloping side that extended to the top. Carson looked around for a good spot. He wanted a bush or tree to help prop him up, but on the other hand he didn't want to have to try digging through roots. Finally, he shrugged and rested his downhill foot against the base of a small bush, extended the pick part of his folding shovel, and began whacking at the dirt to loosen it up.

It was surprisingly well packed, but then it would have to be to hold on this slope. He loosened up the top half-meter or so, then shoveled it out to see his progress and give himself more room to work.

"Anything yet?" came Finley's call from below.

"Nope. Half a meter down and it's still just soil. It does look a bit grayer than the surface. I think your grandfather mentioned that in his report."

"Okay."

Curious about the grayer soil, Carson knelt down to examine it. It looked a bit like volcanic ash. He undid the canteen from his belt and poured a little water onto it, then stirred it with his fingers. It was thick and goopy, a bit like oatmeal, not quite what he had expected. He held up a handful of the goop and tilted his hand. It clung until his palm was almost vertical, before oozing off and falling to the ground. Interesting.

"Are you digging or playing with mud pies?" Finley called again.

"Yes," Carson called back. "I think I've figured out how the soil stays on these steep sides. This lower layer is very sticky when wet. The question is how it got here in the first place."

"Keep digging, maybe you'll find out."

Carson smiled at Finley's impatience. He'd been like that himself once. It was something that had to be unlearned to become a good archeologist, but right now he felt exactly the same way.

He stood up and shook as much of the sticky mud off his hand as he could, then picked up his shovel again.

A few minutes later, the shovel blade struck something hard and made a distinct scraping sound as it slid along something under the dirt.

"I've hit something!" he called to the others below. Carefully, he began to excavate a hole about two-thirds of a meter square and nearly as deep, exposing a layer of stone beneath it. He brushed aside as much of the loose dirt as he could, then poured water to wash off a hand-sized area of the stone. It was smooth, but not polished, and a dark pink, almost grey. *Bingo.*

"There's definitely a smooth stone layer underneath. It doesn't look like anything magmatic. No markings on it though. I'm going to extend my trench downward."

"Need a hand?" Finley called up.

"No. How high above the forest floor would you say I am?"

"About seven meters. Why?"

The pyramid on Chara III had had carvings only up to about five meters. "I'm coming back down. Let's just dig from there. There's more dirt but we'll be closer to anything interesting."

∞ ∞ ∞

There was indeed more dirt around the base of the pyramid. Also more tree roots. Carson outlined a trench starting about two meters above the forest floor and extending down the side of the slope. It was as narrow as he could make it. He didn't want them to have to dig any more than necessary, but it needed to be wide enough for them to work. The resulting excavation was almost disturbingly grave-like.

"This would be a lot easier with a backhoe," Finley said, standing in the trench and heaving out another shovelful of dirt.

"You'd hate some of the digs I've been on," Carson said. "Imagine digging this out a centimeter at a time with just brushes and hand-trowels. We'd be doing that here if I thought there was anything small to find."

"And taking months to do it. No thanks."

"Anyway," Dundee said, "we don't have permission to use power equipment, nor an easy way to get it in here without tearing up some of the forest." He was sitting on the slope above where they were digging, keeping an eye out for predators. At least, that had been his excuse for not taking a turn with the shovel. Carson suspected that with the noise they were making, there were no large animals anywhere within half a kilometer.

"We may ultimately have to do that," he said. "We're not going to hand-excavate a doorway, if we do find one, in any reasonable time. Worst case we could helicopter in a small backhoe. It would probably have less environmental impact than supporting a work crew here for several weeks."

"Then what's the point of this?" Finley said, tossing up another shovelful of dirt. "And isn't it your turn?"

"The point is to see if there's anything worth a proper excavation. I think it's pretty clear this isn't a natural volcanic remnant, but there's no definitive proof yet."

Finley bent down, digging the shovel in again. "Proof? Just what kind of proof do you want?" As he said that, they heard a muffled thunk. Finley, still leaning on the shovel, looked up. "I think I've hit rock."

Carson was already lying down on the edge to look into the trench; there wasn't room for two of them down there. "Okay, lift the last shovelfuls of dirt away from the rock, then brush it clear with your hands." He scrabbled around in his pack and pulled out a flashlight. The shadows in the pit made it hard to see detail. By now Finley had set the shovel aside and was sweeping dirt away with the edge of his hand.

"Wow," Finley muttered.

"What? What do you see?" Despite the flashlight, Finley was blocking Carson's view.

"Hand me the light." Finley was still on his knees, brushing at the stone now with his fingertips. Carson handed the light down and Finley reached up for it, then, moving back from where he'd uncovered the stone surface, shone the beam on it at an angle.

"Is this," Finley said, gesturing with the light, "what you meant by proof?"

Where he pointed, a complicated pattern of shadows threw the engravings on the stone into high relief.

Chapter 38: Rico's Reassignment

Space Guard HQ, Sawyer City

"BOSS? WHAT THE hell is going on?" Rico asked Ducayne when he got over his surprise at seeing him.

"Not what you might think, Rico. We only heard you were here a couple of days ago. Most of what Bannon here—" he gestured at the man Rico had known only as Friday "—may have told you is true. You had us worried. When your body disappeared we thought maybe the Velkaryans had you. Bannon didn't know you were working for us, so he didn't tell us he had you."

"Wait, you said a couple of days ago? Why wasn't I released then? Am I being released? What was with all the questioning?"

"Slow down, Rico. Bannon, can we get those chains off? He doesn't need them."

"Of course."

Rico stood up as Friday, or rather Bannon, unfastened his chains.

"Sorry about that," Bannon said. "It was necessary for yo—"

"For my own safety, yeah, yeah."

"It really was. If you'd decided to make another break for it before we'd explained everything . . . ."

"I get it. And that incident with Meatloaf outside?"

"Meatlo—? Oh, the guard. That was for verisimilitude."

Rico's eyes narrowed. He looked at Ducayne. "This was a test, wasn't it?" he said, his tone accusatory.

"Sit down, Rico, and relax. You have answers coming."

They all sat.

"Well?" Rico said.

"Yes, Rico, the last three days were a test. Don't feel picked on; all our agents go through some kind of test. You did well on

Earth, and I was genuinely sorry when I thought we'd lost you. What happened after that was a monumental fuck-up we're still unraveling, but we think it involved Sawyers World agents operating on Earth." He turned and eyed Bannon.

"I wouldn't know anything about that," Bannon said, all wide-eyed innocence.

"I'm not blaming you, or your organization. I'd probably do the same," Ducayne said.

"Anyway," he continued, "once we realized you hadn't been killed, we put tracers out looking for you. Meanwhile ACTO here was trying to figure out who you were and what you were up to. Eventually the connection was made."

"So you decided to take advantage of the situation and see if I'd turn?"

Ducayne nodded. "Something like that. Things have changed a bit while you were in cold storage. I've got another mission for you, but I wanted to be sure we could rely on you."

"And?"

"Bannon says you passed. It might be different if you were being worked over for real—everyone has their threshold—but neither did you sell out easy. And that was without training. We'll get you some of that before sending you out again."

"Out where?"

Ducayne looked at Bannon, who asked: "Want me to leave?".

"You've probably got this room bugged anyway. No, special relationship and all that, you might as well hear the gist of it," Ducayne said before turning back to Rico.

"You spent some time on Verdigris when you were with Hopkins, didn't you? In fact, I think that's where you first met Carson."

Rico remembered. "It was. And I did. Why?"

"I imagine you still have contacts there? Contacts in the, ah, less savory side of society?"

"You mean crooks and smugglers. I might know a few. Just in passing, mind, I wouldn't normally hang out with unsavory characters myself." Rico grinned and winked at Ducayne. "What's happening on Verdigris?"

"That's what we'd like to find out. The Velkaryans have a big presence in New Toronto, and news out of there is sketchy and filtered of late. There are rumors of arms build-ups and native put-downs."

"The Velkaryans are bastards. And I have a personal grudge against a couple of them. So, what do you want me to do?"

"First, get you out of here and get you back into shape. Several months in a traumapod is no good for anyone. The machines can only do so much to keep up your muscle tone and bone mass."

"No kidding," Rico said, remembering how he'd felt when he'd made that escape attempt from the wheelchair.

"You'll get a full briefing later, but mainly we want you to blend into the background on Verdigris and keep your eyes and ears open. If it comes down to it, maybe kill people and break things, but let's hope it doesn't."

"Sure, Boss." Rico said, although after what he'd just been through, there was a certain appeal to killing people and breaking things, especially if they were Velkaryan, and one Velkaryan in particular.

Chapter 39: Pyramid concealed

Pete's Pyramid

HANNIBAL CARSON FINISHED clearing the dirt off the engraved surface of the pyramid, then used his omniphone to take pictures of them. "Yep, there's our proof." He touched an icon to tag their precise location.

He took a few more pictures of the engravings they'd uncovered, then stepped back. "All right," he said, "let's fill this back in."

"After all that work to uncover it? Are you joking?" Finley demanded.

Carson shook his head. "No. Much as I would love to start excavating this properly, we can't. This was just a quick reconnoiter to verify whether this was a pyramid or the remains of a volcano. We've done that. We need to regroup before we can do a more thorough excavation"

"Okay, we can't stay. But why the trouble of covering it up again? It's not like anyone is going to stumble across this by accident."

"They might. Poachers, wardens, who knows who might come stumbling through here? But they're not who I'm worried about."

"Then who, grave robbers?" Finley asked. Dundee, still sitting upslope on the side of the pyramid, was listening to the conversation but staying out of it.

"It wouldn't be the first time," Carson said, "but no. Velkaryans."

"The political party? Why would they care?

"Political party and religious, or quasi-religious, fanatics. They want access to alien technology, if there is any in there." Carson had to watch what he said. "I've seen them make a mess of archeological sites before. I don't want it to happen to this one." He hoped that would satisfy Finley and Dundee.

"Oh, all right," Finley said, picking up a shovel. "But it's going to be pretty obvious someone was digging here, no matter how you try to disguise it."

"You're right. So, we'll just have to dig in a few other places to confuse the issue. But don't worry, it won't be as deep."

Finley looked disgusted. "I had to say something, didn't I?" He tossed a shovelful of dirt into the hole, covering Carson's boots. "Oops," Finley said, not looking sorry at all.

"Hey!" Carson said as he scrambled out.

"Just trying to get a move on. Apparently, we have more holes to dig."

Carson took it with the humor that was intended. "If I ever have to bury pirate treasure, I'm not inviting you along."

"That's all right. Just remember me if you're ever digging it up."

Chapter 40: Artifacts

Homeworld Security, Sawyer City

TWO DAYS LATER, Carson was back in Sawyer City, the evidence of his quick look now disguised, and the remainder of the Office of Land Management team—he wondered how many of them were legitimate OLM employees versus plants from some other government agency—continuing with their ecological survey. He was at Ducayne's office now to fill in the details after the one word report he'd sent from the field: "Confirmed."

"So it *is* a pyramid," Ducayne said when Carson finished briefing him. "That raises new questions, not least of which is how we get into it before anyone else does."

"I don't see how you can avoid bringing the Sawyers World government in on that," Carson said. "They already know something is up, and it would certainly be much easier with their help."

"Oh, I agree. I'd pretty much already decided that. It would be difficult to keep them out. In fact, they may want to keep *us* out, but I think they'll be cooperative. This just raises the urgency." Ducayne gazed off at the wall behind Carson, then turned his attention back. "But that's my problem, not yours. I have something else for you. Walter Black is back from Chara, and he brought a souvenir."

"He did? What?"

"I'll let you see for yourself. Black is in Lab C with it right now, I'll tell him you're on your way."

∞ ∞ ∞

Lab C, Homeworld Security

Carson found Walt Black examining a large, boxy-looking piece of equipment on one of the benches in the Lab, with alien markings on it. Carson leaned in and peered at it closely, without touching it.

"This came from the pyramid on Chara III?" he asked Black.

"That's right," Black said, "from the hidden room you mentioned."

Carson nodded thoughtfully. "This must have been what they took from the pyramid on Verdigris," he said, "or rather, one like it. It does look like it would fit the empty console we found."

"Probably," Black said. "The room we found it in matched the one you described and photographed, complete to the access shaft off the main corridor, so we assume so."

"Do you have pictures of it *in situ*?"

"Of course. Here," Black put a series of images up on the large monitor on the adjacent bench. They showed a rather stark interior chamber, with stone walls and the ubiquitous low intensity lighting of the style they'd found inside both pyramids. The placement of the dais, or console, was as Carson remembered, but this one had an object on it, the same object now in the lab.

"That's it all right," he said. "I think there are some minor differences, the color of the stone is a little different for one. That may be due to local materials or aging. Maybe even just the lighting."

"Good," said Black. "Our next trick is to figure out what the thing is. We don't want to do anything too disruptive unless and until we have a second one to compare it with."

"Well, we know there's another one out there somewhere," Carson said. "Probably more than one, if we find other pyramids."

"There's a rumor you already know of another pyramid."

"Really? I can't imagine why anyone would think that," Carson said, his tone wry. He didn't know what Ducayne had said about it, if anything.

"Fair enough. Anyway, we had a long debate about even bringing it back here. We studied it on site for as long as we could, but I knew Ducayne wanted it."

"He's not the only one. It certainly doesn't look anything like the Maguffin we found." Carson leaned over it, looking at it closely. There were few obvious controls, but they were labeled. At least, Carson assumed the markings were labels in alien writing. "Interesting."

Black guessed at what Carson was thinking. "That language isn't anything like what's on the walls in the lower chambers, is it? We thought that interesting too. Was your Maguffin labeled?"

"It was, but it basically just had a power setting and an on-off switch, at least that's all I remember. The symbols were close enough to the wall markings that we figured it out. I decided any differences were as much due to style or font as anything else." He inspected the device further. "Look, here, this symbol looks familiar." He pointed to it. "And this one."

"Yes, that's pretty clearly an on-off switch," Black agreed. But this whole section here—" he gestured to a panel covered with writing, what on a human-built device might have been operating instructions "—none of this text corresponded to anything we found elsewhere."

Carson nodded. "I think that makes sense. Assuming they intended the easily accessible areas as a teaching museum, they'd design a language to be easy to learn and understand, although probably borrowing symbols from their own where they made sense. This gear was in a hidden room only accessible if you knew where it was *and* had an access key, a talisman."

"Sure, so they'd just use their own language. But what about that Maguffin? That wasn't intended to be part of the museum, right?"

"Not likely. We only found it because we used the key. But as I said, it didn't have much on the way of symbols on it. We don't generally have long instructions on hand tools, either."

"I can go along with that," Black said.

"You've had longer to look at this than I have. Is there anything that gives even a hint of what it does?"

"Maybe."

"Oh?"

"Look at these symbols here," Black pointed them out. "Does that look like the Pyramid Builder pictograph for gravity?"

The symbol looked something like a tapered corkscrew, or a stylized tornado. "Yeah," Carson said, "it looks like how someone might draw a black hole. Do we really want to be messing with this?"

"Maybe we'll take it to the back side of Selene before testing it," Black said, referring to the moon of Sawyers World.

"That's probably a good idea." Carson pointed out another symbol, one that appeared in several places. "These parallel lines, Marten and I thought they might represent parallel worlds or extra dimensions."

"Yeah, that fits with the lessons on string theory. At least, I think that's what our physicist told me that was. Half the time I didn't understand him, and he was speaking English."

Carson had picked up a bit of this from Roberts. "The theory is that gravity is such a weak force, compared to electromagnetism or nuclear forces, is because unlike those, it propagates into the hidden or 'rolled up' extra dimensions of string theory. I'm probably butchering the explanation. Anyway, that's why we can pump a ton of energy into a warp module without evaporating the ship—it bleeds off as gravity waves."

"Why would anyone put a warp module inside a pyramid?"

"I'm not saying that's what this is." As Carson said that, he found himself wondering if that's what it might really be. The Kesh had pyramidal starships, too big to go faster than light, but from what Ketzshanass had said, you could make a warp bubble much bigger if you were content to go slower than light. But the Chara pyramid was no starship, it was anchored into the rock, and nothing they'd seen inside had looked anything like what a ship might. "No, that wouldn't make any sense. But it does seem like it might have something to do with gravity waves."

"A detector, perhaps?"

"But why?"

"We use gravity detectors to sense ships going in and out of warp, but we deploy them in space where there's less noise, not under a mound of rock."

"Might the rock also help filter noise?" And why was this conversation giving Carson a sense of déjà vu?

Black shrugged. "Not my field. I'd think they'd be worried about normal ground movements, quakes and landslides mucking up the signal. Maybe they had something to compensate for that.

Anyway, it's awfully small for a gravity detector. Ours are huge things."

That was it! Carson remembered now where he'd had a conversation like this—it had been regarding the artifact Tevnar had pulled from a wrecked ship, possibly a Kesh scout, at Kapteyn's Star. From what Carson and Roberts had seen of the wreckage, it would have been mounted at the center of mass of the ship, just where you might want a gravity wave detector. He'd have to pass that along to Ducayne.

"What?" Black asked. "You looked like you suddenly remembered something."

"I did. Not sure I can talk about it though."

"The Kapteyn's artifact? Ducayne briefed me."

"Oh? Then yes, that might be a gravity wave detector," Carson said. "I don't think this thing is, though. Or if it is, it's not the same kind."

"Well, no. One was built by the Pyramid Builders, the other presumably by the Kesh."

So, Black had also been briefed on the Kesh. Carson wasn't very surprised. "That's not what I meant. I meant a different function. We use electromagnetic field detectors and generators in all kinds of gear, everything from motors to radios to ovens, to fabbers and autochefs, but they're all different."

"Ah, I get you." Black paused, his eyes widening. "Wow. Imagine a civilization with the same kind of control of gravity waves that we have of electromagnetic waves and fields," Black said. "They might even have anti-grav and tractor beams."

Carson smiled to himself. He was pretty sure that the Kesh had both, but wasn't going to say anything. He just grunted non-committally.

Black shook his head in wonderment. "It's too bad Algernon Brenke died when he did. Nobody since has had his grasp of warp theory and practice."

"Perhaps it's just as well," Carson said. "I'm not sure we as a species could have handled all that new tech at once. Look at the design of the pyramid museum. A species had to fully understand one level of technology before it could solve the puzzles that led to the next level."

"Good thing we have a master key. It's too bad there weren't any more levels. Although I suppose once the natives got to a certain point, they could just blast their way in."

"Maybe. Although the spacefarers might have booby trapped it. Putting traps in pyramids is a time-honored tradition, and not just in fiction."

"Ha!" Black laughed. "There is that."

Chapter 41: Rico Retrained

Sawyers World, UDT Homeworld Security

. . .*BLAM! BLAM!* RICO lowered his pistol and pressed the switch to bring the paper target he'd been shooting toward him. He examined the torso silhouette. Four holes with a lousy grouping centered near the left shoulder, and another two off where the right ear would be. He muttered a curse. He was more out of practice than he realized. The—months, had it been?—in a traumapod had ruined his muscles and hand-eye coordination.

The last week of rehab and training had helped, but he wasn't yet where he wanted to be. He was also getting tired of the routine, although it beat hell out of the little room Friday, or Bannon, had had him locked up in.

He pulled the target down and replaced it with another, then sent it back downrange. He replaced the empty magazine in the pistol, a Maclaren 10mm, and took aim, cradling his right hand in the palm of his left. *BLAM!* He peered at the target. The hole was up and to the right of where he'd aimed. Well, there was part of the problem. He adjusted his aim and quick-fired three more shots. *BLAM, BLAM, BLAM!* He placed the gun down and pulled the target back again.

The grouping was still lousy, a good ten centimeters between the furthest left and right shots, but at least they were centered on the target. He reached for the switch to send the target downrange again, but was interrupted by the Range Officer's voice over the receiver in his earmuffs.

"Rico, safe your weapon and report to Ducayne's office."

Oh? What was that about? Rico sighed and unloaded the pistol, making sure the chamber was clear. He took it, his safety glasses and earmuffs and turned them in as he left the range, then went to see Ducayne.

∞ ∞ ∞

Rico found Ducayne's office door open and rapped on the frame. "You wanted to see me, Boss?"

"Yeah, come in and have a seat. I hear you've been spending a lot of time on the range."

"You know me, I like to shoot," Rico said as he sat down. "But I'm rusty as hell. Too long in that damned traumapod. I'm lucky to get a ten-centimeter grouping."

Ducayne shook his head slightly and looked at Rico. "I hear you're shooting that at twenty-five meters. You know we only expect agents to qualify at twenty, with more than half the shots at less than ten."

"I used to be able to do that at forty."

"With a pistol? Seriously?"

"Well, with *my* pistol. Zeroed in. Still, I should be doing better, unless you're not maintaining your training weapons."

Ducayne stared at him for a moment, then said, "All right, I'll talk to the armorer. But that's not what I wanted to talk to you about."

"Fair enough. What's up?"

"We've been focusing your training on small arms and unarmed combat, mostly to help you get back in shape from traumapod deconditioning, but I think it's time to give you some more specialized training."

"Like what?"

"You're a smart guy, Rico. Brown gave you a glowing report, and not just because he thought you'd been killed. The tricks you used to get the Blue Book photographs were very clever. We're going to teach you a few other tricks, some of which rely on specialized equipment."

"You mean I get to play with some of your spook toys?" Rico said, ignoring Ducayne's wince at the term. "Sounds like fun."

"It's going to be work. You need to learn some things about starship systems, communications, electronics—"

"I do know some of that, but I'm game. Is there something in particular you have in mind?"

"I might have a mission coming up that you'd be well suited for, although it's not definite yet."

"You mean Verdigris? You mentioned that before."

Ducayne glanced at his desk monitor, which Rico couldn't see. "You've spent quite a bit of time there, haven't you?"

"You know I have. Hopkins did a lot of business there. What's the mission?"

"That's just one of the places I might want to send you. I'll tell you more when there's an actual mission."

"Okay. So what do I do in the meantime?"

"Report to Regina Elliot. She's got a craft and technical training schedule drawn up for you. But keep up with the combat training in your spare time."

Rico looked up at the name. Elliot was easy on the eyes, but as Ducayne's second in command, she was a hard taskmaster. He shook his head. "Spare time? What spare time?"

Ducayne grinned. He had a disturbing grin. "All those months in a traumapod, and you still want sleep? Make time."

Chapter 42: Theorizing

Ducayne's office

DUCAYNE HAD CALLED Jackie Roberts in to discuss physics. She'd been a little surprised at that; she knew Ducayne had his own people with far more advanced physics and astrophysics knowledge than she had.

"I do, but I appreciate your way of translating things into understandable English," he said when she asked. "It's not that I don't understand all the words my scientists use, usually, but they have a tendency to string them together in ways that stop making sense when I try to parse them.

"Let me ask you," he continued, "if you were going to build a —let's call it a faster-than-light radio, even if that is a contradiction in terms—anyway, if you were, how would you do it? Quantum entanglement?"

"Not likely," Jackie said, shaking her head. "We don't know how that works, but what we *do* know about it suggests that it's not useful for communication. There's no way to control the outcome of measuring one particle, so you don't have any control over the state of its entangled partner. We just know that the state isn't resolvable until you do measure it."

Ducayne frowned. "Does that mean there's some factor or something that gets set when a pair is entangled? We just can't detect what that factor is?"

Jackie smiled and shook her head. "No. You'd think that, it's an obvious assumption, but long ago a scientist named Bell proved that such factors, so-called hidden variables, don't exist."

"The guy who invented the telephone?"

"No, that was a different Bell. Anyway, it's weird, but that's not how entanglement works. But why are we talking about this anyway? It's not like you to be purely hypothetical. Do you have evidence that someone has faster-than-light communications? Other than by starship, I mean?"

Ducayne put his elbows on his desk and steepled his fingers. "That's the problem with hiring bright people," he said, as much to himself as to her. "It makes it hard to keep secrets from them." He shook his head and put his hands back down. "No evidence as such, no."

Jackie thought there was more to it. "So, an absence of evidence, but no evidence of absence? Is that what you're not saying?"

"I'm not saying what I'm not saying," Ducayne said with a grin. "But let me tell you a little story about actions and intelligence."

"Okay."

"If someone is watching your actions, they often have a pretty good idea of what you know and when you knew it."

"I think I follow," Jackie said. "If I take an action that reflects some knowledge you thought I didn't have, then I clearly got that knowledge somehow, or I just got lucky."

"Right, and it's never safe to assume an adversary just got lucky. One classic example is during World War II when the Allies could crack the German Enigma code."

Jackie remembered Burnside talking about Enigma back on Tanith, speculating as to what the alien artifact might be. "I've heard of that. There was some kind of decoding machine involved?"

"There was, but it had so many combinations that even if you knew how it worked, the Germans felt confident that it couldn't be broken. But a few bright lads came up with some of the first computers, and some cryptanalysis tricks, and could often crack the messages within hours of their being sent. That project was code-named Ultra.

"The thing was," Ducayne continued, "if the Allies took too many actions based on Ultra intelligence without some plausible other source of information—parallel construction, we call it now—then the Germans would realize that Enigma had probably been broken, and they would have taken steps to make it even harder to crack. Obviously, the Allies wanted to avoid that, so sometimes they let bad things happen, even when they knew they were going to, just because there was no other plausible way for them to have found out about it."

"Really? That's a tough call."

Ducayne nodded, his expression serious. "One well-known example, although there's still debate about it, is the air raid on Coventry, England. The Allies had learned it was coming, and could have warned the residents and intercepted the raid, but at the expense of losing the Allied advantage of reading Enigma messages." He shook his head. "I'd hate to have been in that position. Although by some reports they knew the raid was coming but not *where*. I'm not sure that's any better."

Jackie could only imagine how hard that trade-off had been, but didn't see the connection to what they had been discussing. "What does this have to do with faster than light communications?"

"Sometimes you have to act on the information anyway, and hope that the opposition doesn't figure out how you did it."

"You're losing me." Jackie wondered if Ducayne had some advance information about Velkaryan actions.

"There are some actions that the Velkaryans have taken that, while they could be due to lucky chance or insight, are more easily explained if they have some kind of FTL communication."

Now she got it. But FTL communication didn't require some kind of magic radio. "Wouldn't a ship or message torpedo explain that?"

"Faster than any ship or torpedo I'm aware of. Unless we're just missing some other connection, there's evidence of messages between Earth and Verdigris in less than a day, for example."

Jackie let out a low whistle. That was over ten times faster than a message torpedo. "You're serious?" She looked at Ducayne's face. "Of course you are. Sorry."

"There's not enough data to be certain. That's just what we deduced by analyzing their behavior after the fact. But if they do have something like that, then knowing how it works would help us find out what to look for. Maybe it is some kind of ultra-fast message torpedo, but so far we haven't seen any evidence of that. We think there must be an FTL communication device, or at least a pair of them. But I don't know if it's alien technology they found somewhere, or something their own scientists came up with. Or maybe some combination of the two."

"But given their interest in alien technology, and the gear missing from the Pavonis pyramid, you suspect the former," she said.

"Roberts, if you ever get tired of flying a starship, I've got a desk job for you. You seem to have a talent for analysis."

Jackie shuddered inwardly. A desk job? "No thanks. I like flying."

"I thought you'd say that. But back to the problem at hand. Forget quantum entanglement. It must be something else. What about gravity?"

"That doesn't help," Jackie said. "Gravity propagates at light-speed. And that's ignoring the size of the detector you'd need."

"What about through the so-called hidden or rolled-up dimensions? I know gravity leaks out through those, that's how warp drives avoid cooking themselves. How fast does it propagate through those?"

"Uh, we have no idea, but there's no reason to assume it's other than cee. Although. . . ."

Ducayne spoke again before she could finish the thought. "Then the only way to go faster than light is to generate a warp field?"

She nodded. "Yes. Except it doesn't really go faster than light, it warps spacetime so you're not really travelling as far as you think." Roberts fished around for a comparison. "This is a bad analogy, but consider sound. You can't yell at someone and have your voice travel faster than sound."

"Well, no, but we can make objects go faster than sound."

"Sure, but they're not sound waves. But say you had a long pipe, a hundred meters long, and you yell in one end. How long before the sound comes out the other end?"

Ducayne shrugged. "I don't know; what's the speed of sound?"

"Let's make it easy and call it ten meters per second."

"Okay, then it takes ten seconds to travel the length of the pipe. One hundred over ten. Where are you going with this?"

"Right, bear with me," Jackie said. "Okay, I'm vastly oversimplifying, but now close the ends of the pipe temporarily, just after you yell." She held her arms apart with her wrists bent, palms facing each other, representing the valves at each end of the pipe. "And then you open them again just as the sound gets to the other end." She rotated her wrists to extend her hands, palms facing downward; the valves open. "Same thing, ten seconds, right?"

"Sure. Assuming there's no effect from compression."

"Assume not; I'm simplifying. Now, I'm going to fasten a rocket to that pipe. I yell in one end, slam it shut, fire the rocket, and shoot the whole thing so it travels a kilometer in less than ten seconds." She waved her arms, gesturing as though throwing a length of pipe. "Then open the pipe again and my voice comes out the other end. How fast has my voice travelled?"

Ducayne frowned. "Uh, a kilometer in ten seconds? Or just the length of the pipe in ten seconds? Um. . . ."

"Exactly. As far as the inside of the pipe is concerned, the sound is still travelling ten meters a second. To anyone *outside* the pipe, it just travelled at a hundred meters per second—ten times our hypothetical speed of sound. The warp drive works the same way."

"But, the pipe itself moved faster than sound."

"Right, and with starships, the warp bubble moves—for a rather loose definition of moves—faster than light. Except that it's a bubble of warped spacetime. Einstein never said that spacetime *itself* couldn't stretch or contract faster than light, and in fact cosmic inflation after the Big Bang proved that it could. Alcubierre did the math, others refined it, and Brenke reduced it to practice."

Ducayne sat absorbing this for a moment. Like most people he was vaguely aware of how starships worked, but that didn't mean he could have explained it, even to himself. "So, the only way to make something seem to go faster than light is to change the effective distance; to cheat."

"Exactly." As she said that, she remembered the point she'd been on the verge of realizing when Ducayne had interrupted her. Her eyes widened.

Ducayne beat her to it. "Tell me, then. What is the effective distance between two points in the hidden dimensions that gravity leaks into?"

"Uh. . . ." Roberts tried to remember what they'd said about that in school. "Anything from subatomic distances to nobody knows how far, depending on the dimension. But. . . ." There was another detail. What was it?

"But?"

"Something about the Casimir Effect, but that's electromagnetics." It came to her as she said it. "Oh, right. If the dimension is smaller than the wavelength, it won't propagate at all, the radiation won't penetrate it."

"But it goes somewhere, right? What's the gravitational wavelength emitted by a warp drive?"

"It's complicated. I've never needed to know. Not very short, but I think it's speed and size dependent." Her instructors would have been horrified at that; speed was a very inaccurate term when applied to warp travel, and size wasn't much better. "Or rather," she corrected, "it's warp geometry dependent."

"Which would mean that for some kind of gravity wave communicator, you'd want short gravity waves," Ducayne mused, half to himself. "How small can you make a warp field? For that matter, how small can you make a warp generator?"

"A single warp generator is small, but the field is unstable," Jackie replied. This was basic warp-ship theory. "The warp modules on a starship each contain multiple generators, to average out random Finazzi instabilities and make the whole thing controllable. You also need to route a lot of power to each unit. I think the warp modules on a message torpedo are about as small as it's possible to make them." She looked at him, understanding his real question. "Certainly bigger than any of the alien artifacts we've brought back."

As she said that, and seeing the disappointment on Ducayne's face, Jackie remembered an alien artifact they *hadn't* brought back: the Maguffin, the disintegrator they'd found on Chara III. Their theory of how it might work hinged on the fact that the edge of a warp field disintegrated matter through tidal disruption.

"On the other hand," she said, "however small *we* could make one, I think the Pyramid-Builders made one small enough to hand-carry."

Chapter 43: Investigating the Object

Sawyers World

"HOW IS THE RESEARCH going?" Ducayne asked Black in the lab.

"Not well," Black said. "The device comes on-line and seems to be operating within parameters, but we're not getting anything that looks like a signal."

"Maybe nobody is sending. If Velkaryans have the only two others in the neighborhood, perhaps there's just not much traffic."

"There is that. Also, if they are the only ones out there with active devices, we want to be very careful about sending anything."

Ducayne shook his head. "No, we don't want to send anything at all. It would blow our advantage if they suspect we have one. So, what's the problem?"

"We get powerful signals, but they're either pure noise or not modulated at all. And they come at irregular intervals."

"Are you sure its pure noise? An encrypted signal should look like that." The best encryption techniques made the output appear random.

"pear random.

Black shrugged. "You've got a point. Anyway, I'd like to ask Jackie Roberts some questions. She was there both at St. Jacobs and at Zeta Reticuli."

"So was Carson."

"Carson doesn't have any physics training. Roberts does."

"All right," Ducayne said. "I'll let her know you'd like to talk to her."

∞ ∞ ∞

"Where have you been testing?" was one of Jackie's first questions when she met up with Walter Black in the lab and he'd explained the problem.

"We first powered it up on Selene's farside, just as a precaution. When it seemed safe, we brought it back here to the lab where we have all our instruments. Why?"

"In the Chara system, it was in a pyramid on a mountain with little else going on around it. At Zeta Reticuli, the signal relay would have been from something at the gas giant's L5 point. I'm thinking you may need to isolate it from noise sources."

"Very likely, but what noise sources?"

"You're assuming that it's based on some kind of gravity wave?"

Black nodded. "Yes, of course. And the strongest waves are going to be from a ship dropping out of warp, but that happens well away from the planet."

Something she knew well. "Right. Warp drives aside, where's the noisiest place you can think of to put it?"

"Somewhere there's a lot of mass moving around at high speed." Black paused, realizing what he had just said, and shook his head. "Like near a spaceport," he said.

Jackie nodded. "Any primitive civilization where the Spacefarers set up pyramids would have been well below the capability of moving multi-ton objects around at any speed."

"What about girannos?" Ducayne said, referring to the giraffe-sized rhinos native to Sawyers World, and known to occasionally stampede.

"It would take a herd to equal the mass of even a small starship, and their top speed is what, forty kilometers per hour?" Jackie said. "It might add some noise, but probably not much, and at a very low frequency." As she said this, Jackie remembered the artifact Tevnar had pulled from the alien wreck at Kapteyn's Star. Whatever it was, it was unlikely to be a communicator. While the receiver side might be designed to filter out the ship's own emissions, there would be no way to transmit anything over the high-energy gravitational roar of the warp drive.

"You know," she added, "I'd bet that the Velkaryan transceivers aren't on Earth or Verdigris, but elsewhere in their systems."

Ducayne looked thoughtful. "There is a Velkaryan outpost orbiting Neptune in the Solar system," he said. "Officially it's an independent research facility, studying that planet's unusual system of moons. They think we don't know about their connection to it."

Jackie thought for a moment, then nodded slowly. "That could be a good place. Ships entering Sol space usually come out of warp a lot deeper in-system, between Saturn and Jupiter orbit, above or below the plane. Any effects from Triton or the other moons would be predictable."

"What about in the Delta Pavonis system?" Ducayne asked her.

She thought for a moment. The system was not too unlike the Sol system, with rocky inner planets, a large gas giant and smaller Neptune-like ice giants, plus the usual collection of tiny, irregular bodies. "Yes, the system is clear enough that ships come in pretty deep. They could have a remote station almost anywhere."

"Would a ship passing nearby cause a problem?"

Jackie grinned and shook her head. "No pilot would willingly set their course within five AU of the orbital plane until they've paused to check, and even if they did, nothing in warp is going to be within a million kilometers of a given point for more than about ten milliseconds. A glitch in the signal at most."

"It sounds like we might need to take this out to deep space to test it, then," Black said. "Where?"

"The system barycenter?" Jackie said. "The center of mass of the Alpha Centauri A and B stars," she added, not knowing if Ducayne was familiar with the term.

"That's as good a place as any, I guess," Black said. "If that doesn't work, there's halfway to Proxima."

"Do you need to worry about traffic between here and Kakuloa?" Ducayne asked.

"No. The usual route is to jump a couple of AU clear of the orbital plane first," Jackie said. "North of it for the Sawyers to Kakuloa leg, south for the reverse. The odds are infinitesimally small of a collision even if the ships didn't do that, but it's a hold-over from atmospheric traffic."

"We'll need some kind of remote set-up," Black said. "I'd like to have the ship back off a reasonable distance to minimize any interference at all."

Ducayne nodded. "Requisition what you need. Jackie, are you and the *Sophie* available for this, or shall I put one of our system boats on it?"

"Are you kidding? I wouldn't miss it," she said. "Besides, Carson will be out at his dig. His approval came through."

∞ ∞ ∞

Starship Sophie, *Alpha Centauri system barycenter*

The alien apparatus that Black had brought back from Chara III was bolted to the table in the *Sophie*'s galley. Jackie hadn't considered this complication when she volunteered her ship for testing, but it was temporary; they would only be out here for another day, two at most. It was also necessary; with the warp drive shut down, the *Sophie* was in zero gee.

Walter Black and his team had managed to reverse-engineer enough of the gizmo to tap into its outputs, which is how they'd been able to test it in the first place. That interface now tied in to the galley's monitor screen. The display reminded Jackie of what it had shown when they first entered the Zeta Reticuli system all those months ago.

There was a schematic of the Alpha Centauri system and its planets, although it omitted Proxima. That was too far away to matter. The device was clearly detecting high-frequency gravity waves. The emissions from the warp traffic between Sawyers World and Kakuloa were obvious, if not very localized. The fuzzy blobs representing ships were, on that scale, nearly a billion kilometers across. With current human technology, it took an array of sensors dispersed over thousands of kilometers to both detect and localize such warp signatures. This device was detecting them, but Black hadn't figured out yet how to get it to display their position, or even if it could.

"Well," Jackie said, "as a detector, it beats our current gravity sensors. But why put it in a pyramid?"

"Protection?" Black suggested. "Fixed reference point? I don't know. The builders obviously intended for their pyramids to endure a long time unattended, maybe they had less confidence that orbital sensors would endure."

"But why a detector in the first place, unless they were expecting warp-capable visitors from elsewhere?"

"Which brings us back to the possibility that this is actually a communication device. But know that we know it's working aboard ship, we can go to the next step of the test." Black tapped out a command on the interface's pad, and the monitor display split, with the left half still showing the system diagram. On the right side was a series of traces like an oscilloscope, showing multiple tracks, each with its own noisy signal trace.

"Let me guess," Jackie said. "Each one of those traces is a different signal source?"

"Exactly. Now we just filter out the ships." He tapped out more commands, and, one by one, a warp source on the left side of the screen disappeared. As each did so, a trace on the right, or oscilloscope, side of the screen also disappeared. Eventually, with all the ships on the left gone, there were just three traces remaining. All were of lower amplitude and noisier than the ship traces had been, with one almost a flat line.

"Wow," Black said. "We weren't able to get it anywhere near that clean when testing before. You were right, Jackie, we had too much background noise."

"What are these traces that are left? Ships that are farther away?"

"That's most likely. We have no idea what the detection range of this thing is."

"That will depend on signal strength." Jackie said, stating what was, to her, obvious. "That will have an upper bound, there's a maximum size to a warp bubble. If I had to guess, those might be big cargo or passenger ships travelling between here and Earth. If we look at the shipping schedules we can figure out which ships are where, that would give us an idea of the range."

"That's brilliant. Do you have that data?"

"Sure, give me a minute." Jackie pushed off and glided forward to the cockpit, where she strapped herself into her seat. It would be easier to pull that information up from the ship's main control panel. While the computer ran the schedule search and correlated it with expected current distance from the Alpha Centauri system, Jackie dug into the kind of math problem she hadn't had to do since pilot school: for a warp bubble of a given size, what is the optimum drive frequency? With the search and calculations complete, she downloaded the information to her datapad, unstrapped, and headed back to the galley.

"Got it," she said. She handed the datapad to Black.

"What's this?"

"The five nearest IL- and IC-class ships. There are no X-class within two lightyears, at least none scheduled." These were all large ship classes, several times the size of S-class ships like the *Sophie*. "The other number on each entry is their drive frequency, or at least what it should be."

"Excellent! Let me punch in these numbers and see what we get." He tapped out the first drive frequency, for the IL-class starship *Southern Sky*, and the biggest remaining trace on the scope disappeared. He looked at the datapad again. "So by the schedule, that ship will drop out of warp in a bit over two hours. We're detecting it nearly a tenth of a lightyear away. That's great!"

Jackie was dumbfounded. "We shouldn't have been able to detect it at all."

"Exactly, this detector must be really sensitive."

"You're not getting it. Gravity waves travel at the speed of light. We shouldn't be picking up that signature, from where it is now, for another five weeks."

Black turned to stare at her, his jaw hanging slack. "I. . . You're right." He shook his head. "It must be a signal from a previous trip."

"No," Jackie said. "We'd be seeing a lot more traces if that were the case. Think of how many ships come and go in a month. That signal has to be travelling through a compacted dimension."

"But we can't *detect* gravity waves in the hidden dimensions," Black said, although he didn't sound entirely convinced.

Jackie just pointed to the device bolted to her galley table. "But *we* didn't build that, did we?"

Black said nothing for a moment, just looking from Jackie to the alien device, and back. "Good point, but let's test that. If you're right, the next signal should be the next ship on your list. That's five hours out, a bit over a quarter light year."

He entered the data into his interface device, and looked up expectantly at the monitor. The trace was still there. "Huh, that's odd."

He looked at the interface, then at Jackie's datapad, then back at the interface. "Oh, I missed a digit." He tapped furiously at the keypad on the interface again, and this time the trace disappeared.

Jackie felt a mixture of disbelief and smugness. She wasn't sure she wanted to believe this alien device could do what it clearly seemed to be doing, but if it *was* doing it, she had been right about how it did it. At least, how it did it at a theoretical level; the actual mechanics were still a mystery.

"Try the third one," she said to Black.

"Already on it," he said as he began entering the numbers for the third ship on the list. There was only one, faint signal remaining.

It still remained after he'd entered the data, checked it, re-entered it, and checked it again. "That's not it. Maybe that ship is behind schedule. Let me try the next."

They went through all the remaining ships on Jackie's list, and then Jackie pulled up a few more and they tried those. The last trace still persistently remained.

"There's no way all those other ships are behind schedule, so I think we've established that the range on this thing, at least for detecting ships in warp, is about a quarter lightyear," Jackie said at last.

"I'll go along with that," said Black.

"So, what's that last signal? And where is it coming from?"

Black grinned. "I think," he said, pausing for effect, "that is exactly the signal we're looking for. And my guess is that it's coming from somewhere in the vicinity of Neptune."

"The Velkaryan FTL communicator signal?"

Black nodded. "Either that or we've discovered some new phenomenon, but that's not the way I'd bet."

"From over four lightyears away?" Jackie doubted it. "When we can only detect ships at one-sixteenth that? That's a powerful signal." As she said it, it occurred to Jackie that distances in whatever compact dimension this signal travelled might not correlate to distances in the more familiar dimensions. She felt a headache coming on.

"Or it's being generated more efficiently," countered Black. "It would be designed for communication, not just the side effect of a warp drive."

Jackie had to agree. That was logical. She'd let someone else worry about the dimensional issues.

"What now?" she said. "There's still not much of a signal there, and it's sure to be encrypted."

"Oh, certainly it is. As for what now, I want to record as much of the raw signal as I can. We'll analyze the data back in the lab. Once we pull out the fundamental carrier frequencies we can improve the sensitivity, reject starship noise and the like, which will give us more data to try cracking the encryption."

"Fair enough," Jackie said. "I'll radio Ducayne and let him know."

"Yes, please do. He'll almost certainly recall us, but with the radio lag that should still give me a couple of hours to collect data."

Black was right. Ducayne's reply was simply: "Wonderful. Return to base. New assignment. QD."

Chapter 44: Pyramid Revisited

Pyramid site, Anderson Wildlife Preserve

CARSON DIDN'T KNOW the details, but he was sure that Pete Finley or perhaps even Elizabeth Sawyer herself had wielded some influence to get the small backhoe and an excavation team airlifted out to the pyramid site in such short order. Notwithstanding their claims of being apolitical and having no official role in Sawyers World government, the Original Eight had all managed to amass considerable wealth, holdings, and influence. Not necessarily in that order.

∞ ∞ ∞

"Just how many of these trenches do you need dug, anyway?" Hector Collins, the operator of the compact backhoe, asked. "This is the fourth one, do you even know what you're doing?"

To deliberately confuse the issue, Carson and Alex Finley had arranged for several trenches to be dug, on different sides of the peak and at various locations. Finley intercepted the question before Carson could.

"As I told you before," Finley said, "it's so we can emplace geophones and seismometers to evaluate any disturbance of the magma chamber."

"I still think you're nuts. This thing hasn't erupted in thousands of years, and I don't think it's going to start now. I may not be a geologist, but—"

"Exactly. You're not geologist. Anyway, it isn't about it erupting, it's about what ground movements can tell us about the whole area," Finley said. "But cheer up, your part is almost done. Finish up this trench and you can head back to civilization."

"And not a moment too soon, as far as I'm concerned," Collins said. "It will be nice to sleep in my own bed instead of that tent."

Finley and Carson just nodded agreement, not wanting to argue the point. Carson was certainly no stranger to putting up with much worse field accommodation than this, and while he didn't know all of Alex Finley's history, he was sure that his grandfather had told him a few stories of how rough the first landing team had had it, stranded without knowing when or even if they'd be picked up again.

Carson had made sure the trenches didn't come too close to the sides of the pyramid. He didn't think it would be easily damaged even by the heavy machinery—whatever the pyramid was made of seemed much more durable than ordinary stone—but it wouldn't do for this construction worker to discover what the peak really was. When the work crew had cleared out, Carson and the few others remaining at the site would finish the excavation, at first with the backhoe and then with shovels. He estimated about another half-day of digging. By tomorrow afternoon, they'd be ready to enter the pyramid.

∞ ∞ ∞

Next day

The trench was now excavated down to the door level. Yes, they had found the door. The pit reminded Carson of the pyramid on Verdigris, which had also been partially buried.

The excavation team had been kept small for security reasons. With the door uncovered and opened, it would soon become obvious that the pyramid builders had advanced technology.

The small group—Carson, Dundee, and Alex Finley, the same team as earlier—gathered around the still-sealed entrance to the pyramid. Carson examined the engravings surrounding the doorway. Almost out of habit, he took a few pictures with the omni on his wrist.

"Now what?" Finley asked.

"The carvings form a kind of astronomical puzzle. Solve the puzzle and the door should open."

"You mean we have to know astronomy?"

"The idea was that the natives had to have achieved some level of scientific insight to get in. But I have a key." Carson reached into his pocket and withdrew a small sample case. He opened it and extracted a rounded-square stone.

He held it up. It was the new talisman he had been sent by the anonymous inheritor. He just hoped it worked as well as the first. "I just need to find the keyhole." He scanned the engravings around the opening again, looking for a recess that matched the outline of the talisman. There, on the right side, about shoulder height. He looked back over his shoulder at the others and grinned. "Open sesame!" he started to say as he raised the stone, but his words were drowned out by a short burst of automatic gunfire.

Startled, he almost dropped the talisman as he turned toward the sound. As he fumbled and recovered it, he tapped a quick sequence on his wrist omni.

"Thank you, Doctor Carson. We'll take it from here." Above them, around the edges of the trench leading to the entrance, stood a half-dozen armed men, their weapons trained on the dig crew.

"Who the hell are you?" Carson demanded. He didn't believe these guys were artifact smugglers, they looked far too organized, and they were in uniform. It was not a uniform that Carson recognized.

"Anderson Territorial Police. This is an illegal excavation, you're all under arrest."

"That's bullshit. This is authorized through the Office of Land Management."

"We have no record of that. Come up out of there with your hands up."

Carson didn't believe this. It wasn't out of the question that there was some kind of bureaucratic screw up, especially with the speed and secrecy of their planning. But it seemed unlikely. Were the Velkaryans making a move? That seemed more probable. Still, with the weapons trained on them, he didn't see that they had any other options.

"All right, we're coming."

As they reached the top of the sloping trench, the cops, if that's what they really were, placed wrist ties on each of them and patted them down, confiscating their omniphones and any other gadgets they had, including Carson's multitool. They also relieved him of the talisman.

"What's this?" the man in charge asked. "An illegal artifact?"

"I'm an archeologist with the university," Carson explained as calmly as he could. Losing his temper wouldn't help. "That's part of the university collection, it didn't come from this site."

"Really? Then why are you carrying it around with you?"

"Look, this is authorized. Call the university. Ask for Dean Matthews. Or call the Office of Land Management. They'll explain."

"We'll do that, all in good time. Meanwhile, you three are going to sit tight while I have my men search the area." He turned to two of the others. "Garrett, you and Brady put them in the tent. Secure them to something for now."

"Got it," the larger one of them said, and he and the other gestured with their weapons. "You heard him. Move."

Chapter 45: Briefing Interrupted

Homeworld Defense, Sawyer City

JACKIE ROBERTS RAPPED on the open door of Ducayne's office. "You wanted to see me?"

"Yes, come on in." Ducayne gestured at the two empty chairs in front of his desk. A third chair was already occupied. The man's face was turned away, but Jackie thought something about him seemed familiar.

He turned toward her as she sat down. Was that . . . "*Rico?*" she gasped. "Rumor had it you were dead. It's good to see you."

"Only mostly dead. I've been spending far too much time in traumapods since I met you. Not that it's your fault," he said, and grinned.

"And mostly we won't talk about it," Ducayne added. "Need to know, and all that. But I have a mission for Rico and another agent. She should be here any moment."

"I'm guessing they need transportation," Jackie said.

Ducayne nodded. "I'll fill you in when we're all here."

As if on cue, there was another rap on the door behind Jackie. Ducayne waved the newcomer in. Jackie turned to see who it was.

"Roberts, Rico, this is—" Ducayne began.

"You!" Roberts and the newcomer said simultaneously. It was Avril Boutelle, from the dinner at Rick's.

Ducayne looked from one woman to the other. "So you two have already met." He turned to Rico. "Rico, this is Avril Boutelle. Avril, this is Rico."

"Is Rico a first or a last name?" she asked.

"Yes," Rico said, his tone not inviting further questions.

Ducayne glowered, and said, "And apparently you already know Captain Roberts."

"We were at the same dinner a few weeks ago," Jackie said. "Mutual acquaintances." She was unsure if she should mention Carson's name in front of Boutelle in this context. She also wondered how well qualified Boutelle was to be one of Ducayne's agents. Let's see what the mission is first, she thought.

"All right." Ducayne touched a switch on his desk, and the office door closed and latched.

"No briefing room?" Rico asked.

"You'll all get more details later," Ducayne said. "This is just high level. Simply put, I need to get a couple of people to Verdigris, namely Avril and Rico. Jackie Roberts will provide transportation in her Sapphire."

"I'm known on Verdigris," Jackie said. "Last time I was there they refused landing for the *Sophie*, at least New Toronto did."

"We'll work around that," Ducayne said. "We can discuss it later."

Jackie couldn't wait to hear what he had in mind. "Okay."

"To continue," Ducayne said, "officially, Boutelle will be continuing her xenoanthropological studies of the Verdigris natives. Rico is nominally a guide and bodyguard—"

"Of which I need neither," Boutelle said.

Jackie had to agree that Avril did look capable of handling herself.

"Of course not," Ducayne agreed. "I said nominally. That's Rico's first cover. Second cover is that he's looking up old contacts to get back into the artifact business."

"And the real mission?" Jackie asked, although she had her suspicions.

"It involves someone you know, Jackie. Jordan Burnside."

She had met Burnside on Tanith, in the 82 Eridani system. He'd been Ducayne's resident agent, until rumors of a high-tech alien artifact surfaced, and she'd been sent there to pick it up. As it turned out, a Velkaryan agent named Vaughan had also been on planet and had heard the same rumors. Vaughan had been recalled to Verdigris, and Burnside had followed to investigate. Roberts and Carson had brought the artifact back to Sawyers

World, expecting to rendezvous with Burnside, but Tevnar, his timoan pilot, reported that he had stayed behind on Verdigris.

"You've heard from him?" she asked.

Before he could answer, a shrill tone sounded from the monitor on Ducayne's desk. He turned to it, saying, "That's an emergency signal. Wait one." He looked at an image on the screen, turning it so the rest of them could see it too. It was jerky, a video stream from a handheld omniphone. Carson's voice came through "*Who the hell are you?*" The image briefly showed several uniformed men standing at the top of an excavation, all holding weapons. A fainter voice came through. "*Anderson Territorial Police —*"

"Bullshit!" Rico said abruptly. "I know him, and that voice. That's Reid. He's a Velkaryan, the one who shot me."

Ducayne wasted no time. "Jackie, how fast can you get to Pete's Pyramid in the *Sophie*?"

It took her just a moment to realize what he was asking. "Twenty minutes if I go suborbital, breaking all kinds of regulations."

"I'll clear it with the locals. Rico, arm yourself and go with her." They both rose to leave. Ducayne was already picking up his phone. "I'll have others meet you at your ship, but don't wait for them if they're late. Just go."

Jackie was already running to the elevator. Rico was right behind her.

∞ ∞ ∞

"You're sure that was a Velkaryan?" Jackie asked Rico as they boarded the *Sophie*. She had already triggered its warm-up sequence from her omni.

"Absolutely. His name's Reid. I met with him on Earth, but I didn't know he was a Velkaryan then. Later we exchanged shots. He got the better of it; he had help."

Crap. That wouldn't be good, but if Reid wanted into the pyramid, he might keep Carson alive long enough for Jackie and Rico to get there and do . . . something. There was still no sign of the others Ducayne said he would meet her here. Screw it, let them find their own ride.

She keyed microphone. "Pan. Pan. Pan. Sawyer Spaceport, this is the *Sophie*, declaring an emergency. Life critical rescue mission, I am lifting *now*. All ships, keep clear." *I am so nuked*, she thought, and brought the throttle up.

A panicked voice came over the comm, almost inaudible over the roar of the thrusters. "Sophie, *say again? What is the nature of the emergency? You don't have clearance to—*" The voice cut off abruptly, then came back. "*All craft in vicinity of Sawyer Spaceport, keep clear for emergency traffic lifting straight out. All craft, keep clear.*"

Jackie had pitched *Sophie* vertical as soon as she was a couple of hundred meters above the field, and was now climbing straight up on main thrusters, already passing through 5,000 meters. She keyed her mike again. "*Sophie* has cleared 5,000 meters. Sorry about that, Sawyer."

"*Roger*, Sophie. *Land and report to Control when able.*" There was a pause, and then "*. . . and good luck.*"

Jackie wasn't sure whether he meant good luck with her immediate mission, or good luck when she had to explain her actions to Space Traffic Control. Either way, she'd take it, but right now she didn't care. She had no idea whether she and Rico would get there in time, or what they would do if they did, but Carson was in trouble.

Chapter 46: Pyramid

CARSON FELL IN behind the other two as they were marched up the ramp and toward their field tent. He looked over his shoulder at the closest guard, trying to examine his uniform. He couldn't see any insignia on it, let alone anything suggesting that the guard was law enforcement.

"Face forward," the guard said, cuffing him with the butt of his rifle.

Carson caught up to Dundee, to ask him if the uniforms looked familiar. That earned him a rifle butt from the other guard.

"No talking," he ordered.

The guards ushered Carson and the others into the large tent they had been using as a field office. It was an open-frame tent, and the furniture was all light weight. Carson wondered just what they were supposed to be secured to.

The answer became obvious when the guards ordered the group to sit on the floor in a circle, backs to the center. So positioned, one of the "cops" tied all their handcuffs to each other with additional binder ties.

In theory, Carson reasoned, they could get away if the four of them could coordinate standing up and then walking as a group, but with each of them facing a different direction, and little room to move their legs being huddled together, that was effectively impossible. They had to get the ties loose somehow.

"Stay put. We'll be back," the larger guard said, and the two of them left the tent.

Carson didn't know if there was anyone standing guard at the entrance, that was a secondary issue. He called out, "Hey out there, can we get some water? I'm thirsty!"

There was no response from outside the tent.

"Thirsty, really?" Finley said.

"No, just wondering how alone we are."

"Why, what are you thinking?"

"There are tools in that cabinet to my right. If we can get to it, we can get these bindings off."

"Isn't escaping custody against the law?" Finley said dryly.

"Did you hear anyone say we were under arrest?" Dundee asked.

"If these guys are really police, I'll eat my hat," Carson said. "Anderson Territory is sparsely populated; does it even have its own police force?"

"It does," Dundee said, "but it's like four guys and I know half of them. None of whom are out there. I don't recognize the uniforms, either. They didn't look right. But how do we get to the tool cabinet?"

"We all bend our legs and push up against each other's backs until we're standing. Then we shuffle over to the cabinet."

"Then what? All our hands are behind us, how do we grab and use anything?"

"We'll figure that out when we get there. Okay, get ready to push up." They all bent their legs and planted their feet. "Okay, on three, push up and walk backwards until we're all standing. Ready?"

The others chorused their agreement.

"Okay, one, two, three, up!"

It was easier said than done. Carson got partway up, his shoulders and upper arms pressing against those of Finley and Dundee to his left and right. They were halfway up when someone's foot slipped, and they all went down in a heap of arms, bodies, and curses.

"Crap," Carson said. "Is everyone okay?"

"I'm going to have some bruises, but yeah," Finley said.

"Scraped my wrists on these damned cuff ties," Dundee said. "Nothing serious. Let's try again."

Carson ignored his own bruises and scrapes. "All right. Again. One, two, three, up!"

This time they succeeded, and the three of them were now standing, back to back, in the center of the tent. The cabinet was two meters away.

"Okay, now it gets tricky. You guys have to kind of shuffle sideways and backward, small steps. Ready?"

"Why do I have to walk backward?" Dundee said.

"Because I'm facing the cabinet. Do you want to try turning around?"

"No. Let's just do it."

"Right. Ready? Go." The group managed to shuffle over to the cabinet, like some bizarre spider, without falling over, although there were a couple of close calls. "Stop," Carson said.

"Now what?"

The cabinet stood about chest high, with two doors that opened outward from the middle. A handle on the right door, at waist height, would have to be twisted to unlatch it. There was no way anyone could reach it with their hand.

"Everyone hold still. I think I can do this." Balancing against the others, Carson raised his right knee and used it to push the handle sideways. It turned slightly, but Carson lost his balance and put his foot down to recover. "Damn."

Finley had been watching over his shoulder. "You almost had it. Try again."

Carson did so. This time, with Finley leaning in to help him keep his balance, he twisted the handle far enough to unlatch. The cabinet door swung open. Inside, various tools and other odds and ends sat on open shelves.

"Almost there," Carson said. This time he reached up with his foot and swept it along a shelf, knocking tools to the floor. He looked over the scattered implements. Screwdrivers, a hammer, a couple of wrenches. . .there! Pliers with built in wire cutters. He kicked those away from the cabinet to where there was open space on the floor.

"Okay, now we shuffle over to the pliers and sit down again," Carson said.

"Ah, I see what you're doing," Dundee said. "Clever. Then we can use the cutter on the pliers to deal with these ties."

"Exactly."

Again, it was easier said than done. The shuffling and sitting was easy enough, but trying to pick up the pliers, slip them over a tie and then cut that tie, all without mashing someone else's fingers in the cramped space behind all their backs was no mean feat. It went more quickly once the first couple of ties had been cut and they could move apart. In a few minutes, they were all free.

"Now what?" asked Finley.

"You two should get out of here," Carson said. "Get back to the clearing. With any luck the survey team should still be set up there."

"Then where did these guys come from? And what are you going to do?" Alex Finley asked.

"I think they're Velkaryans," Carson said. "They must have found somewhere else to land, or they managed to bluff their way past the survey crew. As for me, I'm going to get that talisman back." Carson wasn't about to let that remain in Velkaryan hands.

"How?" Dundee said. "They're armed, you're not, and you're outnumbered six-to-one. Let's just get out of here."

"That talisman is literally a key to the pyramid. It acts like a security pass, or at least it did in the other one."

"What other one?" Dundee said.

Finley covered for Carson's slip. "It doesn't matter. If Carson thinks it's important to get it back, then we get it back. You can go, Carson and I will figure something out."

"Didn't you have spare ammo for your shock rifle stored in here somewhere?" Carson asked Dundee.

"Yeah. That other cabinet," he said, pointing. "But if you and Finley are staying, I'll help. That brings the odds down to two-to-one."

"Fine," Carson said. He looked at Dundee. "I don't suppose you have a spare rifle here to go with those shock darts?"

"Afraid not," he said. "But. . . ." He looked around the tent, and eyed the camp cot with its tubular frame. "I think I have an idea."

∞ ∞ ∞

Reid fingered the rounded square stone he had taken from Carson. It didn't look particularly high-tech, just a piece of stone or fired clay with small rounded gemstones embedded in its surface. Engraved lines connected some of them, the way lines on a star chart made constellations. *Or trade routes?* he wondered. He had been briefed on the Betty Hill star map. It was unfortunate that their attempt to get the original had been subverted. He wondered what had become of Rico, and grimaced. *Hope the bastard suffered and died.* Reid's foot, where Rico's shot had hit him, hadn't healed perfectly. There were limits to what a traumapod could do with shattered bone.

No matter. Somehow this talisman was the key to opening this pyramid. Perhaps he should have waited until Carson had opened the entrance, but he hadn't wanted to risk Carson and his team ducking through it when the Velkaryans showed up. Who knew what weapons they might have access to inside? Somehow they had managed to deal with both Hopkins and Maynard on Chara. He examined the talisman more closely. Some kind of remote opener? The gems might be buttons. He tried pressing them in turn, but they neither moved nor gave any other indication that pressing them had done anything. That wasn't it.

"All right," he said to the others. "Check the carvings around the doorway, and on either side. There should be a slot or something that fits this." He held up the talisman to show them.

They fanned out around the door as best they could in the confines of the trench and began checking the pyramid's surface.

Just then Garrett and Brady, the two men he'd sent up with Carson, came back.

"What are you guys doing back here? What did you do with Carson and the others?"

"We cuffed them together in the tent. They're not going anywhere," said Garrett.

"Yeah," Brady agreed. "We figured you might need some help with the pyramid."

"You mean you wanted to see what was inside," Reid said, annoyed. He pointed to Garrett. "You, get back up there and keep guard. Carson's a tricky one."

"But—"

"Do it. *Now.*"

The man sighed. "Yes boss." He unslung his weapon and headed back up toward the tent.

Reid turned to Brady. "In fact, maybe you should go with him. It might be easier if we just persuade Carson to tell us how this thing works."

"Carson won't talk, I've seen his type before. Stubborn."

Reid had to agree. "All right, then bring the young guy too." There were other ways to make someone talk. The younger man was the better bet, the other one had looked even tougher than Carson.

Before the man could reply, there came the distant roar of an aircraft, or a spacecraft leaving atmosphere. Reid looked up, wondering if Carson had somehow gotten a message out. It was unlikely, and even more unlikely that someone could respond that quickly. He looked up, scanning the skies beyond the scattered clouds. There were a couple of bright dots, moving too fast to be aircraft. He hoped the planned *UDT* vs Space Guard wargames hadn't started yet. He had wanted to observe those. Oh well, the pyramid was more important right now.

"What are you hanging around for?" Reid told the man. "Go get them."

As the other turned to leave, there was a shout from one of the men at the doorway. "Hey, I think this might be it!"

Reid turned to look. "What have you got?"

"This recess," the other said, pointing to a rounded square recess amidst the other carvings around the doorway. It was skillfully worked into the design so that it wasn't obvious unless you knew what you were looking at. "Does your stone fit it?"

Chapter 47: Invasion

Alpha Centauri System

THE PLANNED TRAINING exercise began with a display of precision navigation, as ten *UDT* Space Force cruisers dropped out of warp thirty AU beyond a point midway between Alpha Centauri A and B, less than half a million kilometers apart from each other. They had coordinated their final jump from somewhere nearby, within the orbit of Proxima Centauri, to achieve that. Their next step was a series of smaller, cautious jumps toward Kakuloa, with the intention of rendezvousing near Kakuloa's smaller moon, Mahina'uku, before the final assault.

A Sawyers World Space Guard picket, *Ophion*, detected their gravitational signature a half-hour later, and immediately jumped to Sawyers World, broadcasting the information to the waiting Space Guard patrol squad. Those ships then warped to the vicinity of Kakuloa, splitting into smaller groups.

The *UDT* fleet, meanwhile, had also jumped to their rendezvous at Mahina'uku. They weren't ready for what came next.

Two ships of the Sawyers World Space Guard caught the incoming *UDT* force by surprise, taking out the *UDT* ships *Talon* and *Warlock* in a simulated attack. The Space Force hastily mounted a counterattack, knocking the Guard ship *Phorcys* out while the other, *Galene*, managed to escape to warp.

The *UDT* Space Force ships then split up. *Vigilant* and *Vulcain* took up synchronous orbit above the equator north of the Southern Continent. Two other pairs split off into low orbits, with *Scorpion* and *Antares* in a polar orbit, and *Sirius* and *Tonnant* taking up a low equatorial orbit. The final duo, *Viper* and *Velociraptor*, vectored to enter and land in an area of the Southern Continent that would be grassland if Kakuloa had had any grass, but instead was a plain of low scrub vegetation that filled a similar niche.

The *Scorpion* and *Antares*, in polar orbit, ran into trouble over the northern icecap. Three Space Guard ships, *Thetis*, *Dynamene*, and *Cymodoce* came from apparently out of nowhere and strewed orbital mines in their path. The orbital mines were, of course, small simulators for training, and programmed to avoid impact if approached too closely. Instead, they simulated a detonation that would have filled the path of another spacecraft with pellets, at a minimum destroying its sensors and potentially puncturing its hull.

Antares was taken out almost immediately. *Scorpion* returned fire, but it was ineffectual, and the ship succumbed to the simulated mines in short order. Four down, six to go.

On the other side of the planet, the UDT Space Force was faring better. The cruisers, *Sirius* and *Tonnant*, had spotted the Space Guard ships first and laid down heavy simulated fire. The Guard ship *Galene*, which had joined the equatorial group, was crippled. The *SSGS Pherusa* got a few shots off and then warped out to a predetermined rendezvous. The third Space Guard ship, *Glaucus*, managed to put up a fight long enough for the *Thetis*, *Dynamene*, and *Cymodoce* to perform a daring out-and-back millisecond warp jump from polar orbit, placing them at the battle scene where they deployed the last of their mines on a high speed trajectory toward the Earth forces. And then there were four.

The undamaged Guard ships regrouped at a prearranged rendezvous point, then split up to deal with the *UDT* Space Forces in synchronous orbit. By this time, *Vigilant* and *Vulcain* were ready, and managed to take out *Pherusa* and damage *Dynamene* before succumbing to the combined attack.

With no support available from space, the two UDT landing craft, *Viper* and *Velociraptor*, by now on the ground, were forced to yield to the *Amphitrite* and the remaining mine-layers.

The final score: *UDT* Space Force 5, Sawyers World Space Guard 10.

Chapter 48: Pyramid Opened

GARRETT GRUMBLED A bit as he approached the tent. There was no way the prisoners they'd left there could get away. Even if they managed to stand up with their hands all cuffed together, there was no way they could break the ties, and even less chance they could get far through the jungle like that.

Holding his rifle at the ready, he used the barrel to push aside the tent flap. A sudden jolt of electricity spasmed his muscles, and he felt the rifle being jerked out of his hands. He couldn't move to resist and was still wondering what happened when he collapsed to the ground.

∞ ∞ ∞

Carson stepped away from behind the tent flap where he had waited to jab a shock dart into anyone entering. They weren't really designed to be hand-held, but Dundee had shown him how to use them that way. Dundee himself now held the rifle he'd snatched from the guard. Carson shot a quick look around the outside of the tent, and, seeing nobody else, safed and pocketed the other dart he held.

He stepped back into the tent. Garrett was lying on the floor, still twitching as the dart discharged its battery in pulses. "Okay, get that out of him and tie him up," he said to Finley. "And make sure you do a better job on him than they did to us."

"No worries," Finley said, following Carson's instructions.

"So," Dundee said. "One down, but we're still outnumbered, with only one rifle and a bunch of darts. What now?"

Carson grinned. "What else would we do when we're outnumbered and outgunned? Attack."

∞ ∞ ∞

Back at the excavation

As Reid placed the talisman in the socket, he heard a slight rumbling, grinding sound. The door seemed to vibrate sightly, but did not rise.

"What's supposed to happen?" one of Reid's men asked.

"There should be a door panel that slides up. Maybe it's just jammed with all this dirt." Reid gestured to two of his men. "You and you, get something to pry this up with."

The two came back a few moments later with a shovel and a pick, and set to work wedging them into the tiny gap which had opened at the base of the door.

Reid reached up again with the talisman. "Get ready to pry it up." He inserted the talisman. "Now!"

As the door groaned and vibrated, the two leaned into their levers, pulling and prying. Reluctantly, the door edged its way up, slowly at first, then, as some point of friction was passed, quickly rising about twenty centimeters before jamming again.

Then all hell broke loose.

∞ ∞ ∞

This was the opportunity Carson had been waiting for. With one of the fake "Anderson Territorial Police" men secured back at the tent, that left—as far as anyone had managed to count—just five others. With Reid and two of the men in the trench, none of them with weapons beyond a couple of shovels, the group was at its most vulnerable.

That still left two men on guard with rifles, and they had to be dealt with. Dundee had the rifle he'd taken off the tent guard, but using it would instantly alert all the others. Carson couldn't be sure that the men in the trench were unarmed. They may not have their rifles, but Reid almost certainly had a pistol. Their best bet was to take out the two riflemen with stun darts and relieve them of their rifles. They could then cover the other three.

Dundee had taken up a position where he would be able to cover the trio in the excavation. Carson and Finley had carefully crept around either side of the trench, each coming up behind one of the guards.

Carson saw Finley in the trees behind his guard and caught his eye. He gestured to the pit where Reid was ordering the two men with shovels to start prying up the door. Would Finley understand? When the door started to open, that would be the point of maximum distraction. Finley gave a gentle nod, not wanting to attract the guards' attention with movement. Carson just hoped that Finley had truly understood.

"Get ready to pry it up," Reid's voice came from the trench. This was it! Carson held his shock dart at the ready, checking that it was armed, and crept closer to the guard.

"Now!" Reid said, and Carson lunged forward, driving the dart into the small of the guard's back.

The man spasmed and jerked into a rictus from the shock, a grunt escaping his lips as he collapsed. Carson was ready and grabbed the rifle from his hands as he fell. On the other side of the trench, Finley had managed the same.

Below them, Reid had startled at the sudden unusual sounds from above, and jerked away from the door. He looked wildly about, dropping the talisman and reaching for his pistol.

There was a sharp *BANG!* followed by Dundee yelling "Freeze!" A geyser of dirt at Reid's feet showed where Dundee had aimed.

Reid ignored the command and dived to his right as he pulled his pistol free, snapping off a shot at Dundee as he hit the ground. The other two men had dropped their tools, one diving for what little cover there was in the corner of the trench, the other dropping to one knee and fumbling at his waist.

Carson didn't wait to see what the man would pull out. He swung the captured rifle up to aim, just as two other shots sounded, one from Dundee and another from somewhere behind Carson. *What the—?*

Reid yelled in pain. Carson took a quick step sideways, putting a tree between himself and where the other shot had come from. Had he miscounted the guards? The man Carson had aimed at stopped what he was doing and held his hands out away from his body. Reid was lying on the floor of the trench, his left hand clutched over his right forearm which was bleeding from where a bullet had grazed it. His pistol was on the ground a meter away.

"Cease firing!" Reid yelled, pain evident in his voice. "You assholes are in a lot of trouble, shooting a police officer!"

"We'll take our chances with the real police," Carson yelled back.

"They're not real cops, they're Velkaryans," a familiar but unexpected voice called from behind.

"*You!*" Reid gasped out between clenched teeth.

Carson spared a quick glance back. "*Rico?*"

"We thought you might need some help," Rico called back. "Roberts is bringing up the rear. I run faster."

Another shot rang out. Reid had taken advantage of the distraction to grab his pistol. Several shots sounded in reply, and Reid went down again, his right shoulder a bloody mess.

Rico was down too, cursing. Carson couldn't see where he'd been hit. The other Velkaryans had not had a chance to act.

"Kick those weapons away and lie down with your hands on your head." Carson ordered them. It had been many years since Carson had taken anyone prisoner at gunpoint, in his army days, and he tried to remember the drill. The main point was to not let them near weapons, and not to get any of your own men in your line of fire.

"I'm bleeding out here!" Reid said.

"Tough!" Carson said. That was the least of his worries. "Rico, how are you doing?"

"I'm fine," he called back. "Bastard just winged me." The pain in his voice suggested otherwise.

"Okay. The rest of you," he called to the others, "the sooner you cooperate the sooner your boss gets medical attention. You, the one in the corner, get up, keep your hands up, and walk backward up the slope out of the trench."

The man scrambled to his feet and cast a hesitant look at Reid. Reid glowered and muttered at him, "Just go."

The man raised his hands and backed up out of the trench, stumbling a bit on the uneven ground. As he reached the top, Rico stepped forward and tied his hands. Carson saw the Rico's sleeve was blood soaked.

"Rico, take care of that."

"As soon as we have these guys under control," he growled.

They followed the procedure with the next man, leaving Reid still in the bottom of the trench. Just then, Jackie Roberts came out from the brush, breathing hard.

"You started the party without me," she said between gasps, and then "I have *got* to start spending less time in zero gee."

"You should have RSVP'd," Carson said. "We would have waited."

"Next time," she said.

"Jackie, see if Rico needs help. Alex, with me," Carson said, gesturing to him. Finley came around the trench, handing his rifle to Roberts, then joined Carson down in the trench with Reid.

"What now?" he asked.

"Keep your spare dart ready. I'll tend to this guy's wound, but if he even looks like he's about to try something, zap him."

"Got it." Finley pulled the dart from his pocket and armed it. Reid followed the action with his eyes, his glare hostile.

"All right, let me see it," Carson told Reid, who turned to let him look at it.

Reid's forearm had just been grazed, but the other bullet had hit his shoulder, near the end of the collarbone, and it was a mess of blood and torn flesh. Carson couldn't make out an exit wound. He might be just missing it with all the blood, but the bullet could have hit the humerus or the clavicle, breaking the bone and disrupting the bullet. It must hurt like hell, and Carson had to admit grudging admiration for how stoically the man was taking it. At least the blood wasn't spurting.

Carson tore off his sleeve and wrapped it around the arm over the wound, as best he could given the awkward location, and cinched it tight.

"*Aaugh*, shit!" Reid gasped.

"Sorry, but that will hold it for a while. There's a medkit in the tent. Get up."

"What happened to my other men?" Reid asked as he struggled to his feet.

"Stun darts. They'll be fine once they wake up. Sore muscles for a while though. Where's the talisman?"

"I dropped it when the shooting started. Back there in the dirt somewhere. Can I get this taken care of?"

"All right. Alex, you and Dundee take him up to the tent and treat that. Roberts and I will make sure the others are secured and then I'm going to look for that talisman."

"What are we going to do with these guys? We need to call it in."

∞ ∞ ∞

With the other Velkaryans secured and Dundee and Roberts left to cover them, Finley and Carson, accompanied by Rico, escorted Reid back to the tent.

"How are we going to call it in? They smashed the radio, and we don't exactly have omniphone coverage out here," Finley said.

"Carson managed to get some kind of signal out," Rico said, "That's why Roberts and I are here. The rest of the cavalry will probably be along any minute, but Jackie didn't want to wait."

"Yeah," Carson said. "A special addition to my omni after someone tried to hijack my autocab."

They reached the tent and Carson found the medkit. "Okay, Rico, let's see the arm."

"What about me?" Reid said.

"Screw yourself," Rico said. "You're lucky I don't put a few more bullets into you. I owe you."

Carson looked from one to the other of them. "You guys know each other?"

"Yeah," Rico said. "We ran into each other on Earth."

"I should have made sure you were dead," Reid said between clenched teeth.

"Enough!" Carson said. "Rico, you're still bleeding. Let me get this sleeve off and put some quick-clot on it."

He sat Rico down and, with the scissors from the medkit, began to cut away his blood-soaked shirt.

He got the sleeve off and examined the wound. It was nasty. "That must have hit bone. Does it feel broken?"

"Nah, but it hurts like a son-of-a-bitch. But it makes me feel better to know that Reid must feel worse."

Carson reached into the medkit for the quick-clot, and as he did so, Reid sprang up, pushing Finley aside with his left arm, and dashed for the tent door.

Finley and Carson scrambled up and after him, but when they reached the flap, Reid was nowhere in sight.

"I'll go after him," Finley said.

"No, not alone. He's wounded, he probably won't get far."

Carson went back to patching up Rico as best he could with the medkit. At least he had stopped the bleeding, but it needed more attention that Carson was equipped to give it.

As he finished wrapping the bandage, they heard the sound of helicopter rotors from overhead.

"I hope that's our ride," Rico said.

∞ ∞ ∞

Back at the pyramid

It was. The helicopter, actually a high-speed, variable configuration, twin-rotor aircraft that bore a distant resemblance to a century-old Osprey V-22, hovered above the pyramid site. Several armed troops wearing Space Guard uniforms were rounding up the Velkaryan prisoners, and another was talking to Roberts and Dundee.

One came over to them as Carson, Finley and Rico approached. "Mr. Finley," he said, addressing Alex. "Are you all right?"

Carson and Rico turned to look at him. Carson guessed the connection, but Rico wouldn't know. The latter turned to Alex and said, "You must have some powerful friends."

"I suppose so," Finley said, and turned to the Guardsman. "Yes, thank you. I'm fine, but my friend here needs medical attention. There was somebody else, the leader of this group—" he gestured at the Velkaryans who were being rounded up "—but he escaped."

By now Roberts and Dundee had come over to join them.

"That's a shame," Dundee said, not sounding very concerned. "Was he armed?"

"No, why?"

"He was bleeding pretty badly the last I saw him. Leopards can smell that. He won't get far."

Rico laughed.

"All right," the Guardsman said. "I think we're done here. We can airlift you out."

"Ah, no," Carson said. "You'd better medevac Rico here, but the rest of us can get a ride back in Captain Roberts's ship." He gestured toward Jackie.

The Guard looked a little non-plussed, and looked from Roberts to Finley and back. "Ma'am? Sir?"

"I'm parked in the clearing a couple of klicks away. You may have seen it," Jackie said.

"Yes, that's fine," Finley said to the Guardsman. "Something we didn't finish before we were interrupted. We need to do a bit of clean up."

"All right." The Guardsman pulled a small radio free from a clip on his belt and handed it to Finley. "Here. If you need anything, holler."

Finley took it and nodded.

"Okay, men," the Guardsman called to the others. "We're done here. Let's get this show in the air."

∞ ∞ ∞

As the aircraft flew off, Carson said to the others, "All right, where's the talisman?"

They all looked at each other. Jackie said, "Well don't look at me, I just got here."

"Reid dropped it when he got shot," Dundee said. "Check the trench."

"Ah, right."

After a minute of scrabbling around in the dirt, Carson found the talisman. The door was still stuck mostly closed, with just a narrow gap at the bottom. Carson got down and peered under it. There was no way he could wriggle through that gap, and, peering through, it looked like there was a pile of dirt or something behind it. Probably that's what had jammed it.

Carson stepped back and had Finley ready to pry the door up with the pick. With Finley at the ready, Carson applied the talisman to its recess. The door groaned, Finley heaved, and then with a grating sound, the door slid up the rest of the way.

"What the hell?" Finley exclaimed.

Carson looked on in wonder, thinking the same thing.

Behind the doorway, where in the Chara pyramid had been an open passageway, the corridor here—if there was one—was filled floor to ceiling with what looked like solidified mud. Scrape marks on the outer surface showed where the door had rubbed against it while rising. No wonder it hadn't wanted to open.

"Well," said Dundee. "That was anticlimactic."

∞ ∞ ∞

Carson muttered a curse, then after a few moments said, "Finley, give me that pickaxe."

Taking the pick in hand, Carson stepped up to the dried mud filling the doorway and swung at it, overhand. The sharp end dug into the dirt a half meter and stuck. He pried it loose, dislodging a clump of the compacted soil, and swung at it again. Another lump broke loose. He raised the pick again.

"Carson, are you sure that's the best approach?" Jackie said. "What if there's something fragile behind that?"

Carson paused in mid-swing and turned to her. His intended retort of "who's the archeologist here?" died on his lips. She looked somewhat bedraggled, her hair in disarray, and sporting scratches and torn clothing from having run through a couple of kilometers of predator-infested forest to come to his aid. She looked as good as when he'd seen her in the cheongsam. And she was right.

"No, it's not." He dropped the pick. "Although if this is like the others, the passage should go straight back from the entrance. It should be clear."

"And yet it's filled with dirt," Finley said. "Why?"

That was a very good question. "The pyramid seems to have been deliberately buried," Carson said. "Maybe when it was, some mud seeped in around the doorway." But, looking at the entrance, he didn't see how that could have happened. Maybe if the door had been open at the time? But then how did it close, and how far inside had the mud flowed before it did?

He lifted the pickaxe from where he'd dropped it, and, this time holding the head of it in both hands, used the tip to scrape away at the pit he'd already made in the mud face.

"I think you're wasting your time," Dundee said, pounding on the dirt a little way from where Carson was scraping. "This seems pretty solid."

"He's right," Finley said. "We need to come back with the backhoe, or some other specialized equipment. Maybe pressure hoses."

"There's no water around for those," Carson said dejectedly, "but yeah, you're right. This isn't just a thin layer behind the door. I'm going to try digging a bit farther, but the scope of this excavation just got a whole lot more difficult. *Crap.*" He tossed the pick to the ground again.

Roberts came up to him and put her hand on his shoulder. "I know it's not what you wanted, but the fact that your talisman opened the door proves definitively that it's a Spacefarer pyramid and high tech. Whatever's inside can wait."

He smiled at her. "I guess it will have to. Thanks Jackie. And thank you for getting out here so quickly." He reached up and pulled a scrap of leaf from her tangled hair. "That must have been quite a run. I'm glad you didn't meet any leopards."

She grinned back at him and patted the weapon now holstered at her side. "No, the leopards are glad they didn't meet me. I was in no mood to play fair."

Dundee looked at her, pointedly looked at her holster, and said, "I'm going to pretend I didn't hear that, seeing as I'm grateful for you and Rico coming to our rescue. But leave it in the holster on our way to your ship, all right? Cuts down on the paperwork."

She got a sudden horrified look on her face. "Oh, crap! The paperwork!"

"No, I just said don't worry about it," Dundee said.

"Not you," she said, "Space Traffic Control. I busted all kinds of regulations getting here. Shit, shit, *shit!*"

"It was an emergency," Finley said before Carson could say anything. "Even Space Guard came out. We'll get it sorted."

"Easy for you to say," Roberts said. "It's my ship and my license on the line. But maybe you're right. Either way, dawdling here will just make it worse. Come on, gentlemen, if you want a ride back in the *Sophie*, you'd better get your things packed up quickly."

Carson wasn't quite ready to leave. "Dundee, make sure she gets back to her ship safely. Finley, you can go too if you want. I'm going to stay here, maybe try digging a bit farther, and then seal up the site. I'll be fine here alone."

"Are you sure?"

"After the ruckus we made I doubt there are any animals anywhere near here. I can hike out tomorrow. The aircars should still be back at the clearing."

"They were when I landed," Jackie said.

           Alastair Mayer

"I'll come back for you," Dundee said. "I don't want you to have to shoot anything with more than two legs."

"What about terror birds?" Carson asked dryly.

"Not them either, but you won't see any in the forest."

"All right. Now you better gather whatever you're taking. Jackie needs to get back. Oh, and Jackie?"

"Yes?"

"Dinner when I get back?"

She smiled. "As long as it's not food bars around a campfire, you're on."

Chapter 49: Wrapping up

Ducayne's Office

"*CARSON'S HERE,*" THE VOICE came from the intercom on Ducayne's desk.

"Have him wait. I'll just be a few minutes," Ducayne said, and turned back to Regina Elliot. He closed the screen on the post-mission summary she had given him. It was about the *UDT*-Space Guard wargames.

"Well, that was a disaster," he said. "For one, the *UDT* under-estimated just how well-armed the Sawyers World ships are. I guess they don't read our reports."

"Indeed," Elliot said. "But the Space Force still had the edge in firepower. How did Space Guard manage to coordinate their warp jumps so precisely?"

Ducayne shrugged. "Home field advantage. They know this system and their ships very well, so can jump with sub-millisec-ond precision. The Space Force could probably do as well in the Solar System, but not out here in a planetary system they're not familiar with. Accurate charts help, of course, but there's a hu-man tendency to want to verify information like that before act-ing on it. It also helps that the local crews know that this system is mostly empty because orbits between the two stars are unsta-ble. Alpha Centauri has no asteroid belts, but most singleton sys-tems do."

"It has some asteroids, surely?" Elliot wasn't as familiar with the Alpha Centauri system as Ducayne was.

"Yes, and most have beacons on them. The beacons won't help in real time, of course, but they do pin positions down very well. The accurate tracking data lets the Guard predict exactly where they'll be, and since there aren't many, they can pretty much ignore them."

"So you're saying our Space Force would hold its own better in a more crowded system, like Epsilon Eridani or Delta Pavonis?"

Ducayne considered that. Both those systems had a single sun, and had asteroid belts. Two asteroid belts, in the former case. "Maybe. It depends on the opponent and their numbers. I noticed that Space Force seems reluctant to use fast short-range warp jumps in system, but Space Guard had no problem with that."

"The Sol System is a busy place," Elliot said. "Space Force has to generally abide by space traffic control regulations too. That out-and-back warp near Earth would cost a civilian pilot his license and his ship, and get a military pilot grounded pending an investigation."

"There is that." Ducayne shifted in his seat. This whole situation left him uncomfortable. He knew the Velkaryans were up to something, he just wasn't sure what, and the Space Force had to be prepared. "On the other hand, it's a maneuver they should be practicing. If not around Earth, then perhaps Mars or Venus. Or get them more time in the out-systems."

"I don't disagree," Elliot said, "but that's hard to justify. Half the *UDT* thinks the Space Force is just a waste of budget as it is. Of course, they don't know anything about the other spacefaring species out here."

"And I'm sure the Velkaryan-influenced governments aren't helping."

"What do you think? Venezuela has already proposed disbanding the Space Force all together, replacing it with an unarmed search and rescue organization."

"Of course they have." Ducayne shook his head in disgust. "All right, I'll add my comments and forward your report along. Thank you. And speaking of disasters, go ahead and send Carson in."

"Will do," Elliot said as she rose to leave.

∞ ∞ ∞

Ducayne's Office

Hannibal Carson thanked Ducayne for his prompt action in getting help out to them at the excavation, and for somehow smoothing things out with the Sawyers World government.

"Space Guard owed me one, but mostly it was Finley and Maclaren. They have more influence than they pretend. But tell me about the pyramid."

Carson explained what they had found, or perhaps rather what they hadn't.

"I don't get it," Ducayne said when Carson finished. "Why would your Spacefarers go to the trouble of building a pyramid and then fill it in? Did they decide it was unnecessary because the locals had gone extinct? But why go to all that trouble?"

"I don't think the Spacefarers filled it in," Carson said. "I think it was a lot more recent."

"How recent?"

"I'm still looking into whether there's a way to date the fill material, but there are signs a Kesh pyramid ship may have landed nearby about a hundred years ago. That's Sawyers World years, about a hundred-fifty standard years."

"The Kesh? That would put it just about the time our space program was getting started," Ducayne said, looking thoughtful. "What signs?"

After Carson's surprise and disappointment at finding Pete's Pyramid apparently filled in—the compacted muck had extended back as far as he had dug, several meters at least—he had re-examined the unusual features he'd seen earlier in the nearby cleared area, relying on his expertise as a field archeologist. "I found compression of the ground in the clearing, with straight edges to that. There were signs of vegetation recovering after a destructive event, the way it does after a fire or a volcanic ash-fall, but with no signs of either. The rings on the new tree growth give us a pretty good date. It's about the same age as the oldest trees growing on the pyramid itself, a hundred local years."

Ducayne frowned. "Coincidences make me suspicious," he said. "Are you saying that the Kesh both filled in and covered up the pyramid?"

"Somebody did, and something big and heavy landed nearby at about the same time. I can't be certain of what, but a Kesh pyramid ship would fit. Then there's Elizabeth Sawyer's sighting. If it *was* the Kesh trying to hide that pyramid, they would have freaked when the *USS Anderson*, given the choice of the whole planet, landed just sixty-five kilometers away. Of course they'd investigate." Carson knew that the *Anderson* hadn't had much latitude in the choice of landing area, but anyone worried about their proximity to the pyramid wouldn't care.

Ducayne was looking increasingly uncomfortable. "Since you bring that up, there were also the Betty Hill and other UFO incidents on Earth in about that same time frame. Even though most of those could be dismissed as something innocuous, Brown did find a few reports that fit with what we now know about modern spacecraft systems. I'm beginning to think that the Kesh *are* hiding something."

"Only beginning to?" Carson said. "You've always thought that."

"Maybe," Ducayne allowed. "I've always thought it prudent to assume they were, anyway. I think we ought to ask them just what the hell they're playing at. Phrased more diplomatically, of course."

"How? They don't want to make contact." The one Kesh who Carson had talked with, Ketzshanass, had been explicit about that.

"Maybe it's time to return to Zeta Reticuli."

Carson wasn't sure he liked that idea. His previous visit almost ended badly. "They warned us off. Are you sure that's wise?"

"Sure? Heck no," Ducayne said, his expression sour. "But why did they warn us off, do you suppose? What are they hiding?"

"Ketzshanass said it was more of a respect thing. That and lurking degkhidesh automated weapons systems." Carson remembered too well the particle beam attack on Vaughan's ship, and the similar damage to the crashed alien ship they'd found at Kapteyn's Star.

"Perhaps," said Ducayne, leaning back in his chair with his hands clasped below his chin, looking thoughtful. "Any chance they're working with the Velkaryans? Vaughan showed up on Tanith later, after all."

Carson considered this. The Kesh ship had done something with Vaughan's ship, *Carcharodon*, when it had been pursuing Carson and Roberts aboard the Sophie. But Ketzshanass had been adamant about not interfering. Or rather, Carson realized, about not attacking the Velkaryan's ship. Did that mean . . . ? No, that didn't make sense.

"Why would they?" he asked Ducayne. "The Velkaryans are xenophobic, they want terraformed planets for humans. Why would they work with aliens, or vice versa?"

"They don't seem to have a problem using alien technology when they can get hold of it. But you're right, I don't see what's in it for the Kesh. Keep humans off balance, maybe? Again, another reason to ask them outright."

"That sounds confrontational, but the way they're acting . . . do you think they're *scared* of us?"

"If they are, I have to wonder why. But maybe it's just natural caution. I suppose I might do the same thing in their place, but we need answers, not speculation."

"Does that mean you want me to go back to Zeta Reticuli?" Carson asked. "I'm not a diplomat, and I don't know anything about making first contact. Which," he reminded, "the Kesh aren't interested in anyway."

"But you have talked to them before, however briefly, so you might be the best person for the job. And that presents me with a dilemma." Ducayne sat forward, putting his hands on his desk. "I actually had another assignment for you."

"Of course you did," Carson said resignedly. He was about to complain that his recent assignments had had little to do with archeology as such, like being sent to 82 Eridani for a completely unnecessary follow up on what Jackie had been doing there. Although, he had to admit, that had led to investigating the presumed-Kesh wreck on Kapteyn's II. He held his tongue.

"Were you about to say something else?"

"No. You were saying, about a different assignment?"

"Have you had your fill of pyramids yet? Pardon the pun."

Carson eyed Ducayne warily. "That depends," he said, "what did you have in mind?"

"Oh, I think you'll like this one. You've been wanting to follow up on the Spacefarers, the original pyramid builders. Isn't that right?"

"Yes, but I'm also interested in the Kesh. I agree with your feeling there's something they haven't been telling us."

"They haven't been telling us much of anything, so that's hardly a surprise. But that's not really archeology, is it?"

"Unearthing what they've really been doing for the past few thousand years since they developed space flight is."

Ducayne nodded. "You're right, and that does tie in with what I want you to do. Listen, Carson, there's a war coming. No, not with the Kesh," Ducayne hastily added at Carson's expression, "but with the Velkaryans, or at least with some of the territories controlled by them. It's not that the *UDT* wants one, but we can't sit by and let the Velkaryans continue to act on their agenda. On Earth, they would have already had a visit from *UDT* Peace Enforcers, but our Space Forces aren't quite ready for that."

Carson had heard about the outcome of the recent war games, if not the details, and could only agree. "But what does that have to do with me?"

"That goes back to the reason I approached you in the first place, when you were first looking for artifacts like the one you found in that tomb. There's alien tech out there, whether Kesh, Spacefarer, or whoever the degkhidesh are. Maybe others, for all I know; T-Space seems to have had a surprisingly crowded history, and who knows what's beyond that. Better we get our hands on any such tech before the Velkaryans do."

Carson sat forward in his seat. This was getting interesting. "What did you have in mind?"

"You remember that report I had Avril Boutelle working on, regarding pyramids and pyramid-like structures throughout T-Space? She did a very good job. She did mention Pete's Peak. She even found a report from the first survey of Chara III, before the Mennonites set up their St. Jacobs colony, which also mentioned your stone fences and the pyramid."

"She what? Where did she find that?"

"She's resourceful. But she found a few others that weren't in the archeological literature that you referenced for her. Including old scouting survey reports on planets that have been briefly visited but, like Chara III, are beyond the edges of settled T-Space. Of course since you came back from Zeta Reticuli we've suspected there might be more terraformed planets beyond that, but for obvious reasons we haven't gone looking."

"No, the Kesh as much as warned us off."

"Exactly. But there's more. We think we've determined the locations given by the star maps on the valid talismans we've recovered."

"Really?" This might be a good time to mention the Centauri talisman, Carson considered. Or perhaps not. "I assume there's an overlap?"

"Yes. There's your own new talisman of course."

"I—" Carson began. How had Ducayne known?

"I thought it curious that you didn't ask me for a talisman to open Pete's Peak. That was sloppy, but I congratulate you on keeping it quiet. I assume that's how you convinced Pete Finley?"

Carson nodded glumly. "And Maclaren. She confirmed the isotope dating."

"I thought as much. I traced the packages that were delivered to you recently. I'm surprised you didn't tell him the first time you met."

"I hadn't looked at it closely then. I didn't know it pointed to Alpha Centauri. I was going to mention it to you—"

"When you thought I had a need to know? Look, Carson, I'm not saying you did the right thing, but I understand why you did it, and that's not important now. But," Ducayne said, emphasizing the word, "just keep in mind that I'm likely to have a bigger picture than you do, and withholding information can hurt in ways you might not realize. Got it?"

Carson nodded again. "Got it."

"Fine. Now, I was saying about the overlap between talisman star locations and the report Boutelle did. You'll get the details later. Anyway, once I got her report, I overlaid her locations with my own intensity map of known Velkaryan activity, both overt and covert." Ducayne paused, watching for Carson's reaction.

Carson understood. "So, you're seeing some correlation between their activity and known or suspected pyramid locations."

Ducayne nodded. "Yes. Not a hundred percent, of course. There are places where Velkaryan activity is unrelated—on Tanith, for example—and there are possible pyramid locations they don't seem to be aware of."

"Or have already investigated and either found nothing, or have cleaned the place out," Carson said.

"Yes, there is that possibility."

"Where do you want me to go first? Check out the other pyramids, or back to Zeta Reticuli?"

"That's the question. You can't be everywhere at once. I do have a few other people I can put on this, but you have a unique combination of skills. What do you think?"

That was indeed a good question, and Carson didn't have an immediate answer. On the one hand, he liked the idea of checking out Velkaryan-occupied areas first. The time factor there would be more critical, and he welcomed any opportunity to tweak their noses. On the other hand, there was no guarantee that he could find out anything useful, especially if any pyramid had already been plundered, like the one near New Toronto on Verdigris. Conversely, any of the other pyramids—or potential pyramids—could either come up empty or hold a trove of untouched artifacts. But they had already found one of those, on St. Jacobs at Chara, and another one right here on Sawyers World, if they could ever get into it. On the third hand—the gripping hand, as some people called it, although Carson had no idea why—visiting the Zeta Reticuli system again, possibly including the previously-unvisited Zeta 2 Reticuli this time, and asking the Kesh direct questions could settle things a lot quicker. Or it could stir up a lot of trouble.

"What do you think the odds are of finding anything in those pyramids that we haven't found already?" Carson said. "They seem to be mostly teaching museums, and seemed to stop at a tech level we've already passed. The interesting stuff was in isolated chambers, and we already have samples of that."

"Do we? Where's that disintegrator Maguffin you brought back from Chara III?"

"Disintegrated," Carson said, reluctantly. "I see your point."

"And we don't know what else there might be, either within the pyramids or associated with them, even elsewhere in the same system. That ship you found at Kapteyn's Star, for example."

"That Tevnar found, but you're right. All right. I'll need to look at what you have, to prioritize the locations."

"I was hoping you'd say that. I'm going to assign a couple of other people to work with you. I don't mean to go with you, necessarily, but for you to divvy up the targets among yourselves. I'll give you a couple of weeks to sort it all out."

"Can I involve Marten?" Carson asked, referring to his timoan friend and colleague who had been with him at Chara and Zeta Reticuli.

"The Taprobani native? He can go along with you wherever you're headed, yes. It's probably good cover. I'm not sure I want him on his own missions."

"If it's a question of loyalty . . . ."

"It's not." At Carson's raised eyebrow, Ducayne shrugged. "Marten is your friend and he already knows what we're doing, and as a non-human he has no love for Velkaryans. I get that. But because he *is* a timoan, he's going to be at a disadvantage dealing with Velkaryans, and if anything happens to him and a whiff of his involvement with Homeworld Security comes out, that could trigger a diplomatic incident between Taprobane and the *UDT* government. I'd rather avoid that, and not just for his sake."

Carson saw Ducayne's point. "All right. Until I talk to him, I won't even know if he's available anyway. So who are the others you have in mind?"

"Black you already know. He's one. I'll introduce you to the other at a later briefing."

"And for ships? Jackie and the *Sophie,* I assume. Will Black be taking the *Mandragore?*"

"Again, that's for a later briefing. But I have another assignment for Roberts and her ship before that."

"Oh? Anything you can tell me?"

Ducayne started to shake his head, then looked at Carson and said, "Not really. I just need her to take a couple of people to Verdigris for me, and maybe pick someone up. Just a ferry run."

"You mean Jordan Burnside?" Carson had met him on Tanith at 82 Eridani. The original plan was that he would have come back with Roberts then, but instead he had followed a Velkaryan operative to Verdigris.

"Who?" Ducayne said, poker-faced, then "I can neither confirm nor deny—"

"Never mind, I get it. But if it's just a ferry run, chances are she'll be back before we're ready to go out in search of ancient astronauts, whether those are Spacefarers or Kesh."

"Chances are. We can discuss that more later. Meanwhile, I'll get you those reports to look over."

Carson looked forward to it. "That certainly sounds more interesting than grading assignments."

Chapter 50: Dinner

Rick's Café, Sawyer City

"HOW DID YOU GET a reservation at Rick's this time?" Jackie asked Carson after they'd been seated and their orders were taken. Tonight, it was just the two of them.

"It turns out I not only know the owner, through his nephew, but the owner's silent partner. Peter Finley. In fact," Carson said, "I have a confession: this dinner's on him. I couldn't afford this very often on a professor's salary."

"Finley? Why?"

"Partly by way of apology for giving me such a hard time about the nature of his peak, but mostly to thank *you* for coming to the rescue of his grandson, Alex."

"I, well, thank you, er, him," Jackie said. "It wasn't exactly Alex I was coming for, and anyway, I thought Pete had already thanked me."

"Oh?"

"You know I had to report to Space Traffic Control, for blasting straight out of my parking spot at the spaceport and breaking a dozen other regulations to get there quickly?"

"I knew a bit of that, yes," Carson said.

"So I showed up at the STC office, figuring I was going to get reamed and then have my license lifted," Jackie explained, "when an officer from the Space Guard Judge Advocate General's office arrived, tells me not to say anything, and proceeded to defend my actions as an instance of genuine emergency need and with Space Guard approval."

"Convenient."

"There's an understatement. Anyway, the STC official looked at us both, a bit non-plussed, and scanned his files. A minute later he thanked us for coming in, saying that was all he needed to know. File closed." Jackie shook her head. "I don't know who pulled what strings, but I assumed it was either Finley or Ducayne. Or both."

"Given what I know of those two, which isn't much, you may never find out."

"Yeah. I'm grateful, of course, but also a little uncomfortable with people doing me anonymous favors."

"More like someone rewarding you for a good deed. I wouldn't worry about it."

"I said I was uncomfortable, not worried. Anyway, I figure that's another one you owe me." She waited for Carson's reaction, but before he could utter a protest, smiled and winked. "Not that either of us is keeping score, of course."

"I think Rico gets the most credit this time, although you did get him there in a hurry," Carson said.

Jackie grinned. "Fair enough. Anyway, what's happening with the pyramid? Did you get an extended dig approved?"

"That's still wending its way through the bureaucracy, and very slowly because the whole thing is considered secret. There will be some kind of dig, coordinated jointly between Sawyers World and UDT Homeworld Security, but it will be months before anything interesting happens. But I may not be a part of it."

"What?" She put her hand on his forearm. "Oh, Carson, why not?"

He smiled at her concern. "Actually, I may be moving on to something more interesting. I'm not going to go into it here, but there are a couple of new assignments coming up. You'll find out more about them when you get back from your ferry run to Verdigris."

"My. . . ?" Jackie looked momentarily confused, and then realized what he must mean. "Ah, right, the passenger from Tanith. I'm still waiting on some details for that; the last briefing was rudely interrupted." She wagged her finger at him, grinning. "The nerve of some people."

"Hey, *I* didn't pick the timing. Blame Reid," he said. "Anyway, I can't go anywhere until the end of semester anyway. I have classes to teach and papers to grade."

"That should be just about the time I get back, assuming I leave within the next few days. So, is that how you're going to spend your summer vacation?"

"A bit more than that, I think. These are longer-term assignments. I'm going to take a sabbatical."

"So not a university project, then. I guess that means you won't be going with Captain Gupta on the *Chandrasekhar*."

"He doesn't look nearly as good in a cheongsam as you do."

Jackie burst out with a laugh, quickly stifled as she looked around, blushing. "Thank you. I'm just going to go with the compliment and not ask how you have the remotest idea of what he looks like in a cheongsam."

Now it was Carson's turn to blush. "Just guessing. I know what *you* look like, and I'm glad you decided to wear one again tonight. I was hoping you would."

Before she could say anything in response, the waiter arrived with their meals.

∞ ∞ ∞

Sawyer Spaceport

After dinner, and drinks, and dessert, and coffee, all of which were deliciously decadent, they took an autocab back to the spaceport and the *Sophie*. Neither of them said much, basking in the pleasantly full feeling after an excellent meal, and knowing each other well enough to be comfortable with long silences.

The autocab pulled up beside the ship. Carson and Roberts got out and walked to the foot of the boarding ramp. She tapped the control to open the airlock door, and it slid open.

"Carson," she said, "why don't you come aboard. It may be a while before we can get together again. There's coffee, or, though I keep it locked out in flight, the autochef *can* serve liquor."

He looked into her eyes, and almost lost himself before giving up on trying to figure out what she was thinking. He answered honestly. "Yes, Jackie, I'd like that. You're sure?"

"Don't argue with the captain," she said, smiling, and put an arm around him to nudge him toward the ship.

"Who's arguing?" he said as he walked up the ramp.

She followed closely behind, and the two of them squeezed through the airlock together. She gestured toward the galley. "You know where everything is, make yourself comfortable. Take your tie off. And fix us drinks. I just need to check the systems and maybe change." She stepped into the cockpit as Carson went back to the small galley area, loosening his tie as he did so. He heard the airlock door slide shut.

A minute or two later, as he stood in the galley with two drinks in his hands, he heard Jackie call from the forward area of the ship. "Carson, come on up here. Bring the drinks."

As he went forward, he realized she wasn't in the cockpit, but in her own cabin just aft of it. She was standing in the middle of the small room, still wearing the cheongsam. She smiled up at him as he handed her drink to her.

"Thanks," she said, and took a sip. Then she set it down on the small desk beside the bunk. "You know what, Carson? I think I'm going to need some help getting out of this dress."

"Aye aye, Captain," he said, putting his own drink down and then his arms around her.

"Just Jackie, please," she said softly.

They kissed, and then after a while, when they broke it off, Jackie looked at him with those amazing green eyes and said, "I hope you don't mind sleeping aboard tonight."

Epilog

Ducayne's office, next day

JACKIE ROBERTS SAT in Ducayne's office, waiting for Avril Boutelle and Rico to show up so they could resume their hastily interrupted mission briefing.

"Are you all right, Roberts?" Ducayne asked. "You look a little zoned out."

"Sorry, just mentally going over what needed to be done in the *Sophie* before going anywhere," Jackie said hastily, and then realized she should have said *to* the *Sophie*. Oops.

Just then, Avril Boutelle arrived. "Sorry, am I late?"

"Not at all," Ducayne said. "We're just ready to get started. Rico will be here in a moment, but he already knows most of this. Now, where were we?"

"You mean before Jackie and Rico hightailed it out of here?" She looked at Jackie. "Welcome back. I guess it worked out?"

"It did," Ducayne said, "but what we were talking about was a trip to Delta Pavonis III, Verdigris, and to rendezvous with one of my agents there."

"Right," Jackie said. "Burnside. Then you have heard from him?"

"Yes, but not recently. I would like to make contact, see what he's found out, and whether he needs assistance. That's where Avril and Rico come in. They both have already-established covers."

"What about *Sophie* being a known ship?" Jackie said, just as Rico came into the office, one arm in a sling.

"As I mentioned before, we can deal with that." Ducayne looked at Rico. "You know how to do that, don't you? And how's the arm?"

Rico nodded. "I do. And the arm is okay. Cracked a bone but nothing a couple of hours in a traumapod couldn't mend." He fixed Jackie with a glare. "Mind you, Roberts, I seem to end up in a traumapod an awful lot when you're around." He turned to Ducayne. "Maybe Avril and I can get a different ride?"

"But I wasn't even in the same solar system the last time," Jackie protested.

He grinned at her. "I know, and I was joking." He turned back to Ducayne. "When do we leave?"

∞

The story continues in: *The Pavonis Insurgence*

Glossary

Chara: G type star 27.5 light-years from Earth, also called Beta Canorum Venaticum.

Delta Pavonis: G type star 19.9 light-years from Earth, approximately 16.5 light-years from Alpha Centauri. Home star of the planet Verdigris.

Kakuloa: Alpha Centauri B II - terraformed planet orbiting the second largest star (B) in the Alpha Centauri system.

Kapteyn's Star: a red dwarf star about 12 light-years from Earth. It is known to have at least two planets, each larger than Earth, and orbiting in or near the habitable zone.

Kesh: Aliens encountered by Carson, Roberts and Marten at Zeta Reticuli, possessing advanced technology. They neither confirmed nor denied that Zeta Reticuli was their home system, but it is currently (so far as Carson knows) uninhabited.

omni: Short for omniphone - compares to today's smartphones as smartphones compare to walky-talkies. (Look for "Nokia Morph" on YouTube for a nearly-there concept video.)

omniphone: See omni.

parsec: A distance of approximately 3.26 light-years.

Proxima: Also called Alpha Centauri C, a red dwarf star which slowly orbits the two main stars of the system at a distance of roughly 0.2 light-years.

Sapphire: A class of small interstellar ship (S-class), capable of sleeping about six if they're close friends, with a range of just over 20 light-years on full tanks.

Sawyers World: Alpha Centauri A II - second planet orbiting the largest star (A) in the Alpha Centauri system, the first extrasolar planet settled by humans. (See the *Alpha Centauri* trilogy.)

Tanith: 82 Eridani IV - fourth (hypothetical) planet orbiting the star 82 Eridani. In real life, this star is known to have at least three planets, all larger than Earth.

Taprobane: Epsilon Indi III - Third planet orbiting Epsilon Indi, home world of timoans.

thruster: High-efficiency reaction drive, a kind of fusion-powered arc-jet.

timoan: (Analogous to "human") The sentient natives of Taprobane. Descended from the ancestral species of terrestrial mongoose and meerkats the way humans are descended from the ancestral species of monkeys or lemurs.

T-space: Terraformed (or Terraform) space - Usual term for "known space," a spheroid of stars centered on Earth and about 50 light-years in diameter. So-called because many of the sun-like stars within it were found to have planets that were not merely Earth-like, but deliberately terraformed.

Unholy War: A nuclear war which took place in the first half of the 21st century, involving primarily the smaller nuclear powers, purportedly for religious reasons.

Union de Terre: Union of Earth, the successor to the United Nations formed after the events of and immediately after the Unholy War. Typically abbreviated *UDT*, since the English "Terran Union" has an unfortunate acronym.

Velkaryans: Church of Divine Stellar Providence. A group with both political and religious ambitions. A core belief is that God created the terraformed planets specifically for humans.

Verdigris: Delta Pavonis III - third planet orbiting the star Delta Pavonis, so named for its greenish hue and the heavy jungle covering the habitable areas.

warp bubble: The thin shell of highly-curved space surrounding a ship in FTL flight. Based on Van Den Broek's lower-energy configuration of an Alcubierre warp metric.

Zeta Reticuli: A pair of G type stars separated by about 0.1 light-year at a distance of 39.2 light-years from Earth. (Technically, Zeta 1 and Zeta 2 Reticuli)

Acknowledgments

MANY PEOPLE CONTRIBUTED to the creation of this book in one way or another, from the feedback and enthusiasm of readers of the earlier books, to the encouragement from fellow writers to keep at it through some major changes, for which I thank them all. As originally envisioned, the events of *The Centauri Surprise* and the next volume, *The Pavonis Insurgence*, were to be covered by a single book. It soon became clear that the result would be twice as long as originally planned, and far more complicated, so it warranted a split. It also meant this book took a lot longer to finish than I expected it would. The good news is that most of *The Pavonis Insurgence* is already written.

The chapter "Pavonis-b", and in particular the description of the alien vegetation Jackie sees, is partly inspired by David S. Stevenson's *Under A Crimson Sun (Prospects for Life in Red Dwarf Systems)* (Springer, 2013). That book is well worth reading if you're interesting in the scientific possibility of such life, or planetary development in general.

Thanks also to my first readers/editors, Robert, Jill, and (the other) Robert, for their corrections and comments. Any remaining errors are mine, not theirs.

-- Alastair Mayer, Colorado, Summer 2019

Preview: *The Pavonis Insurgence*

As we left Jackie Roberts and the others in Ducayne's office, they were planning a trip to Verdigris, in the Delta Pavonis system, to rendezvous with Ducayne's agent Jordan Burnside. We last saw him in *The Eridani Convergence*, following the Velkaryan officer Klaus Vaughan to that planet. The next novel, *The Pavonis Insurgence*, picks up as Burnside is getting ready to make a rather unconventional landing on that planet....

Burnside

Delta Pavonis system, above planet Verdigris

JORDAN BURNSIDE WATCHED the airlock door slide shut as he drifted away from the *Razgon*. Neither he nor the ship had enough velocity to maintain orbit, but neither were planning on staying. He was headed for Verdigris, the planet below, and the *Razgon* would be leaving the system.

As he drifted away to a safe distance, the ship fired its attitude jets, putting more space between them, then rotated to point itself at Epsilon Indi, nine light-years away.

This should be interesting, he thought. He'd never seen a ship go to warp from this particular vantage point.

The ship held there, not doing anything. Captain Tevnar must be waiting to make sure Burnside's retrofire went without a hitch. That was considerate of her. He adjusted his own attitude so that the retrorocket on his de-orbit pack pointed forward, at the horizon. He could still see the *Razgon* from that angle, good.

His life-support pack was strapped to his chest. On his back was a larger pack which held his deployable heat shield. He activated it.

He felt a thump and then several vibrations as a Kapton bag, in the shape of a rounded, shallow cone, inflated out of the pack. The vibrations changed as the bag filled with quick-setting ablative foam. Between the surrounding vacuum and his suit layers, he could not hear the hiss he imagined. A few moments later he was nestled in the center base of the shield which would, it said on the tag, protect him from the heat of entry. He wryly wondered if there was a guarantee, not that he'd be able to collect on it if it failed. It was time to make planetfall.

The retrorocket was a small solid-fueled motor at the apex of a frame connecting it to his suit and the heat shield. Simplicity counted for a lot in an emergency pack. Its nozzle still pointed at the horizon. Below him, from what he could see, was the swirly green disk of the planet. He hoped that beneath the skyweed lay jungle and not ocean. His nav system said it did. He double-checked that his emergency locator beacon was *OFF*—the last thing he needed was it broadcasting his position—then triggered the retro.

It burst into life in front of him with a physical thump, its exhaust surprisingly faint although the nozzle glowed from the heat. He felt himself pulled toward it as it decelerated him. The *Razgon,* meanwhile, continued in its trajectory, pulling ahead of him rapidly as he slowed. Then, with a faint violet flicker, it winked out. It had gone to warp. He was on his own now, and as the retrorocket burned out, he began falling towards Verdigris.

The attitude jets in the retropack fired briefly, turning him so that the heat shield faced forward. Things were about to get interesting. And hot.

∞ ∞ ∞

Before long he felt the first gentle pressure as the thin upper atmosphere began to slow him, and he noticed a faint orange glow against the dark sky above him, the faint traces of air ionized with the energy of his passage. Then the glow intensified, and he felt its heat radiating back at him as he was pressed back against the foam shield with increasing gee forces.

There was smoke now in the trail he left, then there came a jolt and a chunk of flaming insulation, spalled off the shield, disappeared into his wake. The ride got rougher, and he wondered just how long this particular entry pack had been in storage. *Maybe I should have had Tevnar land me after all.* Of course, the whole point of this was stealth. A meteor could be shrugged off; a landing ship couldn't.

The attitude jets were useless in the thickening atmosphere, and the retro blew off with another thump, dragging his drogue ballute out with it. As it bobbled in his wake, he hoped it wouldn't burn up or melt before it had done its job. But the fiery orange glow was already fading to blue.

The ride was settling down now. Was that the worst of it? Then there came a flurry of green as he fell through a skyweed layer. *I must be getting low. When does the heat shield jettison?* His main parachute couldn't deploy until the shield was gone.

And then it went, with an impact so sudden Burnside thought he must have hit the ground, until he saw the slabs of charred foam blow past him. *It jettisons at five thousand meters*, he remembered.

With a *THUMP* the ballute pulled a bigger drogue chute from its pack and released, and he felt another tug as it deployed, stabilizing and slowing him further. Finally, as he descended through a thousand meters, it extracted his main chute.

Burnside scanned the ground beneath him, or rather, the tops of the trees below. He could see no clearing anywhere that he could get to. At least his spacesuit would protect him from small branches. As he neared the trees he hooked his left foot behind his right ankle and squeezed his legs together. He did *not* want to hit astride a branch. He stretched his arms up alongside the parachute risers. With any luck the canopy would catch in the trees before he hit the ground, yet leave him close enough to it he could lower himself down. He tried to remember how tall the trees typically grew in the Verdigran jungle, but that factoid escaped him.

With a rush the upper branches brushed by him, and as best he could he twisted his body to slip between the thicker branches below. Space opened up around him as the branches thinned, then he felt a strong upward tug as his parachute caught in the tree, the lines stretching slightly as he came to a stop.

Well, now what?

∞ ∞ ∞

The jungle floor was about seven meters below. Too far to just drop, but the parachute harness held a rope he could slide himself down on, once he unstrapped. He looked up at the parachute tangled in the branches above him. It had been still mostly open when it came to a stop, and it was draped over much of the foliage. It would be obvious from the air. That wasn't good.

If it had been one of Covert Services' gadgets, it wouldn't have been a problem. The chute would have been a drab, camouflaged color to start with, and it would disintegrate a matter of hours after exposure to the elements. But this one was part of the standard bail-out pack that Jackie Roberts gave him from the *Sophie* prior to this impromptu visit. The canopy was brightly colored, designed to be highly visible in case its user need rescue. He had disabled the emergency beacon, but that canopy was a giveaway. He'd have to get it down somehow.

He pulled down hard on one riser, then on the other. When he put his weight on the left, it seemed to sag more than the one on the right. Okay, that might work.

Burnside took the descent rope and uncoiled it, then looped one end through the buckle on the right riser. If this worked better than he hoped, he wanted to have some control over how fast he fell. Gripping both ends of the loop of rope in his left hand, he reached up and unfastened the right riser buckle. The strap jerked upwards as his weight, now entirely on the left side of the parachute, pulled it over the tree branches and he started to fall. The ropes slid through his left hand. He grabbed them tightly with both hands, and his fall slowed, then stopped. He was a meter closer to the ground.

He carefully loosened his grip on the ropes, letting himself slide slowly downward as, above him, the right riser of the 'chute rose, the parachute canopy starting to follow the lines and left riser, still attached to his harness, downwards. It was working!

And then it wasn't. Burnside's downward motion stopped two meters above the ground. Looking up, he saw that the lines were now hopelessly tangled in various tree branches, but at least now most of the canopy was below the top leaves. He jerked on the remaining riser a few times, but made no further progress.

He pulled the descent rope loop free of the right riser buckle and then threaded it through the left, letting the ends drop to the ground. After undoing the rest of his harness, he slid down the rope to the ground.

Burnside unfastened and removed his helmet, taking a deep breath. The jungle air was warm and humid, but his suit had been designed to keep him cool in space, not on a planet with atmosphere. Taking the helmet off was a refreshing change.

He pondered what to do about the parachute canopy as he doffed the rest of his suit. There really wasn't much he could do, but he pulled the descent line free. That might come in handy.

As far as he could tell from this angle, more than half of his canopy was now hidden from above by leaves. He'd come through a thick layer of skyweed on the way down, and nobody flying above that would see anything. Hopefully nobody would be flying below it. Skyweed didn't stay afloat indefinitely. The tiny plants—aerophytoplankton—would get washed out by rain, and older plants got too heavy for their buoyancy sacs and winds to keep them aloft. With any luck enough of the weed would settle out over the chute to hide it from view before anyone spotted it.

Either way, he intended to put a considerable distance between himself and his landing area as quickly as he could. He just had to figure out the direction to New Toronto. Fortunately, Verdigris had a navigation satellite system that wasn't bothered by skyweed, and he had downloaded what maps Tevnar had available to his omni. Less fortunately, large sections of those maps were marked with a single word: *jungle*.

New Toronto

Verdigris, New Toronto

NEW TORONTO WAS rapidly becoming the largest city on the planet. Already the regional capital and largest city on the continent, it was both an agricultural and major manufacturing center. The city lay on the shore of a large freshwater lake, some twelve-hundred kilometers from the site where Jean Dubois had first landed in the *Jules Verne*.

Dubois, heir to a billionaire's fortune, had bought the ship—originally built for the 2069 Alpha Centauri expedition but never used because of mechanical issues—and refitted it with the latest solid-state fusion units and the newly available commercial warp units.

It was a bastard design, lacking the warp-induced artificial gravity of the newer ships. Furthermore, as had its sister ships of the first Centauri expedition, it relied on its chemical engines for lift-off from a planetary surface. Still, it was the *Jules Verne*, and Dubois had a certain Gallic pride in it. He was determined to find a new terraformed planet.

Delta Pavonis was known to have an Earth-sized planet in its habitable zone, but while early observations had detected oxygen in its atmosphere—almost a sure sign of life—its color was wrong. Terraformed planets should look mostly blue and white, not green. It was low on the list of places to visit with the new V-class ships.

Even with its upgraded power and warp systems, Delta Pavonis was beyond the *Jules Verne*'s range of ten light-years. Jean Dubois was determined, though, and laid out a course that took him and his crew first to refuel at Alpha Centauri, then at Epsilon

Indi—this was before the *UDT* had imposed restrictions on visiting Taprobane—and finally from there to Delta Pavonis.

The third planet appeared green from space because of vast clouds of aerophytoplankton, now known as skyweed. The *Verne* found a thin patch over what their radar told them was a suitable landing site and made their descent, acquiring a film of scorched brown and green slime in the process. Being a rather irreverent fellow, Dubois named the planet Verdigris.

In a similar vein, he named its mottled-looking large moon after a particular creamy, semi-soft cheese made in his home region of Jura, France, *Bleu de Gex*, although now it was simply referred to as Gex.

His landing site, near the mouth of a large river, would later become the town of Louisbourg. The river itself, two-thousand kilometers long, ultimately drained much of the continent, beginning at a large lake. Given the lake's similarity to a Great Lake of North America back on Earth, he named it *Lac Quebec*.

A few years later, another wave of settlers deemed the shore of that lake an ideal spot, providing easy access to much of the interior of the continent and easy water transport to Louisbourg and thence to the other continent. However, they were no Francophiles. They couldn't change the name of the lake, but since it was about the size of Earth's Lake Ontario, they defiantly named their settlement New Toronto.

Now, several of New Toronto's major industries were owned by Velkaryan interests, and that organization played a dominant role in regional politics. Klaus Vaughan didn't care about the history of New Toronto, he cared that his superiors had ordered him here to resolve slowdowns in the Velkaryan-owned industries, with a particular focus on the production of armed starships.

∞ ∞ ∞

The story continues in The Pavonis Insurgence, *available in hardcover, trade paperback and ebook editions.*

About the Author

Alastair Mayer was born in London, England, and moved to Canada with his family as a young boy. He describes his interest in space flight and science fiction as genetic: his father, Douglas W.F. Mayer, had been an early member of the British Interplanetary Society as well as a science fiction fan (who in fact published some of Arthur C. Clarke's first tales in *Amateur Science Stories*).

Alastair became involved in both the L5 Society (now the National Space Society) and computers, publishing articles in *Byte*, *Final Frontier*, and other magazines, as well as becoming an accomplished scuba diver and a private pilot. In 1989 he moved to Colorado, where he still lives, and where, after working in the computer and satellite networking businesses, he now writes full time.

His short stories have been published in several anthologies and his work has appeared often enough in *Analog Science Fiction* magazine to gain him entry to the "Analog MAFIA" (Members Appear Frequently In *Analog*). Many of his works can be found in e-book format on Amazon, Barnes & Noble, Smashwords, and other e-book vendor sites.

The Centauri Surprise is the fourth in Mayer's Carson & Roberts series, one of several set in the T-Space universe, which also includes the *Alpha Centauri* trilogy and the in-progress *Kakuloa* series.

Visit his web site at www.alastairmayer.org, *which also links to the T-Space Wiki.*